SEPTEMBER AWAKENING

MERRY FARMER

SEPTEMBER AWAKENING

Copyright ©2018 by Merry Farmer

This ebook is licensed for your personal enjoyment only. This ebook may not be re-sold or given away to other people. If you would like to share this book with another person, please purchase an additional copy for each recipient. If you're reading this book and did not purchase it, or it was not purchased for your use only, then please return to your digital retailer and purchase your own copy. Thank you for respecting the hard work of this author.

This book is a work of fiction. Names, characters, places, and incidents are products of the author's imagination or are used fictitiously. Any resemblance to actual events or locales or persons, living or dead, is entirely coincidental.

Cover design by Erin Dameron-Hill (the miracle-worker)

ASIN: B07F6ZM27Z

Paperback ISBN: 9781723738395

Click here for a complete list of other works by Merry Farmer.

If you'd like to be the first to learn about when the next books in the series come out and more, please sign up for my newsletter here:
http://eepurl.com/RQ-KX

❦ Created with Vellum

CHAPTER 1

WINTERBERRY PARK, WILTSHIRE – SEPTEMBER 1880

Lady Lavinia Prior had lived her entire life, twenty-six years of it, on the outskirts of London high society. She lived in a respectable townhouse around respectable people. While she herself was unambitious to a fault—in spite of her mother's constant machinations—she'd managed to make a few friends who were important in the political world and far higher up the social ladder than she could dream of being.

So when she received an invitation from her dear friend, Marigold Croydon, sent from the grand country estate, Winterberry Park, owned by Marigold's influential husband, Alexander Croydon, inviting her to a late-summer house party, she was astounded. The gentry threw house parties all the time, but this was Marigold's first party and Lavinia's first invitation to attend. Lavinia had spent weeks imagining the opulence of such a grand residence as Winterberry Park, but she hadn't truly grasped how massive the Park was. Until now.

As the Croydon carriage that had picked up her and her mother, Lady Ursula Prior, from the train station in town rounded the bend, giving Lavinia her first full view of the estate, she was stunned. The Park was more of a palace than a house, with its three, commanding stories and elegantly shaped towers. The front garden was a masterpiece of landscape architecture, complete with a cheery fountain. And those were only the surface features. Who knew what wonders awaited inside? Lavinia had underestimated her friend's good fortune in marrying a rising star of Parliament.

Her mother, on the other hand, let out a self-satisfied sigh and proclaimed, "It's just as I thought it would be." She added a giddy giggle to her statement and grabbed Lavinia's arm. "This is your chance, my dear. I can feel it in my waters. This house party is the chance we've been waiting for all these years."

"It's my chance to visit with my closest friends," Lavinia said, her voice barely above a whisper.

Whether her mother heard her or not, she went on as though Lavinia hadn't spoken, as usual. "Mr. Croydon is sure to have invited a whole passel of eligible gentlemen to his house party. That must be why Mrs. Croydon wants you here. I'm confident that by the end of the month, we will have found you a baron or a viscount or even an earl to marry." She clapped her hands together as the carriage rolled to a stop in front of the wide stairs leading to the grand front door of Winterberry Park. "This is it, my dear, this is it."

Lavinia fought to keep her benign smile in place. This had been "it" a dozen times before. Every high society ball they were invited to, every musicale hosted by a duchess that she'd managed to wheedle an invitation to, all of the social events of London were Lavinia's big chance to snag a titled husband. And yet, none of the gentlemen who had danced with her or engaged her in conversation were good enough for her social-climbing mother, and Lavinia certainly wasn't good enough for the sort of men her mother set her sights on. The daughter of a baron who had fallen on hard times had no business being courted by a peer, or being addressed as "Lady", but her mother insisted on both, much to Lavinia's embarrassment. The only result of her mother's machinations was a pickiness that had Lavinia convinced she would die a spinster.

Not that she minded. A spinster with good, powerful friends could be an independent woman, which was exactly what Lavinia wanted to be. A woman without a husband and children to tie her down could travel, could become involved in politics, and could be the beloved "auntie" to her friends' children. The single life was precisely the future Lavinia had in mind for herself, in spite of her mother. As the carriage stopped at the base of the wide staircase leading up to Winterberry Park's front door and Marigold rushed out to meet it, Lady Stanhope and Mariah deVere following behind, a thrill of excited possibility struck Lavinia's heart.

"My," her mother exclaimed as a footman in smart livery opened the carriage door for them. "Mrs. Croydon does look stylish in that frock." She glanced over her shoulder to Lavinia as she scooted toward the footman. "Do stand up straight when you're presented, dear, and don't fidget with your trim."

Lavinia pursed her lips to hold her temper in check. "Mama, I haven't fidgeted since I was twelve. And besides, these are my closest friends."

Her mother made a doubtful noise and turned her attention to the footman, who helped her alight. Lavinia stepped down after her, beaming at the sight of three of her closest friends together.

"I'm so glad you've made it here at last," Marigold said, leading the pack as they hurried down the stone stairs to greet Lavinia with hugs and kisses.

"It was a trial of a journey," Lavinia's mother answered before Lavinia could. "But you are so kind to have invited us to such a splendid event."

As soon as Marigold let Lavinia go so that Lady Stanhope and Mariah could hug her in greeting, she turned to Lavinia's mother with a polite smile. "Welcome to Winterberry Park, Lady Prior. I've had Mrs. Musgrave prepare a special suite of rooms just for you."

"A suite," Lavinia's mother exclaimed, eyes bright, a hand pressed to her chest. "Mrs. Croydon, you are too kind."

"I wonder if she'll say the same when she realizes the suite is in an entirely different part of the house than where Marigold's put us," Lady Stanhope said, hooking her arm through Lavinia's in an almost sisterly gesture.

A wave of gratitude and admiration swept through Lavinia. Katya Marlowe, Lady Stanhope, was old enough to be Lavinia's mother. She had three children of her own who were nearly grown. Her son, Rupert, the current Earl of Stanhope, stood on the verge of assuming the duties of the title that Lady Stanhope had carried out for a decade. Her daughters, Bianca and Natalia, were already being spoken of as the debutantes to beat once they had their coming out. And yet, Lady Stanhope considered Lavinia a friend.

"Marigold couldn't possibly have given me a room in the same part of the house as the rest of you," Lavinia said, her eyes wide in disbelief. "Surely she has me secured on some hall with the other single, young ladies invited to the house party."

"Ah," Mariah said, walking on Lavinia's other side as they mounted the stairs and headed into the house. "As it turns out, you're the only single lady in attendance this month."

"Bianca and Natalia don't count," Lady Stanhope added. "No matter what they tell you about their level of maturity and sophistication." Her expression hinted that her daughters were anything but sophisticated or mature.

Lavinia's brow rose. Mariah was a newer friend, one she'd become close to thanks to her connections with Marigold and Lady Stanhope, so she didn't think the young countess would tease her. On the other hand…. "Aren't house parties designed to introduce eligible women and men to prospective partners?" she asked.

Lady Stanhope and Mariah laughed, their faces alight with mischief. "Not when the majority of the gentlemen invited are set to play vital roles in the new parliament this November," Lady Stanhope said, flickering one dark brow. "Marigold told you Alex has been picked by Gladstone to be in his cabinet, didn't she?"

"She did," Lavinia answered, still in awe of how important her friends were.

Mariah leaned closer to her as they passed through the hall and into a large receiving room with tall, French doors that looked out into a garden courtyard. "The men are up to something," she said. "Couriers have been in and out of the house since we arrived a few days ago. Mr. Croydon's man of business, Mr. Phillips, has already been to London and back with special messages."

"If you ask me," Lady Stanhope said, "they're plotting the fate of the Empire in the library as we speak."

"Can they do that?" Lavinia asked, her eyes going round. She instantly cursed her show of naiveté.

"Whether they can or not," Lady Stanhope answered, her handsome features making her appear downright wicked, "they are."

"Oh." Lavinia breathed out the single syllable in awe. It didn't matter how long she'd been friends with Lady Stanhope and Marigold, she was constantly surprised by the power and influence the ladies and their husbands wielded. Particularly after the election in the spring. Their Liberal Party had won a definitive victory, and everyone across the nation was holding their breath and waiting to see what brave new era would be ushered in. Lavinia had high hopes that her circle's particular cause, the rights of women, would be front and center in the new parliamentary session.

But there were other campaigns that needed to be set into motion besides those that would happen in the halls of Westminster.

"Tad, would you please escort Lady Prior and her things to the Rose Suite?" Marigold asked as a particularly handsome footman stepped into the receiving room.

"The Rose Suite," Lavinia's mother gasped, as though she were about to be given a treat. "Lavinia, come along." She made a sharp gesture for Lavinia to come away from Lady Stanhope—whom she did not approve of one bit, in spite of Lady Stanhope being a countess—to join her.

"Oh," Lavinia began, disappointed.

Marigold intervened. "The Rose Suite is especially for you, my lady. I've put Lady Lavinia in a lesser room."

What would have sounded like an insult to uninformed ears made Lavinia smile, especially when her mother puffed herself up and said, "Yes, yes, of course. How very thoughtful of you, Mrs. Croydon." To Lavinia, she said, "Do not wander off or go out frolicking in the garden, dear. You'll spoil your dress. I shall return forthwith to instruct you in the ways and manners of house parties." She turned to the footman and nodded, and within moments was led away.

Lavinia let out a breath, her shoulders loosening. "She's been like that since Paddington Station," she moaned.

Her friends circled around her, leading her out to the

balmy sunshine of the garden courtyard. "She always was priggish and patronizing," Lady Stanhope said.

"You should have heard her lecturing me on the chance I have to snag a husband at this house party," Lavinia sighed as her group was seated in a lovely set of white wicker furniture surrounding a small table that a maid was setting with tea.

"Yes, well, we have other plans, don't we," Marigold said, a glimmer in her eyes.

"The foundation of the plan has already been laid," Mariah added, equally mischievous. "I haven't announced that I'm expecting again to anyone but you." Her cheeks glowed as she smiled at her friends. "Once I make my condition known, I'll begin dropping hints that I would dearly love my friend Lavinia to come stay with me in my confinement and to be a help and a comfort once the new baby is born."

"Aren't you concerned that my mother will remember you have your sister, Victoria, living with you at Starcross Castle and that she'll question why you need me as well?"

Mariah lost some of her smile. "Victoria is still in a black mood, and her spirits are quite depressed. If your mother does mention her, I can say as much." She blinked her way back into a broad smile. "In fact, I could say that you would be of great use in cheering poor Vicky up as well."

"And if your mother attempts to object to that," Lady Stanhope went on, "all we need to do is have Peter impress upon her how delighted he, an earl, would be to have you in his household."

"And how many titled men that will give you a chance to meet," Marigold said with a grin as she poured tea. "Thank you, Anne," she said to the maid, who moved to the side, waiting in case she was needed.

"But the point is not to marry at all," Lavinia said. "The point is to get out from under my mother's thumb so that I can live my own life, for a change." She took a teacup from

Marigold and handed it to Mariah. "I'm more concerned that she will attempt to invite herself to Starcross Castle instead of letting me go on my own."

"I will make very clear to her that the invitation is for you and you only," Mariah said.

Lavinia huffed a wry laugh. "You don't know my mother. I'm convinced that she will march up to the gates of heaven with me and demand St. Peter accommodate me as she sees fit, and then she'd sit on my cloud with me, instructing me how to play my harp for all of eternity."

"We won't let that happen," Lady Stanhope said, plucking a biscuit from the plate on the table between them. "The only force on earth more powerful than a meddling mother is a determined group of friends."

A deep feeling of affection filled Lavinia's gut, causing her to blink away tears. She was the luckiest woman in the world to have such wonderful friends. The only thing that would have made the moment more perfect would have been if Elaine Bond, the new Countess of Waltham, could have been there with them. But Elaine and her new husband, Basil Waltham, had only just returned to Cumbria, and according to the copious and *descriptive* letters Elaine had sent to Lavinia through Lady Stanhope, they weren't in any rush to head south when life in Brynthwaite was so *satisfying*.

The tea Marigold served was the best that Lavinia had ever sipped, and the conversation with her friends was some of the most relaxing and encouraging she'd had for months. She settled back in her chair, ready to face a future that was full of the hope of an independent life. The sun shone down, birds chased each other through the colorful garden beds, and all seemed right with the world.

She was on the verge of closing her eyes when someone opened a window halfway along the house, several yards from them. The stern face of Dr. Armand Pearson, now

Viscount Helm, stared out into the garden for a moment. The sound of men's voices discussing something with passion drifted out, mingling with the lighter conversation of the ladies. Dr. Pearson turned and met Lavinia's eyes. She sucked in a breath and looked away, heat coming to her cheeks. There was something about the man that intimidated her to no end. Perhaps it was the frown he always wore or the restlessness that had enveloped him on every occasion when they'd met. She would have to do her best to avoid the man for the duration of the house party or else she feared she would do something to make herself look like a ninny.

"Ma'am." Lavinia was shaken out of her thoughts as the footman, Tad, strode swiftly into the garden, a concerned frown on his face. He approached Marigold, but glanced to Lavinia as he did. "Ma'am, I'm afraid Lady Prior has been taken ill."

Lavinia sat up straight, setting her teacup on the table. "So soon? We've only just arrived. She was fine on the train."

"She seemed to be settling nicely. She was asking me who the gentlemen of the house party were. I only got as far as Dr. Pearson when she came over funny." Tad glanced at her with a strange look that combined apology and irritation. "She says she's quite ill now and that she needs a doctor."

"Oh, dear," Marigold said, standing. "Anne, fetch the doctor, please."

Lavinia stood as well, the tea she'd enjoyed just moments before suddenly feeling like acid in her stomach. "She wouldn't dare," she breathed, stepping away from the chair and falling in by Marigold's side as they followed Tad back toward the house. "We've only just arrived. She wouldn't dare pull something like this so quickly."

But as they hurried back into the house, Lavinia had the horrible feeling that her mother had already set her matrimonial machinations into motion.

"Gladstone's directive is clear," Alex Croydon said, stabbing his finger on the letter that lay open on his desk in the library. "In order to nip whatever opposition Disraeli's gang throws at us in the bud, we need to come up with a plan of action for November."

"Which is easier said than done, when you consider the monumental work ahead of us," Malcolm Campbell answered as he paced restlessly in front of the desk.

Armand Pearson knew that kind of restlessness and then some. He'd felt it nearly constantly since receiving the news five years ago that his eldest cousin had died, leaving him the sole heir to the Helm title and estate and all that came with it. But instead of pacing, like Malcolm, Armand felt frozen to his spot, unable to move.

"We need to tackle the issues one at a time," Peter deVere said, looming by the side of Alex's desk, glancing at the letter. "Gladstone can't expect us to write an entire agenda for the full spectrum of the Liberal Party's aims."

"Why not?" Malcolm asked with a shrug.

"Because outlining the entire course of action for a new government in secret could be considered a gross manipulation of power and undermining democratic process?" Peter suggested.

"I think he just wants us to come up with a course of action on women's rights," Alex said. "Especially since I'll be too busy in the cabinet to put as much effort into it as I have been putting."

"Which is why we're all here, isn't it?" Rupert Marlowe asked. "To take up your torch and continue to run?" He was the youngest of their group by three decades and likely only there because his indomitable mother had announced she had better things to do than steer the course of the British government. And yet, young Rupert—who was not even twenty—was not the odd man out in the room.

That honor fell squarely on Armand's shoulders. He didn't know what he was doing. Politics was new to him, as was being a viscount. He was a man of medicine, not a statesman. He was in so deeply over his head that he couldn't even see the light above the water. For the thousandth time, he wished his family's solicitors had untangled the Helm inheritance mess by choosing his cousin Mark to be viscount instead of him.

"The first order of our business should be to crush our enemies," Malcolm said, his southern Scottish accent as sharp as his words. "We've already managed to wedge Turpin out of government and into prison. Denbigh has fled to his country estate with his tail between his legs, and word has it he won't be returning to London for the new Parliament. Shayles needs to be next." His voice dropped to a low, menacing growl.

Lord Theodore Shayles was the one bit of politics that Armand had been able to grasp since being forced to take up his seat in the House of Lords. "Last I heard, Shayles was in trouble with his creditors," he said, the only information he had to add to the situation.

"Knowing Shayles, if one source of income dries up, he'll squeeze one of his pimple friends until they burst into giving him whatever money he needs," Malcolm grumbled.

"What a thoroughly disgusting metaphor," Peter said with a smirk. "Apt, though. And what with the income I'm sure he makes from that so-called club of his…."

"What club?" Rupert asked when Alex fell silent and the rest of them merely winced.

"You're too young to know about things like that," Malcolm said, as though Rupert were his own son instead of Katya's.

Alex sent Malcolm a flat look before turning to Rupert. "It's the blackest sort of brothel, disguised as any other club. Most of its activities are horrifically illegal, but thus far, Shayles has managed to blackmail and bribe his way into keeping it open."

"That's horrid," Rupert said, turning pale. "Surely, Scotland Yard could do something."

"We suspect Scotland Yard is on the payroll," Peter sighed.

"I want the Black Strap Club shut down," Malcolm cut through the discussion, his growl feral. "I don't care if it takes a parliamentary act closing all gentlemen's clubs or the destruction of Shayles's personal fortune, I want that man punished for the harm he's caused over the years."

"Yes, of course, we want the same thing," Peter said with a vaguely uncomfortable pinch of his expression.

They all knew why Malcolm had made Shayles his nemesis. Malcolm's deceased wife, Tessa, had been forced into an abusive and disastrous marriage to Shayles before Malcolm was able to help her escape and obtain a divorce. For Alex and Peter, neutralizing Shayles was a matter of principle and a way to remove the chief obstacle to their grander aims. For Armand, Shayles was the reason his life as he knew it was over. Peers were needed to cast votes in Parliament, not to treat the sick, and so his practice had come to a swift and thorough end. Shayles and his cronies were the reason Armand's vote in the House of Lords had become more important than his skill at healing, a fact which had made every day since he inherited a misery.

"We'll have to include the criminalization of prostitution along with our efforts to increase the rights of women, in our agenda for November," Alex said with a sigh. "Though, much as it pains me to say it, I fear it won't be popular."

"Nothing we're proposing to do will be popular until we provide thorough, well-thought-out arguments as to why it is necessary," Peter added, steering the conversation back to the task at hand.

"Whatever it takes," Malcolm snapped. "I'm tired of seeing women suffer needlessly."

Armand walked away from the desk, his mouth pinched in a sour expression. He'd seen first-hand the ravages of the venereal diseases women had contracted through prostitution, and often through marriage to scurrilous husbands. When inheriting his blasted title had precluded him from practicing standard medicine, he'd turned to the only sort of medicine he could, the sort that wasn't considered serious medical pursuit at all, the budding field of gynecology. Even then, he'd only been able to help with research, not treatment. But just a tiny dip in the waters of what women suffered through, without attention or acknowledgement, had increased his frustration. The world told him that being a viscount was more important than being a humble doctor, but he knew differently.

He reached the window at the edge of the room and pushed it open to gulp in a breath of fresh air. It didn't do much to lessen the sensation that he was trapped—trapped in a gilded box labeled "Viscount" with no way to get out. There was so much in the medical world that he still wanted to do, so much more healing that he felt called to. But men with titles were supposed to go on shooting parties, ride horses, and make an idle nuisance of themselves. Peers were supposed to sit on a bench in the Palace of Westminster for days on end, listening to the maddening drone of self-important lords who were convinced they controlled the world. It was a terrible life. It wasn't the life he knew he was born to lead.

Across the garden, a small group of his friends' wives sat taking tea. They had more political influence than he did, even young Lady Lavinia Prior. He studied her for a moment, her perfect, pale skin and her auburn hair, caught up in the latest style under a jaunty hat. She glanced to him for a fraction of a second before looking away, color painting her cheeks. Yes, even timid Lady Lavinia had more of a place in the world than he did.

"Armand, what are you doing over there?" Alex called to him from the desk. "We need your input on these things."

"No, you don't," Armand grumbled, stepping away from the window and walking back to his friends. "You never needed my input when I was just a physician, and you don't need my input now."

Alex sighed. Peter glanced politely in the other direction. But Malcolm glared at him. "Stop your winging and focus on the matter at hand," he barked. "You've had five years to groan about losing your medical practice. Let it go and do your duty to your country by supporting our cause."

"Easy for you to say," Armand snapped back. "You've never done anything besides arguing and spitting in Shayles's eye your whole life."

Malcolm's eyes went wide with indignation. "Oh, and you think that devoting my life to the causes of liberty and equality is beneath your high, medical standards, do you?"

"Liberty? Equality?" Armand sniffed. "What are you, French?"

"I'm Scottish." Malcolm pulled himself to his full height.

"And I'm a doctor," Armand said. He hesitated, debating sharing the news he'd been sitting on for weeks, but the visceral need to let his friends in on the joy he'd been keeping inside was too much. "I've been offered a chance to practice medicine again."

"What?" Peter and Alex said simultaneously.

Armand let out a breath, turning to them. "It's true. I've been offered a position in India. I was contacted by a Dr. Tahir Maqsood, who runs a hospital in Lahore. They need trained doctors there, and they're not so stuffy about society's rules that they faint at the thought of a viscount administering pills and setting broken limbs."

"Dr. Maqsood," Rupert said, tilting his head to the side. "Why does that name sound familiar?"

"Because he's a renowned physician," Armand answered, barely stopping himself from adding, "Like I once was."

"Are you going to accept this position?" Peter asked.

"Very possibly, yes," Armand answered.

"You can't," Malcolm said, frowning. "The duties of that title you inherited call you elsewhere."

"I'm a doctor," Armand insisted. "I was happy as I was, on the verge of opening a practice on Harley Street. I never asked for the title. They should have given it to Mark."

"The judge determined your father was born ten minutes before his," Peter said.

"The records were destroyed," Armand fired back. "It could have been the other way around. They're going off the word of a midwife in her nineties."

"It doesn't matter," Alex cut in before he could take his argument any further. "I'm sorry that it meant you had to give up something you love, Armand, but the title and everything that goes with it was given to you. And right now, our nation needs healing. The law has no provision for reversing the court's decision. Once a viscount, always a viscount. If you don't take up your seat in the House of Lords, it will be vacant, which means one less vote for our cause when it counts. You've been called to help, so help where you are called."

Armand clenched his jaw and stared off at the shelves of books lining the room. He had been called to help. And the cause his friends were fighting for was absolutely worthy. But it wasn't the life he'd built for himself. It wasn't what he wanted.

"All right," he breathed, trying to let go, but only managing to quiet the roar of unfairness within him, not quench it altogether. "What do we need to do to make Gladstone happy?"

Before any of his friends could answer, there was a knock on the door. One of Alex's footmen stuck his head inside.

"Yes?" Alex asked.

"If you please, sir," the man said to Alex, then glanced to Armand. "A guest has been taken ill. Your help is needed."

As if fireworks had lit the sky, joy blossomed in Armand's heart. "Where are they?" he asked, marching toward the door without a second thought. "Take me to them."

"Yes, sir," the footman said, leading him on.

Finally, something Armand felt competent to handle.

CHAPTER 2

*D*read roiled in Lavinia's stomach as she followed Tad through lavish, unfamiliar halls and up a grand staircase decorated with oriental carpets, centuries' worth of portraits on the walls. She wasn't concerned so much for her mother's health as for what sort of mischief she was about to wreak on them all.

"Does she do this often?" Marigold asked as they mounted the top step and turned down a long, well-lit hall.

"Only when she thinks she has something to gain by putting on the act," Lavinia sighed.

Her mother's plaintive groans floated down the hall from an open door, but that wasn't what made Lavinia jerk to a stop. Dr. Armand Pearson had just stepped into the hallway from a staircase at the other end, followed by a second footman. Lavinia's stomach dropped to her toes.

"Is something wrong?" Marigold asked, pausing and glancing back at Lavinia.

Lavinia pressed a hand to her stomach, eyes wide and fixed on Dr. Pearson as he marched toward her. Really, he was marching toward the door to her mother's room, but Lavinia knew better. "She wouldn't dare," she whispered.

Marigold stared at her curiously, but all too soon her expression shifted to understanding. "My, she doesn't like to waste time at all, does she?"

"No," Lavinia sighed and started forward again.

Dr. Pearson had already headed into her mother's room, sparing only a quick glance for her. There was nothing for it but to face the inevitable matchmaking that awaited her around the corner in the Rose Suite. She allowed herself one painful wince before soldiering on.

"Mama, whatever is the matter?" she asked, feigning innocence when she entered the front room, Marigold at her side.

"I don't know, my dear, I don't know," her mother answered. She'd draped herself elegantly on a chaise that sat in a beam of cheerful afternoon sunlight, the back of one wrist pressed to her forehead, in a position worthy of the finest stages in London. "I came over so faint as soon as I was shown to my room."

"It could be the strain of the journey," Dr. Pearson said in a low, clinical voice. He sat on the side of the chaise and took Lavinia's mother's hand, testing her pulse.

"Oh, Lord Helm," her mother said in a suddenly hale voice. "Have you met my daughter, Lavinia?"

It was all Lavinia could do not to cringe where she stood. When Dr. Pearson glanced briefly at her and nodded, a hot blush came to her face. She would die a thousand deaths if the doctor-turned-viscount caught on to what her mother was attempting. But then again, Dr. Pearson was a man of experience. She'd learned through her friends that he was in his late forties, considered the "baby" of his group, and that he had lived a vivid life while practicing medicine. There was no way he wouldn't see what her mother was doing.

"I believe Lady Lavinia and I have been introduced on a few occasions," he said, then went right on to, "Did you feel dizzy before the onset of faintness? Do you feel feverish at all? When was the last time you ate?"

"Lavinia, come closer," her mother said, back to sounding as though she were on death's door. With mortification in her soul and an apologetic look for Dr. Pearson—which she was certain he didn't see—she inched closer. "No, no, dear. Come sit by my side." Her mother patted the chaise.

Lavinia swallowed, praying she wasn't as red as an apple, and slipped to the chaise. She lowered herself to perch gingerly on the opposite side from Dr. Pearson, glad, for once, that the copious material and cage of her bustle prevented her from settling comfortably.

Dr. Pearson lifted his eyes to study her for what felt like an eternity. His expression was grave, though his features were attractive. He'd aged well. His eyes were a deep, crisp blue, and his skin had a healthy glow. His jaw was square and strong, but at the moment, his lips were pursed in irritation. The lines around his eyes and mouth spoke of frustration rather than smiles and laughter. Lavinia began to tremble. He didn't like her, she could tell. He didn't approve of her at all.

"Lavinia, say something to Dr. Pearson," her mother demanded as Dr. Pearson rested the back of his hand on her forehead to check her temperature.

Lavinia opened her mouth, but all that came out was a withered squeak of helplessness.

"Lavinia," her mother scolded in a whisper.

"I'm sorry," Lavinia managed to blurt, staring at Dr. Pearson with wide, frightened eyes. He was ten times greater than her. He'd traveled, seen things, done things. Even though he was clearly aggravated, he had a powerful aura of confidence around him. She wanted to lean toward him and run away at the same time.

And then he met her eyes with a flash of kindness and understanding that sent spirals of heat through her. "It's all right," he said softly. Yes, he knew precisely what her mother was up to.

"I...I didn't know," Lavinia blundered on, face burning with embarrassment. "That is to say, I assumed she would—" She snapped her mouth shut, biting her dry lips. "It's the travel, of course," she said, praying she'd covered her blast of badly-timed honesty well enough.

The faintest hint of a smile touched Dr. Pearson's lips before he turned back to Lavinia's mother. "My diagnosis is that you have overexerted yourself through travel. I recommend that you indulge in a long nap and take tea before—"

"Where is the patient?" a new voice shouted as a squat, balding man rushed into the room. "What seems to be the trouble?"

Dr. Pearson and Lavinia stood simultaneously, glancing to each other in question and then to the newcomer. Lavinia's mother straightened, an odd, offended look twisting her smile into a frown. But it was Marigold's reaction that gripped Lavinia. She'd gone white as a sheet.

"What are you doing here?" Marigold whispered, eyes wide and glassy, pressing a hand to her belly.

"I was told a doctor was needed, so I came," the man said.

"Dr. Miller was just passing in the lane," Anne, who had come in with the newcomer, said. "You told me to fetch a doctor."

"Not this doctor," Marigold said, fury rising in her voice.

In an instant, Lavinia remembered it all—the horrible news that had reached her after Marigold had been in a carriage wreck which caused her to miscarry the summer before, the reports of the doctor who had botched her treatment, resulting in Marigold's loss of the ability to bear children.

Fury replaced embarrassment in Lavinia's gut. "Stay away from my mother," she hissed with a surprising amount of force. She stepped around the chaise to stand between Dr. Miller and her mother, which resulted in her standing shoulder-to-shoulder with Dr. Pearson. "You're not wanted here."

"Oh?" Dr. Miller's expression brightened as though she'd treated him to an inviting smile instead of a threatening scowl. "And who have we here?"

"Tad, fetch Mr. Croydon at once," Marigold ordered, stepping toward the door. "Get out, Dr. Miller."

"Yes, yes." Dr. Miller waved away her order. He glanced to Dr. Pearson and said, "Ladies form grudges so easily. They do not understand the inevitability of unfortunate medical conditions."

Dr. Pearson narrowed his eyes, standing taller. "I know who you are, sir, and I know what you've done."

For the first time since entering the room, Dr. Miller lost his smile. "I am the doctor, sir," he said. "I've been called to treat a patient." He inched closer to Lavinia's mother. "Now, ma'am, what seems to be the problem?"

"I…what…that is…." Her mother gaped like a fish, glancing between Dr. Miller, Lavinia, and Dr. Pearson. "Who are you?"

"I'm Dr. Miller, and I'm here to make you feel better," he answered.

"Oh," Lavinia's mother said, blinking in confusion.

"Get out," Marigold repeated, pointing a shaking finger at the door. "Now."

"Is that any way to treat the man who has been called to your house to treat the sick?" Dr. Miller protested.

"This woman is suffering from fatigue, if that," Dr. Pearson said, moving in such a way that Dr. Miller was forced to back toward the door. "I have prescribed rest and nourishment."

"And who are you?" Dr. Miller asked, attempting to assert himself even as he was forced to step into the hall. Lavinia followed, Marigold just behind her.

"I am Dr. Armand Pearson," Dr. Pearson said.

A knowing grin came to Dr. Miller's face. "I know you. You're that puffed-up, accidental viscount who thinks he's still a doctor."

"I *am* still a doctor," Dr. Pearson argued.

Dr. Miller chuckled. "A doctor with a title, but not a practice. Whereas I have just been appointed to a prestigious position in an exclusive, private practice in London."

"You have?" Marigold asked, incredulous. "Who in their right mind would hire the likes of you?"

Dr. Miller was saved from answering as Mr. Croydon turned the corner from the staircase at the end of the hall. "Miller," he shouted, his voice booming down the hall and making Lavinia flinch. "Get out of my house this instant."

Dr. Miller flinched toward Lavinia. "I'm relying on you to save me, my dear," he murmured.

"Me?" Lavinia yelped, taking a step away from him. That step knocked her squarely into Dr. Pearson, who was forced to grip her around the waist to keep her from tumbling over. His touch sent electric jolts of panic through her, but she couldn't seem to move away from him.

Mr. Croydon marched down the hall like a general going to war. He didn't stop when he reached their flustered group. Instead, he approached Dr. Miller, grabbing a fistful of his lapels and nearly wrenching him off his feet.

"Get out of my house and off my property this instant," he seethed, eyes fiery with anger. "If I get so much as a whiff of you again, I will cut you into a thousand pieces and throw you into the fire, where you belong."

Lavinia was convinced Dr. Miller was about to soil himself. His jaw flapped, and he glanced desperately around.

His gaze fell on Lavinia. "B-but I was just making the acquaintance of this lovely lady."

"You leave Lady Lavinia out of this," Mr. Croydon seethed.

Lavinia hid her wince in her hand.

"Lady Lavinia, is it?" Dr. Miller seemed to perk up a fraction. "I love a red-head."

Mr. Croydon responded with a growl as he jerked Dr. Miller off his feet and propelled him down the hall toward the staircase. "I am giving my staff orders to shoot you on sight," he said as they turned the corner.

They could still be heard—Mr. Croydon threatening and Dr. Miller protesting—for a few more seconds before calm returned to the hall. Lavinia let out a breath, moving her hand from her face to her stomach. She wanted to hide again as soon as she realized Dr. Pearson was staring at her with narrowed eyes.

"You do have red hair," he said, as if just realizing the fact, even though they'd seen each other a dozen times before.

Lavinia still wore her traveling hat, but she managed to touch the chignon at the back of her neck. "Unfortunately, yes," she whispered, voice shaking. There were more important things to consider at the moment than the color of her hair, though. She turned to Marigold, who was still pale and shaking. "Are you all right?" she asked, moving to take her dear friend's hands.

Marigold was silent and still for a moment before nodding slowly. "I will be. I need a cup of tea."

"I'll come with you," Lavinia said.

They hadn't gone more than two steps before her mother's shrill call of, "Lavinia, get back here this instant," snagged her.

Lavinia cringed. Of all things, Marigold smiled, some color returning to her cheeks. "Go on," she said. "I'll be in the garden with Katya and Mariah. Join us when you escape your dragon."

Lavinia nodded, her gut churning all over again. She watched Marigold head down the hall as her mother called, "Lavinia," once more. But when she turned around to face the inevitable, Dr. Pearson was still standing by the door, studying her with a frown.

Swallowing, hand still pressed to her stomach, she moved closer to him. "Please allow me to apologize for my mother, Dr. Pearson," she whispered, darting a quick glance into her mother's room, where she sat upright on the chaise. Lavinia banked on the hope that as long as her mother saw her speaking to Dr. Pearson she wouldn't intervene. "She has ideas," she continued, glancing up into Dr. Pearson's eyes. My, but he was tall.

A faint smile touched his lips. "This is not the first time a meddling mama has tried to tempt me into bondage by throwing her daughter in my path."

Lavinia's cheeks burned with shame and she glanced down, mortified. "Oh."

"I'm sorry," he said with a cringe, reaching toward her, then pulling his hand away. "I didn't mean to offend or embarrass you by saying that. I have a horrible habit of speaking out of turn."

She risked looking at him once more. "Believe me, sir, it is not you who offend and embarrass me." She cast another miserable look at her mother, who seemed to be straining to hear what they were saying.

"I'm sorry for that as well," Dr. Pearson replied, a note of genuine sympathy in his voice. "It must be frustrating to be a woman at the mercy of her mother."

A flicker of hope formed in Lavinia's heart. Perhaps he did understand. "The thing is," she confided, feeling bold but lowering her voice further, "I came here to escape her."

"Oh?" He arched a brow.

"Mrs. Croydon, Lady Stanhope, and Lady Dunsford are three of my closest friends. We've hatched a plot to separate me from Mama so that I can, at last, be the independent woman I long to be."

Dr. Pearson's expression twitched to puzzlement. "You wish to be an independent woman?" When she nodded, he went on with, "Most women I've known wish to marry an important man and to be a mother."

"Not me," Lavinia said. She tilted her head to the side. "I wouldn't mind being a mother, but not now. I want to taste freedom. I want to make my own decisions and stand on my own two feet for once in my life."

Dr. Pearson met her declaration with an indulgent smile. Lavinia was instantly aware that she'd overstepped her bounds. Heat flooded her face once again, and she lowered her head and her hands started to shake.

"I admire your determination," Dr. Pearson said, surprising her. When Lavinia glanced up, there was a distant, almost painful look in his eyes. "There are few things more important than determining your own path in life."

"Yes," Lavinia agreed. She smiled, the funny feeling that Dr. Pearson needed more smiles in his life growing inside her. He met her look with kindness in his eyes. A spark ignited inside her, like someone striking a match to light a lantern that would show the way.

"Lavinia?" Her mother's impatient snap doused the fire and the feeling. "Lavinia, come here at once. Whatever are you saying to Lord Helm?"

"I believe he prefers to be called Dr. Pearson, Mama," Lavinia said with an apologetic look for Dr. Pearson. She stepped toward the door.

"Either will do," Dr. Pearson sighed. "I suppose I should get used to 'Lord Helm'. Or you could call me Armand."

"Oh, no, I couldn't do that," Lavinia said, ducking into her mother's room and away from the odd feelings Dr. Pearson gave her.

She didn't look back, but somehow she knew that Dr. Pearson walked away. "Would you like me to fetch some tea for you, Mama?" she asked, glancing toward Anne, the only servant who had stayed in the room.

"No, no," her mother said, irritated. She paused, then looked to Anne. "On second thought, yes. That would be nice. Fetch me some tea, girl." Anne jumped into action, leaving the room. "And shut the door behind you."

As soon as Anne closed the door, Lavinia's spirits sank in advance of the lecture she knew she was about to get. "Mama," she started, crossing to the chaise.

"That was a golden opportunity, and you missed it," her mother hissed. "I couldn't have set things up for you more magnificently."

"Mama, Dr. Pearson does not need a charity case like me throwing herself at him," Lavinia said, plopping onto the corner of the chaise with far less grace than the way she'd sat while Dr. Pearson was there.

"Charity case?" her mother nearly shouted. "You are anything but, my dear. You are a beautiful young woman of intelligence and talent. Thanks to my instructions, you are perfectly suited for the life of a viscountess."

"Mama, please don't throw me at Dr. Pearson's head during this house party," Lavinia begged. "That's not what I'm here for, not at all. In fact—"

"That is exactly what you are here for," her mother interrupted her, eyes blazing with indignation. "And what is wrong with Lord Helm? He is unmarried, he needs a wife to organize his estate and run his social life, and he is friends with the husbands of your closest friends. It is an ideal match, if you ask me."

"But I don't want to marry," Lavinia sighed, shoulders slumping.

"Blasphemy," her mother gasped.

Lavinia rolled her eyes. "I don't want to marry right now. I want to experience life first. I want to—"

"You will want what you're told to want, Lavinia," her mother snapped. "I have not gone to all this trouble and expense to bring you up right, clothe you fashionably, and ensure that you have made well-placed friends so that you can end up a spinster on a dusty shelf."

"But Mama—"

"Mrs. Croydon is hosting a ball tomorrow night to inaugurate her house party," her mother blazed on. "Along with her guests, half the wealthy, titled people in the country will be in attendance. You do not have to endear yourself to Lord Helm—though I think he is by far the best choice for you—but you will engage yourself to someone by the end of the month or I will not be responsible for my actions."

Her mother's voice took on a pleading, suffering shrillness at the end of her speech, so rather than argue, Lavinia simply sighed. "Yes, Mama," she said, not because she was inclined to follow her mother's dictates, but because she couldn't go on protesting without developing a serious megrim.

"Good," her mother said, patting her hand and smiling once more. "Now, go take tea with your friends. I'm sure they'd counsel you on the same course of action as I am."

Lavinia rose without the heart to reply to her mother. She headed for the door, but once she was in the hall, she leaned against the wall with a heavy sigh. Already she could see that her Winterberry Park holiday wasn't turning out to be the glorious bid for freedom that she'd hoped it would be.

CHAPTER 3

The day after the official start of the house party was as beautiful as anyone could have hoped for, with sunny skies, balmy temperatures, and not a hint of rain in the air. Armand was a fool for not being able to appreciate it, but the gnawing restlessness that had been growing in his gut wouldn't leave him alone.

He was in no mood to socialize with the other guests, or even his friends, as the ball that would draw close to a hundred people from across Wiltshire got underway. The letter that had arrived for him that morning had started a clock ticking in his head and put hope back in his heart.

"*Dear Dr. Pearson.*" He remembered the words as though etched on his soul. "*I am eagerly awaiting your response to the offer for employment at Mayo Hospital. My ship departs from Exeter in a fortnight, and I sincerely hope you will be aboard. I cannot stress the importance of a speedy and definitive reply to this offer as arrangements must be made at once. Yours, Dr. T. Maqsood.*"

Armand sighed as he paced through the flowerbeds lining one wall of the tremendous hedge maze Alex's gardeners had installed that spring. In just two weeks, his life could be restored to normal. He longed to send Dr. Maqsood an affirmative reply with every fiber of his being, but the looming sense of responsibility pressing down on him stayed his hand. Malcolm would likely sail to India after him to drag him home, the same way he'd tracked Basil to Cumbria and forced him to do his political duty. Perhaps there was a way to delay taking up the position in India until after whatever bill his friends needed him to vote for was passed. Though knowing them, once one bill was passed there would be another and another and another. But he had to practice medicine again. He had to.

The sun dipped toward the horizon in the west, and Armand felt his hopes sinking with it. He could cast aside the duties he'd never asked for in the first place and run away to a place where his calling took him and never be forgiven, or he could help his friends and wither inside. Neither choice was palatable.

"Lavinia," he heard Lady Prior call somewhere around the corner of the maze. The sound of her voice made him freeze, lest she find him. "Lavinia, where are you? That doctor is looking for you."

A shiver passed down Armand's spine. He most certainly was not looking for Lady Lavinia. He launched into motion, slinking away into the maze and down a side path to get as far away from the meddling mama as he could.

Not that he had an issue with Lady Lavinia. In fact, he had found her to be surprisingly shrewd about her mother's dealings the day before. He'd barely noticed her in all of their previous meetings. She was shy and lacked the confidence he preferred in women. He hadn't even noticed how vibrant and pretty her hair was until the odious Dr. Miller pointed it out. Armand had caught himself imagining what Lady Lavinia's flame-like hair would look like unbound and spread across his pillow as he'd settled in for bed that night. And, of course, those thoughts had led to others, which had made it impossible to sleep. But to be caught in a web spun by a marriage-minded mother? Not even flaming hair, enticing curves, and soft, pink lips were worth that price.

He rounded a corner of the maze, picking up his pace to outrun the arousing thoughts that nipped at his heels…and other places. But without looking where he was going, he smacked headlong into Malcolm Campbell. Both of them grunted with the impact and muttered a string of curses.

"Armand, what the devil are you doing out here?" Malcolm growled, his brogue thicker than usual.

"I could ask you the same thing," Armand said. "Don't you know there's a party going on?"

"That's precisely why I'm here," Malcolm answered, lowering his voice to a dour grumble.

Armand couldn't stop himself from laughing. "Katya giving you a hard time?" he ventured, falling into step with Malcolm as they wound their way through the maze and away from the house.

Malcolm sent him a peevish look but didn't try to deny it. "That woman is intent on vexing me until I can't see straight. She's like a plague of locusts."

"Ah, so she hasn't let you back into her bed yet," Armand said, his lips twitching with mirth.

Malcolm stopped and glared at him. "I do not…this isn't about…I wouldn't if she were the last…shut up." He hunched his shoulders and marched sullenly on.

Armand caught up to him, chuckling. "Maybe if you were nice to Katya. I hear flowers can work wonders."

"I'm as nice to Katya Marlowe as she deserves," Malcolm muttered. There was still enough light from the sunset for Armand to see his friend's blush. "She needs to get down off her high horse and accept that there are some things a woman should do and some she shouldn't."

"This from the man who professes to be fighting for the rights of women," Armand said, his voice thick with sarcasm.

Malcolm stopped, stepping just enough in front of Armand to force him to stop as well. "I'm doing far more to advance the rights of women than you are. Unless moping about and bewailing your good fortune is considered help these days."

Armand's good humor vanished. "I have nothing to add to the argument that you lot haven't already put forth," he insisted. "What do you want me to do?"

"I want you to put your time in with the rest of us," Malcolm answered, a typically Glaswegian fierceness in his eyes. "And not run away to India so that you can avoid your responsibilities."

"It's not running away," Armand insisted. "I could be of real use there."

"You could be of real use here," Malcolm said, then studied him with narrowed eyes. "You're actually thinking of doing it, aren't you?"

"Of course I am," Armand said, louder than he should have. It grated that his friends might have thought his announcement was idle banter and not a serious consideration. "You all seem to forget that I have been, first and foremost, a physician for over twenty years now. Medicine is all I know, all I love."

"It is not all you know, and love is fleeting," Malcolm contradicted him, though there was a touch more understanding in his demeanor. "The skills you've learned through your practice are ones that can be of use in Parliament."

Armand made a dismissive sound and marched on. "Parliament is a Commons game these days anyhow. The House of Lords is losing its influence by leaps and bounds every year. Mark my words, by the end of my lifetime, it will be little more than a rubber stamp."

"But it still holds sway now," Malcolm argued, marching deliberately beside him. "If it becomes necessary for Peter to introduce our bill advancing the rights of women in Lords—and it very well might be, if Shayles finds a fool willing to replace Turpin and block the issue in Commons—then we'll need more than your vote. We'll need your silver tongue and your reputation to help us in Lords."

"Since when do I have a silver tongue or a reputation?" Armand asked, pausing to face his friend again.

"You always have had," Malcolm told him, as if baffled he didn't already know. "You explain complicated medical conditions to your patients all the time and make them understand."

"I would if I were in India." Armand walked on.

"We need someone with that knack for explanations *here*, to support our bill," Malcolm insisted. "And we need all hands on deck to defeat Shayles." His voice took on a dark edge.

"I know your grudge against Shayles goes far deeper than bills and politics," Armand said, patting his friend's back. "Tessa would be proud of everything you've done to avenge her."

"It's not enough," Malcolm growled with equal parts hate and sorrow. "I can't stop until Shayles is utterly defeated, humiliated, and ground into dust. If we play our cards right, we can enact legislation that will make places like his Black Strap Club illegal. Gladstone has already given his approval for us to introduce bills that curtail the financial dealings of places like that. We could bankrupt Shayles."

"If he isn't already bankrupt," Armand murmured, arching a brow. "Gladstone consented to legislation that will limit gentlemen's clubs?" It seemed outrageously unlikely, given the mass popularity of clubs, indeed their essential nature, to an important segment of the population.

"Shayles's club is no ordinary gentlemen's club," Malcolm said.

"I know that and you know that," Armand went on. "Half of London knows that. But you're never going to prove that the place is a brothel. Shayles has covered his assets, so to speak, too completely."

"I want that place shuttered, burned to the ground," Malcolm continued as though Armand hadn't just said it was impossible. "Regardless of what the rest of you say, I'm including a clause in the plan of action we're sending to Gladstone for the investigation and dismantling of The Black Strap Club."

It was plain for Armand to see that he wasn't going to get anywhere in his argument that Shayles's club was untouchable. Instead, he sighed and said, "Have you hammered everything out, then? Is the plan ready to be sent to Gladstone?"

"Yes." Malcolm nodded. "We outlined everything after you left to take care of that emergency yesterday." He sent Armand a crooked, sideways grin. By the time they'd all reconvened in the smoking room after supper the night before, the tale of Lady Prior's "illness" and plot to throw Lavinia into his arms had reached his friends. They'd ribbed him about it all night. "Tomorrow afternoon, once we've all slept off the effects of this blasted ball, Marigold Croydon is going to pen the official letter, and Alex's man, Mr. Phillips, will take the letter to London post haste."

"Marigold?" Armand blinked.

Malcolm shrugged. "Alex insisted she has the best penmanship of all of us."

Armand chuckled. "More like he's head over heels in love and wants his beloved wife to feel involved in the campaign."

"Probably," Malcolm laughed along with him. They reached the end of the maze, and Malcolm turned to face him. "It's not a bad idea, you know."

"What isn't?" Armand asked.

"Marriage." Armand heaved a long-suffering sigh and rolled his eyes, but Malcolm wasn't deterred. "Hear me out," he said. "You hate being a viscount. You keep going on and on about how it isn't the life for you, how you know nothing about what you're supposed to be doing."

"Right," Armand crossed his arms and narrowed his eyes at his friend, dreading where he was going with his argument. "Which is why I'm taking this position in India."

"No you're not," Malcolm said with a dismissive wave. "You're going to stay here, do what matters to the most people, and marry a woman who knows what she's doing."

"No."

"Lady Prior might be a pill," Malcolm went on, ignoring him, "but I'd bet you all the tea in China that she's raised that daughter of hers, Lavinia, to know a thing or two about running a grand house." He paused. "Actually, I know for a fact that she's been groomed to marry a gentleman, the higher the title the better."

"And how do you know that?" Armand asked, not wanting to hear the answer.

"Her father talks about it at White's," Malcolm shrugged. "And Katya listens to poor Lady Lavinia fret about her mother's expectations all the time."

Armand's brow shot up. "So you're having intimate conversations of that nature with Katya, but you can't be bothered to dance with her and you can't wheedle your way back into her bed?"

"Shut up," Malcolm growled. "This isn't about me, it's about you. You and your blasted stubbornness."

"I think it is about you, all of you," Armand grunted. "And

the fact that you can't leave my life alone." He dropped his arms and marched off along the perimeter of the hedge maze, heading toward the rose garden. "I've decided. I'll reply to Dr. Maqsood in the morning."

"Don't be an idiot," Malcolm called after him. "It's time to trade one life of service for another. So what if you aren't doing what you thought you wanted to do? People still need you."

Armand made a rude gesture to his friend as he turned a corner into one of the side entrances of the maze nearest the rose bower in the center. It didn't make him feel better. The gnawing ball of acid in his gut kept growing and growing, making him feel as lost as ever.

"My lady," Dr. Miller called after Lavinia in a stage whisper. "My lady, slow down. I merely wish to speak with you."

Lavinia groaned and turned another corner in the hedge maze. The horrible Dr. Miller had approached her as if he'd been perched and waiting for her when she'd stepped out of the increasingly crowded ballroom to get a breath of fresh air. He couldn't possibly have been invited to the ball, even though it felt as though most of Wiltshire had been, but that hadn't stopped him from boldly approaching Lavinia.

"My lady, I just wish to make your acquaintance," he whispered on. "We have so much in common. We're both on the rise in the world. An alliance between us would be—ouch!"

A rustling of branches and a thump sounded behind Lavinia. Rather than stop to see what had happened to Dr. Miller, she picked up the skirts of her ball gown—a ridiculously diaphanous thing that showed too much of her bosom and shoulders, but that her mother considered *haute couture*, and whipped around the next opening in the maze. With an entire, thick wall of boxwood between her and Dr. Miller, she followed the maze as it doubled back.

Dr. Miller had picked himself up and was brushing at the knees of his trousers when she reached him, just barely able to see him through the thickness of the hedge. "We have nothing in common and nothing to talk about, Dr. Miller," she insisted in her firmest voice, which was, admittedly, not particularly strong.

Dr. Miller made a confused noise, twisting this way and that before catching a glimpse of her on the other side of the hedge. He let out a wordless exclamation of victory and attempted to part the thick branches of the hedge. Lavinia took a large step back, pressing herself against the opposite wall of the path, but thankfully, the hedges grew far too close together and were far too lush for Dr. Miller to squeeze through.

With panting breaths and a sharp yelp of pain as, presumably, he was scratched, he said, "My new employer assures me that, because of his influence and power, I will be acceptable to the finest ladies of society."

"I don't care what your employer says," Lavinia told him. She swayed forward, only to realize bits of her skirt had been snagged by the branches of the hedge she'd backed into. As she tugged herself free, careful not to rip anything, she went on. "You hurt my friend egregiously. I could never, ever think well of you."

Dr. Miller made a dismissive sound. "Mrs. Croydon's condition was already bad when I reached her. But these things are far too delicate to discuss with an impressionable female."

Lavinia freed the last bit of her skirt with a tug that resulted in a small ripping sound as she snapped straighter. "Your incompetence and your unnecessary intervention mangled her insides irreparably. And don't think for a second that either Mrs. Croydon or myself are too delicate to understand the inner workings of our own bodies."

"Lady Lavinia," Dr. Miller said in a scandalized tone. "This sort of talk is unbecoming. Stay where you are and I will find you. We can speak of larks and roses and kisses," his voice took on a lascivious tone, "and if you are sweet, we can discover whether your hair is red all over."

Lavinia squeaked with indignation. When Dr. Miller stepped to the side in pursuit, she gathered her skirts and rushed on, turning as many corners as she could in an attempt to lose him. She wasn't so ignorant that she didn't know what he meant by his lewd comment. There were distinct advantages to having Lady Stanhope and women who were very happily married as friends. But her flight took her down as many dead ends as open ones.

"Lady Lavinia, please stay where you are," Dr. Miller called breathlessly after her, far enough away to give Lavinia hope, but close enough to fuel her sense of urgent flight. "Have I told you how becoming your gown is this evening?"

Lavinia clenched her jaw and rushed on. What had possessed her to flee into a hedge maze when she hadn't yet explored its paths? The only things that gave her hope were the other, male voices she could just barely make out somewhere else in the maze and the massive rose bower she discovered when she turned yet another corner. It was in the center of the maze and easily stood eight feet tall. The roses weren't in bloom, but the massive ball of greenery was the perfect hiding place.

As nimbly as she could, Lavinia darted toward the bushes. They were less densely packed than the boxwood hedges, but within a second of squeezing between the branches she'd parted with her gloved hands, she knew she was making a terrible mistake. Boxwood branches were like feathers compared to the thorny rose bushes. But she could hear Dr. Miller gaining on her. If she had any hope of shaking him off for the evening, she had to hide, no matter how painful the concealment.

No sooner had she secured herself deep in the heart of the bushes, praying her tiny yelps of pain as thorns raked her couldn't be heard, than Dr. Miller crashed into the opening at the center of the maze.

"My lady? Where have you gone?" he asked.

Through the greenery, Lavinia watched him step first to one side, then the other, in search of her. He frowned, the expression making his flabby face look ridiculous, then started toward one of the many openings that led to the maze's center. But it was too soon for her to breathe a sigh of relief. He must have caught sight of her out of the corner of his eye, because he stopped suddenly and turned squarely toward the towering rose bushes.

"My la—"

"Miller," a louder, masculine shout cut him off. Two seconds later, Dr. Pearson marched into the clearing, fury making him look like a demon straight from Hell. "What are you doing here?"

"I was…I…." Dr. Miller's jaw flapped as he wheeled back from Dr. Pearson. "I'm here with Lady Lavinia," he insisted, thrusting a pointed finger toward the rose bushes.

Dr. Pearson turned toward the bush with a puzzled expression, searching her out. Lavinia's stomach twisted, and when he finally spotted her, caught up on the thorns as she was, her heart sank all the way to her slippered feet.

"What the devil?" Dr. Pearson began. He shook his head and turned back to Dr. Miller. "You have been banned from this property, sir," he said.

"Well, yes, but—" Dr. Miller stammered.

Dr. Pearson took a threatening step toward him. "Do you

want to leave on your own or would you like me to call for my friend, Mr. Croydon, to escort you out?" The way he asked the question made it clear that if Mr. Croydon became involved, it was likely Dr. Miller would leave in a box.

"I'll leave, I'll leave," Dr. Miller said, dancing back as though he were on the verge of soiling himself. "Any girl who would be foolish enough to hide from a legitimate suitor in a rose bush isn't worth my time anyhow."

"Did you do something that made her choose thorns over you?" Dr. Pearson demanded.

Dr. Miller didn't stay around to answer. He whimpered, then turned to flee down one of the maze paths.

Lavinia let herself breath half a sigh of relief before pivoting and trying to make her way out of her hiding place. But it was apparent within two seconds that she had a problem on her hands. "Oh, dear," she said, inching her way toward freedom. If she'd been tempted to think catching her gown on a few boxwood branches was a sticky situation, she'd underestimated the meaning of the term. Her billowing skirt was snagged in at least three dozen places. Thorny branches raked at her gloved arms and the exposed parts of her chest and shoulders. The height of the bushes meant that her hair was caught as surely as her clothes. She could barely raise an arm to shelter her face from the scratching thorns. "Oh, no."

"Here, let me help you," Dr. Pearson said, striding toward her.

Lavinia's heart beat double time as he drew near. She would have sagged in mortification if it weren't that the slightest bit of movement dug thorns into her. "You must think me a right ninny," she said, her voice tiny and pitiful.

"What did he say to you that was so offensive you would jump into a rose bush?" Dr. Pearson replied.

She had to admire him for understanding and not judging

her, but the anger that laced his words set her to trembling. He reached into the bush, his hands gently brushing back branches and untangling her as best he could. Together, they managed to free her enough that she could begin to inch into the clear, but it would take far, far longer to get out than it had to get in.

At last, their eyes met. The question about Dr. Miller was still sharp in his exasperated expression. She only hoped it was still all for Dr. Miller and not for her stupidity.

"His comments were unrepeatable," she said at last, when she could bear his censure no longer. She lowered her eyes and tilted her head. As she tried to free her hair, it pulled loose of its careful style, sending pins flying.

Dr. Pearson made a noise that sent shivers down Lavinia's spine. He was furious. His arms slipped farther around her, plucking at thorns and branches and doing his best to free her, but it was like being rescued by a ravenous tiger, and with all the pricks the bushes had given her, she must have smelled of blood.

"I'm sorry," she said, barely above a whisper, as he shifted her farther into the clear. At least her face and arms were extracted from the thorns.

"It's not your fault," he snapped, sounding aggravated all the same. "Miller is a bounder and a charlatan."

"I can't disagree with you there," she said. A loud rip sounded as she tilted toward him. "Oh!"

One strong arm closed around her waist, supporting her. "You certainly have landed yourself in a muddle."

"I'm sorry," she gasped. "I'm so, so sorry."

"Miller is the one who should be sorry," he insisted.

He shifted his weight, sliding part of his body between her and the bushes, and reached around to tug the snagged parts of her skirt free. Rip after rip sounded, making Lavinia wince. The heat of his body wrapped around her, blocking out the chill of the descending evening. His crisp, masculine scent filled her nose. It struck her in a rush that she was tangled in him now as much as she was tangled in the bushes. One of her arms was slung over his shoulder as he bent around her, his face closer to her shoulder. If she wasn't mistaken, he drew in a long breath. She shivered, heating even more.

He shifted positions, positioning his foot between hers, which curled them closer together. "Almost there," he said, voice strained. The hand around her waist moved lower, and he lifted her slightly as another loud tear rent the air. She gripped his lapel with her free hand to keep her balance. "We're almost—"

"Lavinia!"

Her mother's shout caused both Lavinia and Dr. Pearson to jump. He closed his arms around her as he jerked away from the bushes. Her skirts were torn to shreds and her hair tugged and scattered around her as she burst free of the bushes. She was forced to lean against Dr. Pearson or crumble to the ground at his feet.

"You bounder," her mother continued to shout, her eyes bright with excitement. "You cad! What have you done to my precious little girl?"

"Mama," Lavinia hissed, attempting to right herself. Torn pieces of her gown had snagged on the buttons of Dr. Pearson's coat, and somehow he'd gotten a mouthful of her hair that he was having a hard time wiping away. "Keep your voice down."

"Rape," her mother shouted instead, her face positively glowing. "My dear girl has been compromised. Oh, rape! Rape!"

"Lady Prior, if you would please keep your voice down," Dr. Pearson hissed. "Nothing of the sort has happened. I was simply assisting Lady Lavinia in—"

"Her reputation is ruined," her mother bellowed on, louder and with even more excitement in her eyes. Not excitement, glee. "You've soiled her beyond repair."

The thud of footsteps running toward the center of the maze sounded all around them, and within moments, Lord Malcolm, Mr. Croydon and Marigold, and Lord Dunsford and Mariah, along with a few other guests Lavinia didn't know, poured into the clearing.

"You wicked, wicked man," her mother shouted on as Dr. Pearson hissed and sputtered in his attempt to calm her. He had not, however, bothered to let go of Lavinia yet. "My Lavinia has been ruined by your salaciousness. Whatever shall become of her now? However will her honor be restored? What shall we do?"

Lavinia had a horrible feeling that she knew exactly what would be done.

CHAPTER 4

*A*rmand pressed his fingers against the bridge of his nose where it met his forehead and squeezed his eyes shut, praying his headache would go away. Both the pain behind his eyes and Lady Prior.

"This is an outrage," the old windbag continued to rail, appealing to the disturbingly large crowd that was flooding into the open center of the hedge maze. Was nobody in the ballroom dancing? "My poor girl is ruined."

"She is not ruined, Lady Prior," Armand sighed at last. The only way he was going to escape the awkward situation intact was by facing it head-on.

"She must be," Lady Prior insisted, appealing to Alex. "Just look at her."

Everyone assembled glanced to Lady Lavinia in the dying sunlight. The poor woman's dress was torn in multiple places. Even in the dim light, faint, angry scratches stood out on her skin. Her hair had spilled out of its style and framed her frightened face and pale shoulders. Most damning of all, in the tug-o-war to free her from the rose bushes, one side of her bodice had been pulled askew, exposing far more of the plump mound of her breast than she must have been aware of. Armand tried not to stare at the half-circle of dusky areola that peeked above the ruined neckline.

He cleared his throat and stepped in front of Lady Lavinia, shielding her from the others, then nodding to her bodice. Lavinia glanced down, then gasped as she tugged her bodice back into place. As she did, she peeked up at him with tears in her eyes, as though she knew something he didn't. The one thing Armand knew beyond a shadow of a doubt was that poor Lavinia was not complicit in anything that was happening to them.

Armand gritted his teeth and turned back to the others. "Lady Lavinia was being pursued by Dr. Miller," he said, glancing particularly at Alex. Alex instantly tensed, balling his hands into fists and searching the growing darkness. Armand went on. "She was forced to attempt to hide from the man inside the rose bush." He flung an arm out at the bush to emphasize his point. "I happened across her in distress. After chasing Dr. Miller away, I attempted to extract her from the thorns. That is all."

"Yes," Lavinia insisted, stepping up to his side. "I swear to you, Mama, that is all."

But Lady Prior snorted and brushed away the truth with a wave of her hand. "A likely story. No daughter of mine is foolish enough to throw herself into a rose bush to escape a suitor."

"He wasn't a suitor," Lavinia hissed, both angry and miserable. "He was…he was inappropriate with me."

"You see?" Lady Prior turned to the curious onlookers. "She confesses that the doctor was inappropriate with her." She pointed to Armand.

"No, no, that's not what I meant," Lavinia protested, but already her shoulders were dropping and Armand could hear the defeat in her voice.

Armand watched her with equal parts pity and horror. Lavinia sent another apologetic look his way, as though she knew what was coming and how it would tangle them. He cleared his throat and made a last effort to explain. "I assure you, my coming to Lady Lavinia's rescue was entirely innocent. I simply wanted to help."

"Help yourself, you mean," Lady Prior said, raising her voice and picking up steam all over again. "You saw a beautiful, innocent young woman in a vulnerable position and you swooped in with your lust and depravity. I saw the way you were holding her." She pivoted toward the others. "It was a passionate embrace, I tell you. He was kissing my poor Lavinia's neck and trying to remove her gown."

"No!"

"I was not."

Armand and Lavinia protested at the same time. Armand glanced to his friends, appealing to their rationality and good sense.

But rather than jumping to his defense, Malcolm had his head together with Peter. The two of them wore amused, calculating grins as they discussed the situation behind their hands. Marigold Croydon had her arms crossed as she studied the scene with thoughtful eyes.

"We demand satisfaction," Lady Prior said when the silence had gone on too long.

"Satisfaction?" Armand blinked at her. "Who would you suggest I fight a duel with?"

"No, no." The impossible woman shook her head and clucked, as though Armand was being purposely difficult for not instantly understanding what in Hades she was talking about. "You've compromised Lavinia's honor," she explained with all the precision of an Oxford lecturer. "That means it's your responsibility to marry her in order to restore it."

Armand's eyes snapped wide and a chill ran down his

back. "Marry her?" He glanced to Lavinia, alarmed. Unfortunately, the poor woman didn't look remotely shocked by her mother's pronouncement. In fact, she drooped as though she'd been waiting for the suggestion to be made from the moment the confrontation started. When she lowered her head farther and gulped in a breath as though staving off a sob, twin shards of compassion and aggravation sliced at Armand's insides. On the one hand, he remembered how she had told him not two days ago how eager she was to build an independent life for herself. On the other, was he really such a horrible choice for a husband?

As soon as the thought hit him, he shook sense back into himself. "I'm not inclined to marry," he said, pulling himself to his full height. A tiny moan from Lavinia had him deflating again in a moment. "It's not you," he said in a soft voice, just for her. "It's just that…." He stopped himself from telling her he intended to be on a ship bound for India in two days' time. Instead, he said, "I've been married to my work as a physician all these years. I never considered matrimony. It isn't any reflection on your worth."

She glanced suddenly up at him as if he had, in fact, told her she wasn't worthy. Her lower lip wobbled and her eyes grew even more glassy. Armand let out a breath of defeat. Everything he said or did was wrong, just like the last several years of his life.

"I'm sorry," he began, "but—"

"I think you're going to have to marry her," Malcolm interrupted.

Armand froze, the muscles in his back clenching so fast and so hard that pain flared through him. He turned a furious glare on his friend.

Malcolm merely shrugged, his eyes dancing with mirth. "There's nothing for it," he went on. "You've compromised the woman's honor."

"Yes," Peter agreed, having a hard time not chuckling as he spoke. "It's a time-honored duty, after all, to marry a woman whose honor you've impinged on."

"But I haven't done anything," Armand argued, raising his voice in spite of the part of his mind that urged calm. "I was merely trying to help her get free of the rose bush."

"You have to marry her," Lady Prior said, as though declaring victory. "Even your friends say so." She treated those friends to a grateful smile.

"It isn't fair to Dr. Pearson," Lavinia appealed their audience. "If he doesn't want to be married, he shouldn't be forced into it. And neither should I," she added in a voice so small Armand wasn't sure if anyone other than him heard it.

"I think it's for the best, dearest," Marigold said, coming forward and sliding her arm around Lavinia's shoulder. She leaned closer and whispered something in Lavinia's ear. Lavinia's face pinched and crumpled, but then she let out a breath, her shoulders sank, and she nodded grimly, lowering her head.

Armand had the terrifying feeling his fate had just been sealed. "I don't think Lady Lavinia, or the rest of you, fully understand the situation," he said, jaw tight, staring directly at Malcolm. The man should know better after what they'd been talking about not an hour earlier. He was leaving England. He was abandoning his title and lands immediately. Malcolm knew that.

Then again, Malcolm *knew* that. He likely also knew what it would take to change Armand's mind, even if by force.

"Are you going to explain the situation to her?" Malcolm asked, daring Armand to confess all.

Armand refused to let his wily friend cow him. "Yes," he said. "Yes, I will." He turned to Lavinia, offering his arm. "Lady Lavinia, would you be so kind as to accompany me out of the maze so that we may discuss this matter?"

Lavinia swallowed. She pulled away from Marigold and made a weak attempt to square her shoulders and face him. Her eyes glistened with tears, and she nodded. "Yes." She took his arm.

Armand felt terrible for her as he escorted her away from the onlookers in the center of the maze. Behind them, he heard Lady Prior squeal with delight and Alex say, "Search the maze for signs of Miller. If you find him, flay him alive."

"I wouldn't want to be Dr. Miller," Armand said, attempting humor in a situation where there was none. At least, not to him.

"I expect you frightened him off long before the others came along," Lavinia said, her words filled with exhaustion. She glanced up at him as they turned a corner in the maze, taking the easy path that would dump them out at the far end of the hedges. "Thank you, by the way. I don't think I was given the chance to say that."

Armand answered with a wordless hum of acceptance. The two of them were silent as they made a few more turns, then followed a long corridor out into the open. The moon was rising over the hills as they walked into a clearing far enough from the maze that he would see anyone who attempted to come after them to eavesdrop. The breeze had picked up, fluttering the torn pits of Lavinia's gown. She shivered, rubbing her arms. Armand hesitated, knowing every move he made would be judged, but gallantry won out. He unbuttoned his coat, removed it, and settled it around Lavinia's shoulders.

"I know you don't want me," she blurted all at once. "I know that this was all a wicked, wicked plot of my mother's. She's been trying to marry me off to a gentleman for years now. I'm so ashamed that her plots have actually borne fruit. But I promise I'll be a good wife to you."

Armand was so stunned by her outburst that even though his mouth dropped open, no words came out.

"I won't get in your way," she went on, sniffling and wiping at her eyes with the sleeve of his jacket. "I can manage your house and represent you well in society. And I'll give you children, if that's what you want." Her voice nearly disappeared at the suggestion, and he could see the flash of fear in her eyes. "We may have been pressured into this, but I won't let you down." Without further ado, she burst into tears.

"Don't cry," Armand said, his heart squeezing and adding to the pain in his head and his back. He felt as lame and useless as a ship without a rudder. He couldn't bloody well stand there and let the poor woman weep, but if he followed his instinct and took her into his arms to comfort her, it would be the nail in their mutual coffin. "I know that you had no part in setting this up, if that makes you feel better."

She glanced pitifully at him. "You do?"

He nodded.

"That does make me feel a bit better. I would hate for you to go forward believing I'd deceived you." She took a quick breath, then rushed on with, "I promise you that I'll never lie to you. I'm not like my mother that way. I believe in honesty in all things. I swear I won't become manipulative like she is."

A stab of guilt piled on top of the morass of emotions Armand wrestled with. She deserved the same promises she was making to him. She deserved to know about his plans for India. Perhaps he could reply to Dr. Maqsood, beg him to delay sailing, or to allow him to sail to Lahore on his own in a few months. He could marry Lavinia, get her settled at Broadclyft Hall and…and what? Abandon her along with his title, estate, and other responsibilities? Walk out on her when she most needed a friend? It would be better for him to jilt her now…and ruin any chance she might have for another offer of marriage, if the story of the two of them being caught together made it past the grounds of Winterberry Park. And with so many spectators, that was a distinct possibility. Lavinia had told him she longed to be independent, but he doubted the isolated life of a fallen woman was what she'd had in mind.

At long last, he dropped his shoulders and let out a heavy sigh. Her mother had sprung the trap with devastating efficiency. "We're not going to be able to wiggle out of this, are we?" he asked.

Lavinia lowered her head and shook it. "This is what my mother has been waiting years for. She's not going to let it go."

"And I have the sinking suspicion my dear friends are keen on the match as well."

She sniffled, wiped her nose, and tilted her head to the side. "As Marigold said, it makes perfect sense. We are close friends, you have been friends with her husband for decades. It completes the set, so to speak."

"Is that what Mrs. Croydon whispered to you?" Armand asked, one brow raised. Lavinia nodded. "Are we a tea service, then?" She wrinkled her brow in confusion. "A matched set? And now all the pieces have been assembled?"

A wry twist pulled at the corner of Lavinia's soft lips. "I feel rather like a shattered sugar bowl at the moment."

He didn't know why, but something about the comment and her attempt to make light of things pierced Armand's heart. Risks be damned, if he was going to have to marry the woman anyhow, the least he could do was provide some comfort for her. He stepped toward her, taking her into his arms and rubbing her back bracingly, to give her strength.

"We'll muddle through," he said with a resigned sigh.

She leaned her weight into him and let out a breath as she rested her head on his shoulder. A flash of fear and protectiveness zipped through him. He knew she wasn't happy with the situation, and yet she trusted him enough to turn to him for support, physically if nothing else. Given how Miller had behaved toward her, she should have been shrinking from him in terror. Perhaps marrying her wouldn't be so bad after all.

"That's an encouraging sight." Malcolm's comment—a little too much glee in his tone for Armand's liking—pushed them apart. Lavinia gasped and took a step back, seeming to shrink into Armand's coat as the party of his friends and Lady Prior approached them from the edge of the maze. "So, we can send off for a special license right away then?" Malcolm went on. He elbowed Peter in the ribs as though the two were fifteen years old and sharing a bad joke.

"Oh, this is glorious," Lady Prior gushed, speeding forward to hug her daughter. "I knew this house party would be our opportunity. I just knew it."

"Mama, please," Lavinia muttered.

"We shall get started with wedding plans immediately," she said, looping an arm around Lavinia's waist and steering her back toward the house.

Armand opened his mouth to stop them and ask for his coat back but thought better of it. He sighed and ran a hand through his hair instead.

"Katya will be happy to hear of all this," Marigold said, flanking Lavinia's other side, along with Mariah, as they headed back to the house.

"Lady Stanhope," Lady Prior snorted. "She's probably inside, flinging herself at men half her age."

"She probably is," Malcolm grumbled as the ladies turned a corner and disappeared into the dimming twilight.

Peter came up behind Armand and thumped him on the back. "So you won't be able to flee the country after all," he said with a smile. "There's nothing like marriage to teach a man where his true responsibilities lie."

"I'm not defeated yet," Armand muttered, starting back toward the house. Malcolm and Peter walked on either side. Armand glanced around and said, "I suppose Alex went hunting for Miller?"

"Miller and Gilbert Phillips," Peter answered.

"Why Phillips?" Armand asked.

"To give him an extra task tomorrow," Malcolm said, grinning impishly. When Armand raised a questioning brow at him, he went on with, "Phillips was already slated to take our letter outlining the plan for the new parliamentary session in November to Gladstone. Seems that now Alex wants to task him with picking up a special license for you while he's in town."

Armand nearly tripped over his feet. "You weren't joking, then?"

Malcolm assumed an air of mock seriousness. "I never joke about matrimony."

Peter laughed. "Might as well get it over with sooner rather than later, eh?" He thumped Armand's back again. "You'll like being married to a younger woman. It's amazing what it does for your vitality and outlook on life."

Armand narrowed his eyes at his friend. He suspected that *vitality* was the reason Peter was now expecting his second child within eighteen months of marrying Mariah. Something told him Lavinia wouldn't be quite so biddable in bed. Although if she was….

"I love it when plans come together," Malcolm cut short his thoughts. His friend was in far too good a mood. Katya had better watch her back. "Armand here is about to discover the joys of married life and Parliament is shaping up to plan. Once that letter gets into Gladstone's hands and he approves of our plan of action, we'll have Shayles and his lot running for their lives."

"It's hard to say which of those two things is more important," Peter said. "Love or politics."

"Tricks, you mean, not love. Love is a long way off," Armand mumbled. He just hoped his friends hadn't maneuvered him into the biggest mistake of his and Lavinia Prior's lives.

CHAPTER 5

It was over. Everything Lavinia had hoped her life would become was ruined. As ruined as the basket of fractured pieces of porcelain that sat on the folding table in the center of her circle of friends. Two gloomy days after the ball, the skies had opened up with rain—which seemed all too poetic, given the circumstances—so rather than strolling through the gardens or running pointless errands into the village, Marigold had all of her female guests scattered throughout the morning room, working on various craft projects. Her footmen had erected temporary workstations by setting folding tables between the clusters of sofas and chairs that usually decorated the room. Lavinia was supposed to be constructing a mosaic tile using the bits of shatter plates and teacups, but it seemed like a pointless exercise when there was no way she could piece her dreams back together.

"There," Bianca Marlowe sighed, holding up the disc of plaster onto which she'd glued dozens of porcelain bits. "Don't ask me what it is or what it's good for. I've fulfilled my social obligations." She plunked her creation carelessly on the table and turned to her mother. "Now may I go to the library to read?"

Lady Stanhope arched one of her dark, razor-sharp brows at her eldest daughter. "My dear, you have a great deal more to learn about manners before I turn you loose on the world."

Lavinia would have spontaneously combusted and ended up as a pile of ash if Lady Stanhope were her mother and had looked at her with such censure, but Bianca merely huffed again and flopped against the back of the sofa where she sat beside her mother and sister.

Natalia, Lady Stanhope's younger daughter, held up the plaster square she was working on and, in a sickeningly sweet voice said, "Look at mine, Mama. *I* know how to participate politely." Although the fact that she stuck her tongue out at her sister didn't help her argument.

Lady Stanhope rolled her eyes and shook her head. "Pray that you only have boys," she said to Mariah, who sat across the table from Lady Stanhope, flanked by Marigold and Lavinia. "Girls are far too difficult when they reach that delicate age." She turned her narrowed eyes on Bianca.

"I'm nearly eighteen," Bianca said, tilting her chin up. "I'm not delicate at all."

"You said it," Natalia muttered.

Bianca glared at her sister with a look that made her appear strikingly like her mother. She reached for the pot of paste she'd been using, grabbing the brush and flicking it in Natalia's direction. Natalia shrieked loud enough to distract everyone in the room as thick, white goo covered her face and bodice. "Mama," she shouted, then growled at Bianca, "I'll murder you."

"Stop it this instant," Lady Stanhope shouted, grabbing

each of her daughters by their wrists as they rose, looking like they would come to blows. "Honestly," she hissed. "Don't make me regret inflicting the two of you on Mrs. Croydon and her party."

To their credit, both Marlowe girls looked instantly contrite. "Sorry, Mama," they muttered, almost in unison.

Lady Stanhope pursed her lips as she glanced between the two of them. She turned to Bianca and said, "Take your sister up to your room and help her clean up."

"Yes, Mama," Bianca said. She jerked her head toward the door, gesturing for Natalia to follow her.

As soon as the two young women had left the room, Lady Stanhope groaned and rubbed her temples. "If Robert hadn't already been in his grave for fifteen years, I'd murder him for inflicting those two on me."

"She doesn't mean that," Mariah said, her lips twitching with amusement.

"I don't mean it," Lady Stanhope agreed, dropping her hands to her lap. Her eyes narrowed. "Except when I do." She shook her head again. "I can't decide if it's worse when they're at each other's throats or when they're up to no good, plotting against the world as though they were the Furies."

"You're in luck, then," Marigold said. "There were three Furies, not two."

Lady Stanhope made a strangled sound as she reached for the basket of porcelain shards. "It's terrifying to think, though, that when I was Bianca's age, I was on the verge of marrying Robert."

Lavinia's spirits sank all over again at the mention of the "M" word.

"I can't imagine entering a marriage at that age," Marigold said, gluing a final bit onto her mosaic, then sitting back. "You can't have wanted to marry that young."

Lady Stanhope shrugged. "I had no choice in the matter. My parents arranged everything." She gave up searching through the basket with an irritated huff. "It didn't help matters that I was with child before my nineteenth birthday."

Lavinia let out a lamenting squeak before she could stop herself. She'd barely let herself think of babies, even though she'd told Dr. Pearson she'd give him children if he wanted them. But she could be a mother by the same time next year.

"There, there." Lady Stanhope rose from her sofa and shifted to sit beside Lavinia on hers. "Everything turned out right in the end for me, more or less, and it will for you as well."

Lavinia turned mournful, doubting eyes to Lady Stanhope. "Everything is ruined."

Marigold and Mariah exchanged knowing looks before Marigold said, "What is ruined, dearest?"

Lavinia felt like an ungrateful child who had been handed a luxurious, marzipan tart when all she wanted was a common sweet bun. She owed it to her friends to explain, even though they were likely to laugh at her. "I wanted to be a modern, independent woman. Instead, I'm about to marry a man nearly twice my age whom I barely know."

"You're about to marry an exceptionally kind viscount who I would trust with my life," Marigold corrected her, putting down her mosaic. "I have trusted him with my life."

Lavinia felt more like a heel than ever. But the bitterness had entered her soul and wouldn't be so easily rooted out, so she said, "You sound like my mother."

"Dear, no one sounds like your mother but your mother," Lady Stanhope said with an arch of her brow. "At least now you'll be free of her."

"Yes," Mariah added. "And wasn't that the point of this entire house party?"

"I thought the point of the house party was so that your husbands could plot and mold the incoming government," Lavinia said, refusing to be comforted.

"It is," Lady Stanhope said. "And soon you can say your husband has a hand in the new order of things too."

Lavinia fixed Lady Stanhope with a flat look. She wasn't amused by the comment, and yet as morose as her soul felt over the whole thing, a spark of excitement flared at the idea that she would be included in the innermost circle.

"If independence is your aim," Mariah went on, the only one of them still working on her mosaic as she spoke, "then you're far more likely to achieve true independence as the wife of an influential man."

"She speaks the truth," Marigold agreed, pulling the basket of broken pieces toward her. "Single women are like children in the eyes of society."

"And besides," Lady Stanhope said, rubbing Lavinia's back. "Armand has been studying medicine and anatomy for years, including female anatomy. I'm quite certain that he knows enough of the workings of things to have you crying out in ecstasy for divine intervention once he beds you."

Mortified by the suggestion, Lavinia buried her hot face in her hands and groaned.

"Oh, come now. You're too old to be cowed by such things," Lady Stanhope went on. She paused, then said, "But come to me for advice on your wedding night instead of going to your mother. She'll have you terrified. I'll share a few tricks that will have Armand cursing himself for not dropping to one knee and proposing the first time he met you."

"Is it the thing with the…you know?" Marigold asked. Lavinia peeked through her fingers in time to see Marigold make a swirling motion with her fingers.

"Sweeting, that technique is amateur compared to what I have in mind," Lady Stanhope answered.

"Ooh! Do tell." Mariah put down her mosaic at last and scooted closer to Lady Stanhope, her eyes alight with mischief and excitement.

"Well," Lady Stanhope leaned in, eyes sparkling with wickedness. "If you reach back—" she made a cupping gesture with one hand "—and grab hold right when he's—"

"Stop." Lavinia stood abruptly, covering her ears. "I can't hear this right now."

Lady Stanhope straightened, grinning. "Believe me, if you're open to experimentation, your married life will benefit."

"I never asked for a married life at all," Lavinia insisted. "I'm not prepared for this, and you're giving me advice on how to please a man I hardly know in intimate ways?"

"Dearest, I know it seems difficult now, but I can assure you that you will appreciate Katya's advice on these things," Marigold insisted, reaching for Lavinia's hand. "Intimacy of every sort is vital to a marriage."

"I. Don't. Know. Him," Lavinia snapped out each word. In a funny way, it was easier to feel angry about the situation than it was to nurture the sharp fear that had lived in her gut during the three days since the debacle in the maze.

"She does have a point," Mariah said, coming to Lavinia's defense in a way that made her want to weep with relief. "We all know Armand well, but to Lavinia, he's a complete unknown."

"But he is a good man," Marigold insisted. "I honestly believe you're in the best of hands. Otherwise, I would have fought against this union tooth and nail."

"And I'm only teasing you about bedsport because it galls me more than anything to see young ladies going into marriage with an ingrained fear of it," Lady Stanhope assured her. "It aggravates me to no end that sexuality in women is all but erased these days instead of embraced. Why, if we educated young girls as we should, they would be comfortable with—"

"I'm sorry, Lady Stanhope, but I don't want to hear this right now," Lavinia said, breaking away from the attempted comfort of her friends. "I know that this is something you care deeply about, and perhaps some other time you can educate me until your heart's content. But not now."

She marched away from her friends, feeling miserable for being rude to them, sick because of everything that was happening to her, and lost because she had no control over it. Her friends were probably right about everything—about Dr. Pearson's character, about the independence marriage could bring, and about the pleasures of the marriage bed. But Lavinia hadn't asked for any of it. It didn't matter how beautiful or pleasurable the cage was, it was still a cage.

If it hadn't been raining, she would have fled outdoors, losing herself in the garden or the woods that stood on the far edge of Winterberry Park. As it was, she was forced to stomp through the halls to work off the excess energy of her anger and heartache. She didn't know the house well, but at least it was large enough for her to stretch her legs and feel the thump of her heart against her ribs as she pushed on and on.

She walked to the far end of the house and was about to turn and march back to the other when the sound of male voices stopped her.

"There's just so much to do," Mr. Croydon seemed to be in the middle of lamenting. "The world is changing so quickly, and if Gladstone wants us to keep pace with that, he'll have to agree to the course laid out in our letter."

"But we won't know what he thinks of it until we receive a reply," Lord Dunsford said.

"We should have had a reply by now," Lord Malcolm seemed to cut in to whatever else Lord Dunsford was about to say. "Two days was plenty of time for Phillips to take the train into London, deliver the letter, receive a reply, and get back here."

"He has to obtain a special license as well," Dr. Pearson added in a low grumble, sending tingles through Lavinia's limbs that made her hands and feet go numb. He didn't sound any happier about their union than she felt.

"I haven't heard anything from Phillips," Mr. Croydon said. "Which is unusual. He generally telegraphs if there's any sort of trouble."

"He hasn't telegraphed, so we have to assume the delay is on Gladstone's end," Lord Dunsford went on. "So while we wait, we need to be sure we have all our soldiers in order."

"You and your military metaphors," Lord Malcolm said, though he sounded amused.

"We're waging war," Lord Dunsford went on. "War against outdated ideas, war to make the world a better place for the women we love."

"And like any good war, the tactics we use and the strategies we employ are key," Mr. Croydon said.

"Which is why we have to take out Shayles first and foremost," Lord Malcolm said.

The others made various noises of agreement and impatience. Lavinia inched closer to the door, wondering what expressions they wore or why Lord Shayles was so important.

"While I agree that Shayles has got to go," Mr. Croydon began, "Gladstone will tell us how far we—"

He stopped, and Lavinia realized a fraction of a second too late that it was because she'd stepped too close to the doorway. She could see all of the men now. The room was some sort of masculine sitting room and smoke filled the air from the pipes Lord Dunsford and Lord Malcolm were smoking. Mr. Croydon appeared to be pacing in the middle of the room, while Dr. Pearson leaned against the frame of a window at the opposite end of the room, glancing sullenly out at the pouring rain. Of course, if she could see all of them, they could all see her.

"Lady Lavinia, is there something we can help you with?" Mr. Croydon addressed her.

Caught without a clue about what to say or do to explain herself, all Lavinia could do was step into the room, twisting her hands together in front of her. "I…I was just passing by, and I thought your conversation was interesting," she said, feeling small.

Dr. Pearson pushed away from the window and marched toward her. "We're just discussing politics," he said. "I'm sure you wouldn't be interested."

"On the contrary," Lavinia said, taking another bold step into the room. "I have been following the work Mr. Croydon has been doing in the House of Commons closely these last few years. Although, I agree that you will have an uphill climb to pass the reforms to the rights of women that you wish to pass."

All four of the men blinked at her. Lavinia only cared about the surprise in Dr. Pearson's eyes. He watched her as though he had no idea who she was, which wouldn't have bothered her, except that he was her fiancé. Lady Stanhope's hints and gestures and mischievous smile came back to her. Good lord, she would have to go to bed with this man. She would have to spend the rest of her life with him.

Her nerves bristled, and before any of the men could speak, she blundered on with, "You'll probably have to extend the franchise before you grant more rights to women.

And deal with Irish Home Rule. But if you give more working men the right to vote, chances are you will secure Liberal control of Parliament for years to come, which will enable you to concentrate on less popular but equally necessary reforms." She blinked, noticing that the men were even more astonished now than when she'd opened her stupid mouth. She clasped her hands together so tightly her knuckles went white and lowered her head. "Or…not."

A thick silence filled the air along with the smoke from Lord Dunsford and Lord Malcolm's pipes. Lavinia began to tremble. She was afraid to look at Dr. Pearson, afraid to see what her soon-to-be, stranger of a husband must think of her impertinence.

"You know, she has a point," Lord Dunsford said at last.

Lavinia glanced up as the other men turned to Lord Dunsford. At least Dr. Pearson didn't seem angry with her.

"Extending the franchise is a far easier goal than securing the rights of women," Lord Dunsford went on. He shrugged and gestured with his pipe. "Not that I'm suggesting we scale down our efforts to pass the women's right's bill in the least, but perhaps a two-pronged attack of progressive legislation will leave Disraeli and his lot, including Shayles, fighting a battle on too many fronts to mount an effective defense."

"I'm not giving up my efforts to see Shayles hung, drawn, and quartered," Lord Malcolm said.

"You won't have to." Mr. Croydon resumed his pacing. "In fact, there may be a way to come at him specifically from more than one angle."

Lavinia slowly let out a breath as the shock of her entry subsided. She would have expected the gentlemen to see her as far more of an unwelcome intrusion, but they continued on as if she weren't there. No, that wasn't it. Rather, they continued as if she were a part of the group.

"Gladstone wants the Irish question sorted," Mr. Croydon

went on, "but it has the potential to consume everything else if brought to the fore."

Dr. Pearson continued his journey across the room to Lavinia as though he didn't care at all about Irish Home Rule. "Is there something you need?" he asked in a quiet voice, coming so close to her that Lavinia swore she could feel his heat, as the others continued their debate.

Lavinia shook her head tightly. "I had to get up and move around."

He hummed, arching a brow. "I know the feeling." His mouth pulled into a wry smile. That mouth would have every right to kiss hers whenever he wanted soon.

Lavinia's knees wobbled, and her insides felt odd. She couldn't think of a thing to say in reply. But as it happened, she didn't have to. A brief commotion in the hall was followed by the study's door flying fully open as Mr. Phillips and her mother burst in on them.

"This is fortuitous," her mother said, clapping her hands together. "The two of you, here together." She smiled from Lavinia to Dr. Pearson and back again. "Mr. Phillips has returned from London."

Lavinia's throat constricted and her heart raced. "Mr. Phillips?"

Mr. Croydon's man of business marched straight past her, handing Dr. Pearson an envelope before moving on to Mr. Croydon. "Did you receive my telegram, sir?" he asked, looking as grave as if someone had died. "Only, I was surprised when you didn't answer immediately."

Mr. Croydon and the others were instantly on the alert. "No. We received nothing. Has something happened? Do you have a reply from Gladstone?"

Mr. Phillips raked a hand through his ginger hair, looking as though he were about to be led to the gallows. "Your letter went missing, sir," he said.

Lavinia wasn't entirely certain what he meant, but anxiety pooled in her gut all the same. Lord Dunsford and Lord Malcolm leapt to their feet, setting their pipes aside. The only one in the room who didn't appear deeply alarmed was Lavinia's mother.

"Missing?" Mr. Croydon asked. "What do you mean?"

"I had the letter when I left Winterberry Park, obviously," Mr. Phillips said. "But when I arrived in London, it was gone."

"Gone?" Lord Malcolm demanded, glowering so ferociously that Lavinia shrank away from him. Dr. Pearson edged closer to her, as if protecting her.

Mr. Phillips let out a wary breath. "I'm sorry, sir. I searched everywhere for it. Dr. Miller helped me search the train car as well."

"Dr. Miller?" Mr. Croydon asked, his eyes narrowing and his voice hoarse with loathing.

"I know it wasn't ideal," Mr. Phillips went on. "But I figured any help would do. As near as I can figure, the letter must have fallen out of my case when I switched trains in Reading."

"If that letter falls into the wrong hands, if the opposition learns what we're planning or, God forbid, the press gets hold of it, we're doomed," Lord Dunsford said.

"It's not as though the letter contained treason," Lord Malcolm said, shaking his head as though his friend were overreacting.

"No?" Mr. Croydon stared at Lord Malcolm as though he were daft. "The letter is a point-by-point outline for the new government's policies and instructions on how to best implement them. It proposes ways to bypass standard parliamentary procedure in a way that renders election results pointless."

"It merely contains suggestions," Lord Malcolm argued.

"It's a blueprint for corruption," Mr. Croydon insisted.

"I knew it was a bad idea to put our plans in writing," Lord Dunsford said. "In the wrong hands, this could cast a shadow of corruption over our government before it's begun. It could lead to Gladstone's very first vote being a vote of no confidence."

"Oh? Really?" Lavinia's mother said as though she were watching a play. "How exciting."

"Mama," Lavinia hissed in an attempt to silence her. Her heart bled for her friends' husbands. It seemed as though they were in real trouble.

"With any luck, the letter has already been soaked and crushed and relegated to the rubbish bin," Lord Dunsford said, though his expression was still alarmed. "Did you have a chance to speak to Gladstone about its contents?" he asked Mr. Phillips.

"I did," Mr. Phillips said. "I telegraphed right away, as soon as I reached Paddington, then headed straight to Gladstone's house. He is aware of the situation."

Mr. Croydon must have seen what Lavinia could plainly see, that Mr. Phillips was eating himself up inside with guilt over what had happened. "It's all right, Gilbert," he said, moving to clap Mr. Phillips on the back. "I know you would never be deliberately careless."

"Which is why something feels wrong in this whole thing," Dr. Pearson said. He spoke quietly, and Lavinia wasn't sure if the others heard him.

"I was able to obtain the special license for Dr. Pearson, though," Mr. Phillips went on, nodding to the envelope in Dr. Pearson's hand.

"Which is all that mattered," Lavinia's mother said with a cheerful sigh. "You gentlemen can sort out your political knots later, but we have a wedding to see through now."

"Now?" Lavinia gaped at her mother.

Her mother stared right back, as though Lavinia were the one being unreasonable. "Yes, of course now. I've had the local vicar on notice since the morning after the ball." She turned to Dr. Pearson. "He's ready to perform the ceremony immediately."

CHAPTER 6

Armand was in the process of opening the letter Phillips had handed to him, but when Lady Prior spoke, his finger slipped on the edge of paper he was tearing, causing a short, painful cut. "I beg your pardon," he said, blinking at the incomprehensible woman.

"Rev. Fallon is ready to perform the wedding immediately," Lady Prior repeated, adding a self-satisfied giggle at the end.

Armand glanced to Lavinia, his nerves bristling. But rather than finding a hoped-for expression of outrage and a determination to put a stop to things, Lavinia's initial expression of shock was fading quickly into morose acceptance.

She met his questioning gaze with a barely perceptible shrug. "When Mama sets her mind to something, it is impossible to get her to budge an inch."

A swell of irritation turned Armand's stomach. Shades of that moment he'd been told he was a viscount and his medical practice as he knew it was over gripped him once again. "Marriage is not something to be entered into lightly," he said, trying to quell his anger by focusing on Lavinia alone and reminding himself she was as much a victim as he was. "Rev. Fallon will say as much when he performs the ceremony."

"You can't get out of things now, Lord Helm," Lady Prior scolded him, using the title he hated.

"Might as well get it over with," Malcolm said with a sly wink.

"Don't worry, you won't have to stand up alone," Peter added.

Armand glared at his friends. The only glimmer of hope and help in the room came from Alex. "Our letter to Gladstone has gone missing and the telegram you send informing me of the fact never arrived?" he said to Phillips. "Something is terribly wrong here."

"Yes," Armand agreed. "We should get to the bottom of this foul play instead of worrying about weddings."

"But if you take an hour to relocate to the church so that the ceremony will be performed, you will have one less thing to worry about," Lady Prior argued. She stepped toward the door, gesturing for Lavinia and him to follow. "Come along."

Armand didn't move. "It's most likely that Miller had something to do with the letter's disappearance." He tried in vain to focus the room on what really mattered.

"I half suspected as well," Phillips said, clearly suffering with responsibility for everything that had gone wrong. "I attempted to search his belongings, but I found nothing. And once we reached London, he vanished before I could question him further."

"Miller is certainly involved then," Alex said in a menacing voice.

"Yes, well, Dr. Miller is not present," Lady Prior said, growing annoyed. "Mr. Phillips has brought your special license, and Rev. Fallon is waiting. Hurry along."

"Mama, please," Lavinia hissed, marching to her mother's

side. "The gentlemen have matters of vital importance to deal with. This is no time to push your plots."

"My plots?" Lady Prior burst with indignation. "Lavinia, do you not remember the way this horrid man desecrated your honor not three days ago?"

"My honor was not—"

"Are you willing to stand by and let the scoundrel get away with debauchery?"

"It was a misunderstanding. No one was—"

"Justice must be served, and it must be served immediately."

"Mama, please stop." Lavinia seemed near tears.

Armand sighed. He was cornered, captured, and conquered. The least he could do was to make things easier for his bride.

"Very well," he said, sending a preemptive glare in Malcolm's direction. Sure enough, his friend was grinning shamelessly over the scene. Armand crossed to Lavinia, offering his arm with an apologetic look. "Since your mother appears unwilling to give you a moment's peace until we stand before the vicar, let's get it over with."

"How romantic," Malcolm muttered behind him.

It wasn't romantic, not in the least. Ladies as young and sweet as Lavinia deserved romance and sentiment in their marriages. He had barely begun, and already he was failing miserably. Worse still, Lavinia seemed resigned to her fate, and not in a contented way. She took his arm without looking at him and let him lead her into the hall, following her giddy mother as she practically sprinted for the front hall and the door.

"I'm sorry," he said when her mother skipped far enough ahead of them not to hear.

"No, I'm sorry," Lavinia answered in a hollow voice. "I'll never forgive her."

The comment stirred something completely unexpected in Armand's chest. He was reminded of the brilliant ease with which she'd commented on their political machinations minutes ago, before things fell apart. Lavinia seemed so young and innocent by outward appearances. She was demure and perfectly behaved. But a few times now, Armand had seen flashes of something under the surface—backbone, intelligence, cleverness. Though everything else was out of his control, at least he might have the pleasure of discovering who his bride really was.

Word spread through the house like a flood that the wedding was about to take place. Though Lady Prior was so eager to see the thing done that she refused to let Lavinia escape to her room to change into a fancier gown, by the time they made it halfway down the path that led to the road into town, Marigold, Mariah, and Katya, Katya's daughters, Rupert, and little James Croydon with his nursemaid caught up with them. As they reached the road, Marigold's maid, Anne, sprinted to meet them with a bouquet of orange and gold flowers. They made such a scene walking into town that several of the people whom they passed on the road dropped what they were doing to follow.

By the time they reached the small parish church, a trail of two dozen people stretched behind them. As Armand suspected, Rev. Fallon wasn't quite as ready to perform a wedding as Lady Prior had led them to believe. He was, in fact, up to his elbows in soil as he worked in the vicarage vegetable patch. His twin toddlers rolled around in the mud with him while his tall and decidedly pregnant wife hung the washing on a line nearby.

Rev. Fallon flinched at the sight of the mob that had invaded his lawn and pushed himself to his feet. "Good gracious, what's all this?"

Lady Prior charged to the front of the pack before

Armand could open his mouth to apologize. "We are ready for you to perform the wedding, Rev. Fallon."

Rev. Fallon blinked, glancing from Lady Prior to Armand and Lavinia, and then to his wife. "When you said to be ready to perform the ceremony on a moment's notice, I had no idea you meant *a moment's notice*."

"What else would you think I meant?" Lady Prior asked as though he were an idiot.

Armand clenched his jaw. Was there no end to the woman's rudeness? He cleared his throat and addressed Rev. Fallon directly. "If it is too much trouble for you to throw together a marriage ceremony without preparation, we understand."

To Armand's disappointment, the man shook his head, still baffled, and said, "No, no. The particulars of the marriage ceremony are fairly standard." He glanced to Lady Prior. "You said something about there being a special license?"

Armand held out the envelope that he still hadn't fully opened. As Rev. Fallon took it, Armand, yet again, glanced toward Lavinia apologetically. She returned his look with a tiny shrug of her shoulders and an attempt at a smile.

Rev. Fallon opened the envelope and took out the certificate it contained. He glanced over it quickly, his brow shooting up. "Surprisingly, this is all in order, down to the parish and the priest. Well done, whoever obtained this."

Of all the ways Gilbert Phillips could have sought to prove that he was, in fact, highly competent, in spite of losing their letter to Gladstone, it had to be this.

"Move along, then," Lady Prior said, shooing Rev. Fallon toward his church.

It was ridiculous. The whole thing was a farce. Lady Prior barely gave Rev. Fallon time to wash his hands and don his vestments. Mrs. Fallon rushed to help him prepare, but that meant she had to bring their twins into the church so that someone could mind them. The twins weren't happy about leaving their sunshine and mud, and cried during the entire thing. It didn't help that Malcolm and Peter whispered back and forth throughout the entire ceremony, making jokes at Armand's expense. In fact, the only time when the church fell completely silent was when Rev. Fallon asked if anyone knew of any impediment or reason why Armand and Lavinia shouldn't be married. Not a soul said a word.

"Do you, Armand Nathaniel Pearson, Lord Helm, take this woman, Lavinia Charlotte Prior, to be your lawfully wedded wife?" Rev. Fallon asked at last.

Armand's gut roiled. How had he landed in this position, stripped of his medical practice and everything he loved, punished with a title he had no idea what to do with, and maneuvered into a marriage with a beautiful but hapless younger woman that he'd never asked for by a woman with ambitions that outstripped his own by far? The only thing that stopped him from calling an end to the entire thing and marching out of the church and straight down to Exeter to find Dr. Maqsood and beg him to depart for India immediately was the sudden fear and tender hope in Lavinia's eyes as she waited for his answer. He couldn't let her down. This wasn't her fault.

"I do," he said with as much strength as he could manage.

Malcolm and Peter did a terrible job of hiding their school-boy-worthy sounds of glee. Katya made a sound of disgust, and Armand caught her rolling her eyes at Malcolm out of the corner of his eye.

Rev. Fallon smiled benignly and went on. "And do you, Lavinia Charlotte Prior, take this man, Armand Nathaniel Pearson, to be your lawfully wedded husband?"

"I do," Lavinia answered, almost too softly to be heard. In fact, Rev. Fallon had to lean in and glance at her questioningly to make sure he heard. "I do," Lavinia repeated with a little more strength.

"Good." Rev. Fallon stood straight again, nodding. "Then by the power invested in me, I now pronounce you man and wife."

It happened so quickly that Lavinia barely believed it had happened at all. She floated through the wedding ceremony as though she were watching someone else's life from a distance. It certainly couldn't have been her life. She was meant to be a woman who stood on her own two feet, who devoted her life to her friends and to the causes she believed in, not a wife.

The full truth of the situation came home to her when Rev. Fallon attempted to omit the first kiss and to end the ceremony.

"No, no, no," her mother protested. "They must kiss to ensure the union is sealed properly."

Lavinia snuck a sideways peek up at Dr. Pearson, her husband. He returned the look with a wry grin and, if she wasn't mistaken, the slightest roll of his eyes. That ironic expression was all it took. A ghost of a laugh slipped out of her lungs, and with it, far more of the burden of misery she'd carried with her to the church than she would have expected. She might have been molded and twisted into the form of femininity that her mother approved of, she may have been manipulated into a marriage she didn't want to a man she barely knew, but now that she was married, her mother couldn't rule her anymore.

Dr. Pearson—she supposed she would have to get used to calling him Armand now—cleared his throat as she turned toward him. She did her best to meet his kiss bravely, tilting her head up to let him know she could bear it. To her surprise, his lips were soft on hers, and rather than feeling invaded and overrun, as she'd expected to, a thrill of promise swirled through her. It couldn't be all bad if his kiss made her feel like that, could it?

"At last," her mother breathed, far too loud to be anything but gauche. Lavinia jerked away from Armand, too angered by her mother's declaration of victory to enjoy the moment. "My dearest daughter, married at last. And to a viscount, no less." She added a squealing giggle to the end of her pronouncement and clapped her hands. "We must return to the house to celebrate."

Lavinia glanced once more to Armand with an apologetic knot in her gut that was becoming far too familiar to her. How could a man who had been forced into marriage ever be happy with his wife? She let him escort her back through the church and outside, knowing she had her work cut out for her.

Much to her mother's disappointment, once they reached Winterberry Park, Mr. Croydon refused to let the swollen crowd of curiosity-seekers who had attended the wedding stay to have a party. He and Mr. Phillips had chosen to stay behind in an attempt to mentally retrace Phillips's steps to figure out what happened to the letter to Gladstone. Both men were in a foul mood when the newlyweds returned. Lord Malcolm and Lord Dunsford seemed to put aside their high spirits and their teasing to focus on business, escorting Rupert Marlowe down the hall as though explaining the situation to him, and, unsurprisingly to Lavinia, Armand joined them.

"I'm probably the last person you want to waste your afternoon with anyhow," he told her with a wry, tired grin as they paused in the hallway.

Marigold and Lady Stanhope had taken James out to the back lawn, the Marlowe girls had run off into the garden, and Mariah had gone to the nursery to fetch little Peter so he could join them. Her mother was attempting to bully Mrs. Musgrave into putting together a wedding feast. Lavinia felt at loose ends.

"Go on," she said, trying to smile. "It's far more important for you to deal with business right now." She paused, then added. "I'm deeply concerned about this letter of yours. Did it contain anything that could be used against you or the Liberal Party?"

Armand sighed and ran a hand through his hair. "I must confess, I didn't see the final draft."

"You didn't?"

"I...I haven't been paying as close attention as perhaps I should." He shuffled his feet, making Lavinia wonder what was eating at his conscience. "I've had other things on my mind."

"Then go," she said, managing a smile at last. "We'll see each other again at supper."

He took her hand, raising her knuckles to his lips as a goodbye. A flutter hit her stomach at the sentimental gesture, and she turned to head out to the garden to join her friends, feeling as odd as though she'd slipped through Alice's looking glass.

She had barely seated herself in one of the wicker chairs out where the children were playing when her mother barged into their midst, grabbing Lavinia's wrist and attempting to wrench her out of the chair.

"What are you doing idling here?" her mother demanded. "You have much to do."

"Unhand her," Lady Stanhope stood and rounded on Lavinia's mother.

"I beg your pardon," her mother snapped, eyes wide.

"Lady Helm deserves far better than to be manhandled by a mere baroness." Lady Stanhope fixed her mother with a look so full of righteousness that it made the handsome angles of her face seem almost demonic.

Lavinia's mother gaped, her jaw flapping, speechless, for a change. It took Lavinia a few seconds more to realize that "Lady Helm" referred to her. "Good Lord," she gasped as it hit her. She outranked her mother by a great deal now.

"I'm simply attempting to guide my daughter through her new duties," her mother finally managed to say. She turned to Lavinia. "You need to direct a maid to gather and pack your things and to move you from your current room into Lord Helm's room."

"Good Lord," Lavinia exclaimed again, her eyes growing rounder. Was that what Armand expected of her?

"There's no need to worry," Marigold intervened, pausing in her play with James. "As it happens, Lavinia's room is only two doors down from Armand's. She can keep her things right where they are and use her current room as a dressing room."

Lavinia stared hard at her friend. Armand was just two doors down from her? That seemed highly irregular for a house party. Almost as though her friend had hoped something would happen. She'd walked into a larger trap than she'd thought.

"I think I need to lie down," she said, rising. She started for the house, but her mother stopped her.

"We have important matters that need to be discussed," she said, fixing Lavinia with a peculiar look. "Matters of an intimate nature."

Lavinia winced, the headache she was about to fake coming on for real.

"Perhaps there are better people present to have that particular conversation with the viscountess," Lady Stanhope said, her lips curling into a wicked grin.

"Do you mean a harlot who has opened her legs for more

men than even Her Majesty's Exchequer can count?" Lavinia's mother snapped.

Marigold clapped her hands over James's ears and cleared her throat, staring angrily at both women in turn.

"Better that than to receive a horrific miseducation from a woman whose fruit has withered and died on the vine," Lady Stanhope fired back.

Lavinia's mother shrieked in offense. "Why you vile, disease-riddled, barely better than a common—"

"Say it," Lady Stanhope dared her, crossing her arms and grinning as though she'd scored game-winning points.

Lavinia's mother pressed her lips together, her round, red face and her high-pitched hum making her look and sound like a kettle about to boil. At last, she squeaked, "Whore."

"I'm leaving," Lavinia burst, turning and fleeing before anyone else could stop her or use her as a pawn in their own wars and nonsense.

She'd made it back into the house before realizing Mariah had come with her, little Peter in her arms. "This hasn't been the best of days for you, has it?" she asked.

"No," Lavinia sighed, turning a corner to mount the stairs that led to the hall where her—and Armand's—room was.

"Well, allow me to help you by saying this much," Mariah went on, reaching Lavinia's side. Her lips twitched slightly, and she rushed on with, "Men are turgid and women are viscous, and if you let it, the marriage bed can be the greatest adventure of your life."

Lavinia paused on the landing to stare at her friend, utterly baffled. "I beg your pardon?"

Mariah giggled, her cheeks going pink. "It's what my mother told me before my wedding," she said as they continued up the next flight of stairs at a slower pace. "She described the male member as 'turgid' and the corresponding female parts as 'viscous' when advising me what to expect on my wedding night."

Lavinia blinked rapidly. "Well, that's...certainly...interesting." They reached the hall and continued on toward Lavinia's room. She shook off her bafflement at the description of marital relations and said, "Elaine has been writing to me all summer long with shockingly explicit details of how much she enjoys married life. She's rather prone to indiscretion, I'm afraid."

"Is she?" Mariah laughed. "I only met her briefly on a few occasions, but I can certainly see how that would be true."

"So none of you need fear that I am completely ignorant about how a man and a woman make love." She paused in front of the door to her room, her cheeks flaring hot. "I'm going to have a difficult time looking Lord Waltham in the eye next time I see them."

"At least someone has been honest with you about things," Mariah said, shifting her baby in her arms.

Lavinia shook her head. "Knowledge is one thing. Knowing how to apply it to a situation in which you are expected to do—" she swallowed, "—those things with a man you barely know, a man who likely resents the way in which you ended up in his bed in the first place…."

Mariah rested a hand on Lavinia's shoulder. "I'm sure if you asked, Armand would put off consummating the marriage."

"What's the point?" Lavinia sighed. "If my mother suspects everything is not exactly as she wants it to be, she'd likely bring a chair into our bedroom and watch to be sure an heir to the coveted viscountancy is conceived post haste."

Mariah made a squeamish sound and exchanged a horrified look with baby Peter, who chose just that moment to raise his head and look at his mother. The timing was almost comical enough to make Lavinia smile.

"No," Lavinia repeated with a resigned sigh. "I'll go to my husband's bed tonight and do what British wives have been required to do since William the Conqueror claimed England as his own. And in the morning, I'll pick up whatever pieces are left of my dreams and figure out how to piece together a future."

CHAPTER 7

The only thing more torturous than supper that evening, with Lady Prior gloating and implying at every turn that Armand—her son-in-law—would certainly provide an even finer feast, better decorations, and more interesting guests, was the teasing he received when the gentlemen retired to the study for cigars and brandy.

"I bet India's the furthest thing from your mind now," Peter told him, slapping him on the back and handing him a large tumbler of brandy. "You've got far more pleasant duties to attend to now."

"I haven't given up on India," Armand grumbled, taking the glass and gulping its contents. In fact, he'd sent off a letter to Dr. Maqsood that afternoon, informing him of his marriage and asking if there was any way to delay his departure for Lahore.

"What's this about India?" Rupert asked, breaking away from the small group of male guests closer to his age who had started a game of cards to join the older men.

"Dr. Pearson here was contemplating running away from

home to cure cholera on the subcontinent," Malcolm said, fixing Katya's son with a particularly intimidating stare.

"Oh," Rupert said with an uneasy laugh. "But I suppose that's out of the question, now that you have a wife," he said to Armand, then darted a look in Malcolm's direction. "A man's first and most important responsibility is to his wife. It is his foremost concern to keep her happy and healthy."

"You don't say?" Malcolm narrowed his eyes at the young man.

On any other day, Armand would have been tempted to find amusement in the confrontation. They all knew that Rupert had a spark in his eye where Malcolm's daughter, Cecelia, was concerned. Armand suspected that was the reason Cece had stayed in London with friends instead of joining the rest of them in Wiltshire, at Malcolm's insistence. But in that moment, being lectured on the responsibilities of a husband by a man who wasn't even twenty was not how Armand wanted to spend his evening.

"My primary responsibility is to my patients," he said. "I took an oath to the effect. Excuse me."

He stepped away before Peter could continue to tease him or Malcolm could glower at him. He valued his friends, but they were just as responsible for landing him in a situation he didn't want to be in as Lady Prior, and at the moment, he wanted nothing to do with them. He set his tumbler of brandy on a table as he crossed the room to where Alex was brooding near one of the windows.

"I'm going to bed," Armand told his friend, not caring if he was being rude. "Just thought you'd want to know in case of any midnight strategy sessions."

Alex glanced up at him with a troubled frown. "It had to have been Miller, but why?"

Armand blinked at the incongruous change of subject. "Who took the letter?"

"Yes," Alex repeated. "But what would he want with it? Miller is an incompetent country doctor. He has nothing to do with politics. Why would he steal a letter bound for Gladstone?"

As much as he knew he should care, the only emotion Armand could conjure up over the matter was jealousy that a bumbling moron like Miller would still be allowed to practice medicine when he was blocked from it at every turn. "Perhaps it was a genuine mistake. What would Miller even do with a letter like that?"

"I don't know," Alex sighed.

Armand paused for a moment, wishing there was anything he could do. But his whole life seemed caught up in the webs of other people's machinations, leaving him hanging and helpless.

"I'm going to bed," he repeated, then turned and marched out of the room.

Irritation seemed to follow him as he made his way through the halls of Winterberry Park. The sensation of being a lion trapped in a cage was utterly unhelpful, but he couldn't escape the frustration. He'd had a clear vision of what his life would be. He would help people, care for the sick, and make them well. He wasn't supposed to be a viscount or a politician or a husband. But every time he came close to escaping his circumstances, another door slammed.

In echo of his thoughts, after entering his bedroom, he slammed the door shut. A sharp, feminine gasp from the bed startled him as acutely as a gunshot. Lavinia sat on one side of the bed, pillows propped up behind her, a book in her hands.

"Good heavens. What are you doing here?" he asked as soon as he recovered from his shock. His heart continued to race, though.

"It's our wedding night," Lavinia answered, her voice

shaking and her face turning beet red. As she closed her book and set it aside, Armand could see her hands shaking.

Bloody hell. She didn't actually expect him to claim his marital rights over her, did she? Not that the comfort of a willing pair of arms around him wouldn't be exactly what he needed to soothe his disgruntled spirit.

"I'm not sure the events of the day truly qualify as a joyous wedding day," he said, moving to sit on the bed so he could remove his shoes.

"Don't let Mama hear you say that," she said.

He let out a wry grunt before he could stop himself. "Sorry," he said over his shoulder. "I don't mean to disparage your mother." Although, in fact, he did.

"She deserves it," Lavinia said with a sigh, surprising him. Armand tossed his shoes aside and twisted to face her. "My only consolation in this whole farce is that I now outrank her," she said, picking at the coverlet.

She had lovely hands, small with long, narrow fingers. A sudden memory of her playing the piano and singing at an event Alex had hosted in his London home hit him. She played well and had a pretty voice. She looked quite fetching with her vibrant, coppery hair loose around her shoulders as well. But her face was so sad. Her soft, angelic features were all turned down, as if she didn't want to be where she was any more than he did. Everything about her touched his heart in ways he didn't understand.

He rose from the bed, crossing to the wardrobe and throwing it open to stave off the rush of desire he felt for her. "You don't have to sleep in here with me tonight if you don't want to," he said without looking at her, unbuttoning his coat and shrugging out of it, then hanging it in the wardrobe. He unbuttoned his waistcoat next. "Just because we've been forced to wed doesn't mean we're forced to bed."

"I considered that," she said. "But there doesn't seem to be any point in delaying the inevitable."

He removed his waistcoat and hung it as well, then went to work on his tie. "There is every point if you aren't ready for...." He glanced toward her and knew she understood without him having to embarrass them both by finishing the sentence.

Lavinia shrugged, her gaze glued to the coverlet, her cheeks like two ripe apples, ready to be picked. "I'm as ready now as I'll ever be."

Armand doubted that. Instinct told him she'd be far readier to be intimate with him if they'd had weeks or months to get to know each other better. But she was the only person in all of Winterberry Park who he didn't feel was laughing at him or making unreasonable demands of him. She was as much a victim as he was. He debated his options as he took his nightshirt from the wardrobe and crossed into the screen that shielded a chamber pot and a washstand containing a basin, a full pitcher of water, and his toiletries. It gave him a moment to think as he washed up and quickly brushed his teeth. If he was going to go through with a wedding night consummation, at least he could make himself physically less repugnant.

Lavinia had gone back to reading her book, but she gasped a second time when Armand came out from behind the screen. He couldn't help but feel that he was sailing into another disaster as he climbed into bed with her.

She set her book aside, then faced him. "All right. Tell me what I'm supposed to do."

A wry grin tugged at the corner of his mouth. "You're supposed to live the life you want to live. You're supposed to follow your passions and pursue the things that interest you instead of being pushed around by an ambitious mother and tricked by manipulative friends."

She stared at him, then blinked. "No, I mean what am I

supposed to do to make love to you?"

Intuition told him she understood he'd been joking, but that she was too overwhelmed to be anything but dead serious. He sighed. "Are you absolutely certain, beyond a shadow of a doubt, that you want to consummate this marriage, such as it is, tonight?"

She lowered her eyes and bit her lip. Her brow furrowed just enough to hint at how intelligent she truly was. "I don't want to exist in a state of limbo," she said at last, looking up at him with what felt to Armand like a great deal of effort, and an even greater amount of courage. "If I'm going to be your wife, then I should be your wife fully. I don't want to give anyone the opportunity to question or conjecture, or to tell me I'm not really what I am."

Her words lodged deep inside of him. They settled in the part of him that didn't know if he was a physician or a viscount, a healer or a politician. They whispered to him that, if all else failed, at least he could know he was a husband.

"All right, then," he said, feeling as though he was letting go of something he'd been holding onto with all his might. "Let's just rearrange these pillows and lie down. There's really not much to the whole thing."

It was another white lie. There could be a great deal to sexual intimacy, but for the time being, his only concern was hurting her as little as possible.

Lavinia seemed to grasp at least the basics of what she needed to do. She shifted to her back and didn't fly into a panic when he positioned himself above her. They both still wore their nightclothes, which, he hoped, would work to their benefit to minimize embarrassment.

"Are you, um, aware of the mechanics?" he asked once he was settled between her legs, his face less than a foot from hers.

"Yes," she answered with a quick nod, resting her hands on his sides.

He couldn't help but be aroused by their proximity and the faintly floral scent of her skin, but his body's reactions hadn't felt so awkward since he was a very young man dealing with his first public erection.

"There might be a little bit of pain," he said, heating with embarrassment as much as passion.

"I know," she said.

"If I can make it less, I will."

"I trust you."

His breath caught in his throat and his heart thundered in his chest. She did trust him, even though she had no reason to. He could see it in her eyes, in the innocent way she looked up at him. The weight of the responsibility he felt toward her pressed down on him, but it didn't feel as burdensome as it could have. She was his wife, she was beautiful, intelligent, and innocent, and she trusted him.

He dipped down to kiss her. It seemed as good a place as any to start. The last thing he wanted to do was overwhelm her by groping her in intimate places, but a kiss, gentle and reassuring, could start enough of a fire to see them through what needed to be done. Blessedly, she responded with openness, letting him lead the way and following willingly. Her hands moved along his back as he tasted her, filling him with an overwhelming sense of acceptance.

He brushed a hand down her side, reaching for the hem of her nightgown and inching it up. Every tiny movement on his part seemed to cause a reaction in her. She tensed, then relaxed, held her breath, then let it out. In spite of his determination not to take liberties with her, he kissed her neck, nibbling at her ear, and slipped his hand under the bunched fabric of her nightgown to test what the petal-soft skin of her breast would feel like against his palm. Each tiny advance left him aching for more, but he forced himself to hold back. It was the most difficult thing he'd ever done, though. Her body fit so well against his. Her unschooled reactions and the innocent catch in her breath as he tugged his nightshirt out of the way of everything important had him as hard as a rock in record time.

He wanted to explore every inch of her body with his hands and mouth. He wanted to suckle her breasts in ways that would leave her panting with pleasure. He wanted to part her legs and taste the sweetness of her honey in ways that would make her come with thundering force, but fear of scaring her off forever kept him strictly in check. The greatest liberty he allowed himself was sliding a hand between her folds to make certain she was ready for him. He couldn't stop a groan of satisfaction when his fingers found her wet and ready.

As quickly as he could, both to spare her as much pain as possible and to satisfy himself before he got carried away, he positioned himself and then entered her. She gasped and tensed, just as he expected she would, as he held himself carefully inside of her.

"Are you all right?" he panted, the urge to move in her almost overwhelming.

"I...I think," she answered. "It feels so strange."

"Did I hurt you?" he asked, praying she would say no.

"A little," she answered, clinging to him. "It's already going away."

"Good. We won't have to go through that bit ever again." He moved his hips subtly, answering his body's pleas for pleasure and release. "I need to move now so we can finish," he said, picking up his pace.

"All right," she said, breathless as she began to move with him.

He wanted so much more as he moved inside of her,

setting a pace that would finish him off in a hurry, but for her sake, he felt as though he needed to get it over with as soon as possible. Fortunately for her, he felt like a man half his age, racing for climax at lightning speed. His mind conjured up images of how things could be between them when she was eager and hungry for him. But it was the reality of the excited sounds she began to make as his thrusts turned feverish that sent him over the edge. Pleasure burst through him, and he came with a force that left him feeling wrung out and unified with her.

He took only a moment to sag on top of her as all energy left him. She felt perfect wrapped around him the way she was, before he pulled out of her. His heart reveled in it along with his body, but for her sake, he rolled to the side as soon as he felt able.

"There," he panted, arranging his nightshirt, and then the coverlet over top of them. "That wasn't so bad."

"No, it wasn't," she answered, moving as though putting her nightgown in place, then turning to her side facing him.

He blinked as he studied her, wondering if he was imagining the warmth in her voice or the spark in her eyes. She hadn't actually enjoyed their pitiful excuse for love-making, had she?

"I'm sorry about all of this," he said, reaching out to brush the side of her face with the back of his hand. "I won't let them make a laughing stock of us."

She smiled sleepily, sending arrows of emotion through him. "Thank you."

She closed her eyes, letting out a long, deep breath.

For the first time in years, the frustration that gripped every part of his body and soul loosened, and the voice in the back of his head whispered that perhaps he was the luckiest man in the world after all.

CHAPTER 8

"*Dear Elaine.*"

Lavinia glanced up from her parchment and sent a covert glance around the drawing room. Outside of the tall windows, the skies were stormy, and rain lashed at the panes. Bianca and Natalia were playing tag with little James Croydon at the other end of the room. Lady Stanhope and Marigold were arguing over a new story that they'd read in *The Times* that morning, Mariah and her husband still hadn't come down to join the party, and the other guests, whom Lavinia hadn't had the time to get to know, were either reading or working on embroidery. Everyone was engaged, but that didn't stop Lavinia from feeling guilty for confiding her tumultuous thoughts to Elaine on paper instead of answering the curious, wheedling looks Lady Stanhope and Marigold had been giving her all morning. It had been obvious from the moment she and Armand walked into the breakfast room together that her friends were desperate to gossip about what had transpired the night before, but Lavinia would rather have died than spoken her thoughts aloud.

Which was why she thanked God for paper, ink, and Elaine.

"I don't know where to start," she continued writing in a small, stiff hand. *"If my letter of two days ago reaches you before this one, which I trust it will have, then you know all about how I was literally entangled into marriage with Armand Pearson. What you will be shocked to hear is that the wedding took place yesterday, thanks to the blasted efficiency of Mr. Croydon's man, Mr. Phillips, and my mother's dogged determination."*

Thunder clapped outside, rattling the windows. Lavinia glanced out into the garden with an impatient huff, as though the weather, too, were trying to wedge its way into her private thoughts. She shifted in her seat, a twinge of soreness reminding her just how married she was.

"I have been up to my ears in advice these last few days," she wrote on, *"and I have had nothing but knowing looks and coy smiles this morning, after spending my first night in Dr. Pearson's bed. It is as if the two of us have been unwittingly providing the entertainment for the house party, like monkeys dancing to an organ-grinder's tune. And I am sick of it, I tell you."*

Her pen scratched across the paper, leaving an angry blob of ink as punctuation showing her frustration. She sighed in irritation and took up a small piece of flannel to clean the metal pen nib before dipping it in the ink and continuing.

"The worst of it is that I don't have nearly as much to gossip about this morning as I thought I would. After your letters, after Mama's attempts at education, and after Lady Stanhope's insinuations, my experience of consummation was…."

She glanced up, staring out the window, at an utter loss for words. How could she possibly describe the event with Armand the night before? Uncomfortable? Brief? Disappointing? None of those words began to do justice to the maelstrom of emotions that had overcome her. They were completely inadequate to explain the intense closeness or the unexpected camaraderie she'd felt with Armand's body inside of hers. The storm of entirely new sensations she'd felt was as demanding as the thunder raging outside Winterberry Park, but unlike the morning's bluster, her experience with Armand had been all too short. He had finished just as she was getting started. She'd lain awake for hours, listening to the steady sound of his breathing and reliving every second of their intercourse. There had to be more to it than that. Otherwise, why did her friends go into such raptures of smiles, giggles, and blushes when whispering about their husbands? Perhaps she was just…wrong.

"…*my experience of consummations was—*" she reread her words, then finished with, "*—interesting.*"

Thunder boomed once more, close enough to cause Lavinia to flinch. Her pen slipped across the page, and once more, ink splattered the parchment. Frustrated, she jabbed the pen into its holder and snatched up the letter, crumpling it into a ball. Teeth clenched, she rose and marched to the fire, throwing the ball of paper into the flames with as much force as she could manage. She didn't feel like writing anyhow. The trouble was, she didn't feel like doing much of anything. There wasn't much for a dancing monkey to do when the music wasn't playing.

"Lavinia, there you are," her mother said as she swept into the room.

Lavinia's stomach pinched, and she crossed her arms and turned away, facing the fire. But, of course, there was no escape from her mother.

"What are you doing in here?" her mother accosted her. "Your husband is in the library."

Lavinia's face flared hot. "He is engaged in political conversation with the other men," she said, frowning with uncharacteristic boldness. Her mother attempted to grab her sleeve, likely to push her toward the door and down the hall to the library, but Lavinia resisted her.

Her mother jerked off balance when she failed to capture Lavinia. She blinked in surprised as she turned back to face her, then pursed her lips. "A new bride's place is with her husband. You need to go to him at once."

"He is busy, Mama," Lavinia insisted. "An important letter went missing, and it is of vital importance that the gentlemen locate it or, if they cannot, that they determine a way of conveying the information it contained to Mr. Gladstone as quickly as possible."

Her mother made an undignified noise and brushed the argument away. "What's important is that Lord Helm compose an announcement about your marriage to be sent to *The Times* for publication." Her eyes lit up like the flames that danced in the fireplace beside them. "He must host a ball to honor the occasion as soon as we are all back in London. More than one ball, at least. I must make a list of my friends to invite." She rubbed her hands together in glee. "Won't Mrs. Turpin be green with envy when she learns that my daughter is a viscountess. Although it would be wrong to gloat when her husband has landed himself in prison." She paused, then giggled. "That won't stop me, though."

"Frankly, Mama, I am not in the least bit interested in hosting parties of any sort," Lavinia said, her sour mood making her bolder than she ever would have dared to be.

She attempted to step around her mother and head to the door. Lady Stanhope and Marigold stood as she did, proving they'd been eavesdropping on the conversation. Knowing her friends, they'd probably been watching her out of the corner of their eyes all morning. When her mother attempted to follow her to the hall, they jumped into action, crossing the room to flank her as though they were her guards.

"And I suppose you plan to get involved in my daughter's affairs again, do you?" Lavinia's mother snapped at Lady Stanhope.

"Your daughter clearly wishes to be left to her own devices today," Lady Stanhope said in a surprisingly steady voice. "I assume it is because she has delicate thoughts she needs to sort out on her own." Lady Stanhope raised an eyebrow at Lavinia in question.

As aggravated as she was with her friends for meddling in her life to begin with, she was grateful that Lady Stanhope understood without her having to spell it out. She nodded slightly, then attempted to walk on.

"What utter nonsense," her mother said, grabbing her wrist to stop her. "Delicate thoughts?" She made a scoffing sound. "I've always counseled her that the best way to cope with those thoughts is to close her eyes and think of the beautiful children she will have when it's all done."

"Mama, please," Lavinia hissed, her face heating even more.

"If I were in her place, I would be picking out names and choosing the finest schools for the dear, future little ones to attend. The eldest son will, of course, be named after his father. He is to inherit the title, after all, and—"

Lavinia stormed off before her mother could say another ridiculous, smug, self-congratulatory word. That didn't stop her mother from chasing after her, though, Lady Stanhope and Marigold scrambling to keep up.

"A Christmas ball would be a wonderful thing," her mother said, sounding far too excited. "What is the name of Lord Helm's London house again?"

"He doesn't have one," Lady Stanhope said.

Surprisingly, that made her mother stop. "Doesn't have one? That is preposterous."

"The townhome went to his first cousin, as consolation

for not inheriting the title after the confusion of the line of succession," Lady Stanhope said.

"Confusion? What confusion?" Lavinia blinked.

Lady Stanhope sent a wary look to Lavinia's mother, as if she didn't care to drag the story out in front of someone who might make it gossip.

"I'd forgotten about that ordeal," Lavinia's mother said. She turned to Lavinia. "Lord Helm's father was a twin. Apparently, the records detailing which brother was born first were destroyed in a fire. Since there were three older brothers, the family assumed it wouldn't matter who was born first. Except that it did end up mattering, because the three older brothers and their male issue all predeceased the twins. The Viscount Helm who died five years ago was the only child of the second son. When it came to it, the courts had to go on the word of the elderly midwife who delivered the babies, and she declared Lord Helm's father was the first-born of the twins, and, therefore, the rightful heir."

"But there's a chance the other twin's son should have inherited the title instead?" Lavinia asked, a burst of hope for Armand—and his longing to continue practicing medicine—filling her.

Lady Stanhope shook her head. "The courts decided what they decided, and they never change their minds. Whatever the truth might be, Armand is the viscount, and that's not going to change."

"And his cousin was given a house in London as consolation?" Lavinia wondered who the cousin was and if the consolation had been enough for him.

"Lord Helm must purchase a new London house right away." Her mother made a rapturous sound, breezing on before Lavinia could ask the identity of the other potential Viscount Helm. "Oh, it will be heavenly to choose and outfit a London home. It must be located on one of the grander squares, of course. Grosvenor Square is my favorite, of course. A guest suite overlooking the park would be divine."

If Lavinia hadn't already expected her mother had no intention of leaving her alone now that she was married, she would have frozen in horror. Instead, she picked up her skirts and quickened her pace in her flight down the hall. Of course, she never should have expected the organ grinder to give up the monkey just because it'd found a mate.

She only had a vague idea of where she was going as she turned a corner and started down the hall in Winterberry Park's east wing. Whatever political conundrum the men were attempting to solve had to be less stressful than her mother's constant pecking and her friends' pointed concern. But when she finally reached the door to the library, she wasn't prepared for what met her.

"...not as though I even wanted a wife in the first place," Armand was shouting at his friends. "And if the lot of you hadn't pushed me into it, I wouldn't be saddled with one. How do you expect me to—"

He stopped, his mouth hanging open, as all eyes, including his, landed on Lavinia in the doorway.

Lavinia hadn't expected to be welcomed with open arms and romantic kisses, but her nerves were stretched so taut that Armand's words hit her like a lightning bolt. Her vision narrowed and her head swam as she felt the blood drain from her face. She whipped around, intending to bolt, but her mother, Lady Stanhope, and Marigold had caught up with her.

"I did not raise you to run from me when I am attempting to speak to you, young lady," her mother scolded, forcing her to backpedal farther into the library.

"How dare you speak to Lavinia like that?" Lady Stanhope snapped.

All Lavinia wanted to do was flee the room and run until

she imploded, even if she had to run through the storm to do it, but her mother continued to push her deeper into the library. Armand strode to meet her, but whether to shield her from her mother's ire or to tell her how he truly felt about having been forced to marry her she had no idea.

"Interfering in a family matter, are we, Katya?" Malcolm jumped forward, meeting Lady Stanhope.

"Stay out of this, Malcolm. You don't know what's going on," Lady Stanhope snapped.

"We were discussing important business here," Mr. Croydon said, his temper clearly short.

"How dare you speak to me that way?" Lavinia's mother glared at Mr. Croydon. "I have had just about enough out of everyone today. Lavinia may be married now, but she is still my daughter and should do as I say."

"No one wants to be treated like a child," Marigold began, jumping into the fray.

Lavinia was inches away from pressing her hands to the sides of her head and sinking into a ball on the floor when Armand's arm closed gently around her, guiding her away from the crush of people in the center of the room and over to one window. Whether real or imagined, the noise of the row died down as the sound of the rain on the windowpanes grew louder.

"Forgive me for what you overheard," Armand said in a voice as soft as the distant thunder. "It wasn't what it sounded like."

"I know you didn't want to marry me," Lavinia replied, keeping her head down, unable to summon the courage to look him in the eye.

"And you didn't want to marry me," he reminded her. His hand slipped under her chin and he nudged her to look up at him. "But here we are."

Lavinia swallowed. "I'll go back to sleeping in my room.

And when you're ready to leave, I can stay here, or I can visit Mariah and Lord Dunsford at Starcross Castle."

His expression pinched with confusion. "You don't have to do that."

"But…you just said…you don't want…." Her heart hurt too much to finish.

He let out a weary breath. "Malcolm was giving me a hard time for not devoting more of myself to our group's political cause. Alex is beyond anxious about our letter being waylaid. And Rupert, bless him, keeps asking the sort of inane questions that a young man who wishes to impress older men he has always viewed as father figures ask. It all became a bit too much for me. I was blaming them for cornering me far more than I was complaining about you."

"Are you sure?" Lavinia asked, cursing the tremble in her voice.

"Yes," he said with a tired smile. "We're the wronged parties here."

He was attempting to reassure her, but she was all too aware that he was implying their marriage was wrong. And he was correct. It was wrong. But they were stuck with it.

"Lord Helm," her mother started up once more, turning away from the argument that was still raging between Lady Stanhope and Lord Malcolm to march to Lavinia and Armand's corner of the room. "What is this I hear about you not owning a townhome in London?"

Armand sent Lavinia a brief, wary look before stepping away from her—she hadn't realized how close he was standing—and facing her mother. "I have a small flat in Kensington, but that is all."

"Oh, that won't do," Lavinia's mother said, clicking her tongue. "That won't do at all. We must purchase a townhome as soon as possible. I don't suppose it could be decorated in time for an autumn soiree, but—"

"I'm sorry, madam. We?" Armand blinked at her.

"Armand," Mr. Croydon interrupted from across the room. "We really need to finish discussing what to do in case the letter falls into the wrong hands."

"Yes," Lavinia's mother said, nodding to Armand without a hint of shame and without a bit of consideration for Mr. Croydon's interruption. "You don't expect me to let my daughter live just anywhere. I intend to be fully involved in every aspect of the selection, staffing, and decoration of wherever she lives. She must have a lifestyle that befits her title."

"Armand." Mr. Croydon started toward them. "We need to get to work."

"Don't you insult my son like that, you jumped up, Scottish bog monster," Lady Stanhope's shout sailed above the rest of the roiling, argumentative conversations.

"And that's another thing," Lavinia's mother went on. "I forbid you to have anything to do with that shameless tart once you begin entertaining as Lady Helm."

"Mama, it isn't your place to—"

"Hold your tongue, girl," her mother snapped. "You must—"

"Stop," Armand shouted, in perfect concert with a clap of thunder outside. He held up his hands. "Will everyone please just stop talking for two seconds."

The room fell blessedly silent. Lavinia's heart thumped so hard she was certain everyone around her could hear it. She waited for Armand to go on, clenching every muscle in her body tight. But Armand let the silence draw out so long that everyone else grew visibly uncomfortable. He stared at all of them, an incredulous look in his eyes, daring each one to be the first to say something.

At last, when Lavinia was sure she would burst, he shook his head and lowered his shoulders. "This is intolerable."

Her mother started in with, "That's what I—"

Armand cut her off with a raised hand and a glare. After another uncomfortable silence, he reached for Lavinia's hand. She found herself clinging to him before she was aware of moving.

"I am leaving Winterberry Park and I'm taking my wife with me," he said at last in a tone that brooked no nonsense. "I am taking her home to Broadclyft Hall, and none of you—" he glanced pointedly at Lavinia's mother. "None of you," he repeated with emphasis, "are coming with us."

He turned to Lavinia. It was clear that he'd reached the end of his rope, but behind his utter lack of patience, she had the impression he was asking her if he was making the right move.

Lavinia held her breath. Everything seemed wrong. Her mind seemed at war with itself. She couldn't form a thought to save her life. But as the rain drummed against the window behind her, as the warmth of his hand in hers began to infuse her, pinpricks of sense cut through the cloud of her confusion. Because what she felt pulsing through her wasn't what she was supposed to be feeling. It wasn't what her mother would want her to feel. It wasn't polite or proper or amiable. She felt relief—bone-numbing relief that brought her close to the edge of tears. Relief that she could finally get away from her well-meaning but intrusive friends, the house full of strangers, both high and low, and most of all, her mother.

"I'll find Anne and ask her to pack my things immediately," she said in a quiet voice, meant only for her husband to hear.

His whole body relaxed, and a smile softened his features. "I'll tell Mr. Noakes to have my carriage ready as soon as the rain stops."

Lavinia's mother recovered slowly. "But you can't just leave," she said, blinking rapidly.

Armand ignored her, offering Lavinia his arm. When she took it, he turned to Alex. "I'm sorry. I know there are important political matters at stake, but you gave me this responsibility, and I intend to take it seriously."

It wasn't an ideal comment, but Lavinia was willing to accept anything that got her out of Winterberry Park as soon as possible.

Mr. Croydon looked as though he might argue that he wasn't the one who pushed them into marriage, which was true, but he backed off. "Go. I'll send Phillips to help you pack."

"Thank you." Armand nodded.

"You can't just leave," Lavinia's mother tried one more time.

Once more, she was ignored. With a final nod to Lavinia, Armand escorted her through the room, through the gauntlet of their silent friends, and on to the hall without looking back.

CHAPTER 9

*A*rmand didn't regret leaving Winterberry Park for an instant. Not when he and Lavinia were forced to delay their departure as the storm lasted into the evening, not when his carriage became stuck in the mud left by the storm well after dark, and not when the rain picked up again in the middle of the night as they rolled out of Wiltshire, through Somerset, and into Devon. He was relieved to have the debacle of Alex's house party behind him and to get back to normal life, whatever that was.

As uncomfortable as the carriage was, and as much as it made him wish he'd taken the train instead, he didn't regret the way Lavinia had finally given in to exhaustion, slumped against him, and fallen asleep. He rather liked the way he was able to brace himself in one corner of the carriage, his feet propped up on the opposing seat, and position Lavinia in his arms for her maximum comfort. She felt good in his embrace, right and comforting. She was so tired that she slept deeply, in spite of the cramped conditions and the bumps and ruts they'd ridden over.

He could have whipped himself for the things he'd said in

Alex's library. He'd seen the second he turned around that Lavinia had been hurt by his words. He was a damn fool for using his marriage, however he'd entered into it, as a weapon to attack his friends. He didn't feel as though his apology was enough either. Just because he hadn't chosen to marry didn't mean he wasn't determined to make the best of it. The more he reflected on the whole debacle, the more he realized that he actually did have a choice. No one had held a gun to his head, just a great deal of fuss and unpleasantness. He could have said no. He could have walked away, just as he'd walked away from the house party when it became too much for him. It was his own desire not to cause a scene that had landed him where he was now. That and Lavinia's innocent, pleading eyes, her sad, soft mouth, and the silken flame of her hair. Perhaps she wouldn't mind coming to India with him.

She stirred as the carriage jolted, sucking in a breath and moving against him. Morning sunlight shone around the edges of the shades Armand had lowered to block out the light, hoping to buy her more sleep. She lifted her head and blinked blearily, looking like she might fly into a panic of confusion.

"It's all right," he said, rubbing her back. "We just turned off the main road and onto the lane that will take us home. Rest a little longer, we'll soon be there."

Their eyes met for a moment in the dim light. He smiled to reassure her, and she nodded, then rested her head against his shoulder once more. Armand's chest seemed to swell and tighten at the same time. He settled his arms around her, reveling in the feeling of her body against his. It didn't matter that they were both fully dressed and wrinkled from traveling, it felt wonderful to simply hold her like that. It was just the two of them for the first time, no noise, no mothers or friends fussing over them, no demands. Just silence, warmth, and a comfortable hint of arousal.

He wasn't sure if Lavinia fell asleep again or if she was simply silent, but as they made another turn, from the lane to the gravel drive leading up to Broadclyft Hall, she drew in a breath and struggled to sit straight. Armand helped her, righting himself as he did, and pulling up the shades to reveal the dew-kissed world outside.

"There it is," he said with resignation as the massive edifice of Broadclyft Hall came into view. "There's the pile of stones I inherited."

Lavinia drew in an awed breath and pressed herself against the side of the carriage, peering out at the home.

"It's new, as far as grand country houses go," he explained, shifting closer to her and peering out to see what she saw. "The original estate burned to the ground in the eighteen-thirties. My grandfather had this wonder built in its place. It took a good ten years for the whole thing to be finished." He paused as the carriage turned onto the curving part of the drive that wound around a garden with a fountain in the center that faced the house's wide front steps. "I remember spending Christmases here as a boy. Grandfather was so proud of his creation that he would pull out all the stops and invite half of Devon and Cornwall to lavish holiday parties. I think there's something like thirty bedrooms in the house."

"You *think* there is?" Lavinia turned to him. "You don't know for sure?"

He smiled sheepishly. "Is it ridiculous for a viscount not to know how many rooms his country estate has?"

She paused, her eyes saying yes, but answered, "No."

Armand's smile grew, as did the warm pulse of feeling in his chest. The carriage lurched to a stop, then bounced as the driver hopped down. A moment later, one of his footmen opened the door. The young lad flinched in surprise as he noticed Lavinia.

"Good morning, Maxwell," Armand nodded, straightening his hat and moving to step down from the carriage, then turning to offer Lavinia a hand.

"Good morning, sir," Maxwell answered, stepping back and assuming a ready posture, but glancing to the front door with a touch of desperation in his eyes.

Armand focused on helping Lavinia down from the carriage, then offered her his arm before saying, "I know, I know, Maxwell. I didn't send notice that I was coming home. But we departed Winterberry Park under extraordinary circumstances."

"You didn't inform your staff that you were on your way home?" Lavinia whispered as they started up the stairs toward the front door.

"Is that wrong?" Armand asked.

Again, Lavinia paused, subtly biting her lip, and while her eyes once again said "yes", she said, "No."

Armand couldn't help but chuckle. "I might have mentioned that I am a terrible failure as a viscount."

Before Lavinia could answer, the front door opened and his butler, Mr. Bondar, rushed out to meet them, looking startled. "Sir, we weren't expecting you."

"I know, Bondar. It is entirely my fault. But I was eager to bring Lady Helm to her new home," Armand said.

Mr. Bondar's eyes widened. "Lady Helm, sir?" he asked in his broad, Yorkshire accent.

Armand reached the top step, where Mr. Bondar stood, and thumped the man on the arm. "It's a long story, Bondar. Could you have Maxwell bring our things in?"

"Yes, sir." Mr. Bondar nodded, then gestured to Maxwell.

Armand escorted Lavinia into the house, watching her with a smile as she took in the grand front hallway. His grandfather truly had a flair for the grandiose. The front hall was as large as the entrance to any museum and just as finely decorated. A lavish, curving staircase led up to the first floor, which stood higher than most first floors, since the ground floor of the house contained a vast ballroom, a portrait gallery, and a library designed to strike awe into guests. Armand was surprised to find he was actually looking forward to giving Lavinia a tour of the place.

"Your lordship, welcome home."

Armand turned to find his housekeeper, Mrs. Ainsworth, hurrying across the hall toward them. "Thank you, Mrs. Ainsworth." When the woman glanced to Lavinia with as much surprise as Mr. Bondar had, Armand went on with, "Allow me to introduce my new bride, Lady Lavinia Helm."

Mrs. Ainsworth nearly tripped over herself as she closed the final distance of her approach. "Your new bride?" she exclaimed before recovering herself enough to say. "Congratulations on your marriage, my lord, my lady." She smiled at Lavinia with pink cheeks and wide eyes, half shock, half joy.

"How do you do, Mrs. Ainsworth?" Lavinia greeted the woman with a surprisingly poised smile and nod, considering not fifteen minutes ago she'd been asleep in the carriage.

Mrs. Ainsworth continued to gape at Lavinia for a moment before remembering herself and dropping into a respectful curtsy. "Forgive me, my lady. This is all so unexpected."

"Yes," Lavinia answered with a flicker of her eyebrow. "It most certainly is."

Mrs. Ainsworth rose from her curtsy and met Lavinia's expression with a flash of wisdom in her eyes. Armand could feel an instant rapport between the two women, which was a relief. Mrs. Ainsworth was seventy if she was a day, had managed the house through three viscounts, and knew how to navigate the kind of transition that a new mistress of the house would bring.

"I regret that the household is not prepared for your arrival, my lord," she went on, glancing past Armand and Lavinia to where Maxwell was bringing in Lavinia's trunk while the two other footmen, Les and Carl, rushed out to collect the rest of the baggage. "Your room is prepared as always, my lord, but would you like the maids to make up the chamber across the hall for Lady Helm?"

Lavinia blushed and lowered her head slightly at the question. Armand fought the impulse to tell his housekeeper that a separate bedroom wouldn't be necessary, that he intended for his wife to share his bed. Sense and concern for Lavinia's feelings held him back, though.

"You might as well," he said tactfully, stealing a glance at Lavinia. "It's better to have options."

Again, Armand had the feeling that Mrs. Ainsworth had seen everything and knew all. She nodded sagely, sharing another quick, silent exchange with Lavinia. "I'll have Sophie get started on it at once."

"In the meantime," Armand turned to Lavinia, "you can freshen up, change clothes, or even take a nap in my room, if you'd like."

"Thank you," Lavinia said with a smile. "Although once I've changed, I should consult with Mrs. Ainsworth about the running of the house." She turned to the housekeeper. "I have so many questions."

"I'm sure you do, my lady, and I shall endeavor to answer them all to the best of my ability," Mrs. Ainsworth answered, somehow managing to convey that she had many questions of her own without breathing a hint of those words.

"I'd like to give you a tour of the house," Armand began, letting go of Lavinia's arm.

Before she could answer, Mr. Bondar approached. "My

lord, since you have returned, there are a few things we should discuss. Estate matters."

Armand let out a breath, removing his hat and pushing his fingers through his hair. "Yes, of course, Bondar." He sent Lavinia an apologetic smile. "I hate to abandon you to duty when you've only just arrived."

"It's all right," she said, her eyes bright with the newness of everything around her. "I'm certain your staff is kind and competent and that they will do an exceptional job of welcoming me to Broadclyft Hall." She nodded to Mrs. Ainsworth, who beamed under the compliment.

The warm pulsing in Armand's chest grew and spread. Lavinia's was the cleverest answer he could have imagined to his apology. It was clear at a glance that she'd won both Mrs. Ainsworth and Mr. Bondar over in an instant. She was winning him over again and again with each new moment they spent together. He found himself reluctant to part from her. But his blasted duty called, and it would do no one any good to ignore it.

He took her hand, raising it to his lips for a ridiculously sentimental kiss. "We'll see each other later for luncheon."

"We will," she echoed.

Armand let her hand go and stepped away, studying her for a lingering moment before turning to head off toward his study with Mr. Bondar. For the first time since taking ownership of Broadclyft Hall, he felt as though he'd come home.

It was the oddest feeling that Lavinia had ever experienced.

"So with three footmen, four upstairs maids, a kitchen maid, scullery maid, and hall boy, not to mention you and Mr. Bondar, and Mrs. Piper, the cook, you have enough staff to handle the workload of a house this size?" she asked as she and Mrs. Ainsworth finished their tour of the house by taking a seat in the housekeeper's private sitting room.

"Yes, my lady," Mrs. Ainsworth nodded, smiling at the curious kitchen maid, Ellie, who immediately brought in tea. "Though we have been known to hire temporary help from the village when the viscount hosts a party."

"Has the current viscount hosted a party in his tenure?"

"No, my lady." Mrs. Ainsworth fixed a cup of tea for her. "Though I wouldn't mind seeing that change. House parties are a challenge, but they are also a lark."

"I shall give it some thought."

Yes, the feeling was strange indeed. Lavinia sipped her tea, finding it delicious and not too sweet, the way her mother always prepared it for her. Mrs. Ainsworth was old enough to be her grandmother, but she had spent the entire morning deferring to Lavinia and asking her opinion on things. Clearly, the woman was delighted to have a mistress again. No one had stood over Lavinia's shoulder, telling her what she should do or what questions to ask. And, remarkably, she had known precisely what to ask.

She felt respected. She felt competent. She felt important.

"Begging your pardon, my lady," Mrs. Ainsworth said once she had her own cup of tea. "There is already a great deal of speculation downstairs about how you and Lord Helm came to be married. We were given no indication that he was even thinking of changing his situation."

Lavinia grinned, unsurprised that the servants were already chattering, though she hadn't been in the house for more than a few hours. The giddy sense of freedom that filled her chest made her far more generous about details than her mother would ever have approved of.

"In the interest of preventing the spread of untrue stories, I will admit that my marriage to Dr. Pearson was sudden and unexpected on all sides." She rested her teacup in its saucer, her cheeks heating. "My mother has been intent on marrying me off to a titled gentleman for years. She saw her opportunity last week when Dr. Pearson was attempting to extricate me from a rose bush. He was only trying to help, but Mama used what she saw to accuse him of impropriety and to demand he marry me immediately to make up for what she imagined was ruining me."

She finished her explanation and peeked up to see what Mrs. Ainsworth thought. The older woman wore an expression of surprise, and a fair amount of amusement. "Well, we can't go telling the housemaids that story," she said, setting down her tea. "Could we tell them that you and Lord Helm have been acquaintances for quite some time, and that unbeknownst to us, arrangements were already in place for your nuptials at Mr. Croydon's house party? Heaven knows it wouldn't be the first time Lord Helm has left the rest of us in the dark."

Lavinia's mother would probably faint at the frank way Mrs. Ainsworth spoke, but Lavinia found herself smiling broadly. "If you think that would be best, then you have my permission to share that version of things. I am glad I told you the truth, though."

"And I'm glad I can be here to ease what I'm certain is a startling change," Mrs. Ainsworth said.

In spite of her smiles and delight, Lavinia was seized by the sudden urge to cry. What would her life have been like if her own mother had been as understanding and compassionate as Armand's housekeeper? It was a heady feeling to be embraced so warmly. Perhaps her mother had unintentionally done a wonderful thing by pushing her into Armand's arms. And perhaps her friends were right when they hinted that she could be just as happy and free married under the right circumstances as she could maintaining a stalwart, single life.

"Mrs. Ainsworth, Mrs. Ainsworth," the youngest maid, Cherry, said, bursting into the room. The moment she saw Lavinia, she nearly shrieked in fright and froze on the spot.

"Is that a proper greeting for your new mistress?" Mrs. Ainsworth scolded her, but not with malice.

"I'm sorry, my lady," Cherry said, dipping into a low, clumsy curtsy. "Good day, my lady. At your service, my lady."

"Hello, Cherry," Lavinia greeted her.

Cherry snapped straight and turned to Mrs. Ainsworth. "We've guests, ma'am. They've just arrived. Unexpected like."

Lavinia's heart squeezed to a stone in her chest. It couldn't be her mother, could it? She wouldn't dare show up on Armand's doorstep less than twenty-four hours after Lavinia broke away from her.

Her fears were eased somewhat as Mr. Bondar marched into the room. "Lord and Lady Tavistock are here to call, my lady."

A whole different sort of panic filled Lavinia. "Lady Tavistock?" She set her tea on Mrs. Ainsworth's desk and stood. "How does she know I'm here?"

"Begging your pardon, my lady," Mr. Bondar began, "but she doesn't. Lord Tavistock informed me that he and his wife were simply passing by as part of a day trip, and they thought they'd stop by to see if Lord Helm were home."

"We must invite them to luncheon," Lavinia said, taking charge on instinct. "Lady Tavistock is an important woman in political circles in London."

Mr. Bondar and Mrs. Ainsworth exchanged looks, then turned to Lavinia for guidance.

"If she is someone whose favor you wish to gain, we'll do our best to impress her," Mrs. Ainsworth said.

They all set to work. Mr. Bondar returned upstairs to

assist Armand in whatever way butlers assisted their masters while Lavinia ran through a quick course of action with Mrs. Ainsworth and Mrs. Piper.

Exhaustion didn't matter. The impossibility of entertaining Lady Tavistock within hours of arriving in a new home and within days of assuming a new title and position in life was irrelevant. Lavinia had a duty to her husband to fulfill, and she was determined to do it to the best of her ability. As soon as things were settled downstairs, she rushed to Armand's bedroom, tidied up her hair and clothes, made sure she was presentable, then flew back downstairs to the sitting room where Armand was entertaining the Tavistocks. She smiled and greeted Lady Tavistock with modesty and as much grace as she could muster, answering her surprise and delight over finding Lavinia married so unexpectedly with every appearance of felicitation and ease. When luncheon was served, she drew on every lesson in how a titled lady should deport herself to see that her guests were happy and satisfied.

By the time Lord and Lady Tavistock departed, Lavinia was beyond exhausted and she couldn't stop shaking as she thought of the disaster such a sudden call to entertain could have caused. But there was little time to think about it. Mrs. Ainsworth had questions about her wardrobe and how to send for the rest of her things from her mother's house. And while Armand had the look of a man who wanted to spend time with his wife, they barely had a chance to see each other before Lavinia practically fell into his bed that night. She was so worn out that she couldn't bring herself to care that she was sleeping with a stranger yet again.

Fortunately, Armand seemed as exhausted as she was and in no mood for awkward intimacy.

"You were dazzling today, you know," he said as they

settled into the large, oak bed and its voluminous quilts and featherbeds.

"Hardly dazzling," Lavinia said, too tired to measure her words. "We had guests. I did what I was supposed to do to make sure they felt welcome."

"I would have made my apologies and turned them away," Armand said, sounding more like he was talking to himself. He plumped the pillow behind him, then flopped onto his back, pulling the covers up to his chin. "How did you know exactly what to do for the Tavistocks?"

Lavinia's answer was delayed by a long yawn. "Mama spent years drilling social etiquette into me. Lord Tavistock is a peer. We are in the country rather than town. Cold meats and soup wouldn't have been my first choice, but they were sufficient based on what we had on hand. If we host a supper party, service should be *a la Russe*, with two kinds of fish, three savory vegetable dishes, a roast...." Her words faded into half-asleep rambling as a gentle darkness closed around her.

She snapped awake again at the sensation of Armand's arm closing around her, pulling her back against his chest.

"Is this all right?" he asked, snuggling against her.

Lavinia was suddenly wide awake. The heat of Armand's body encircled her like a teasing promise. The firmness of his muscles was both a curiosity and an unexpected temptation. The part of him she'd found curiously delightful as it invaded her on her wedding night nestled against her backside in a state of half-excitement. She caught herself wishing he'd move his hands just a smidgen higher, toward her breasts, or a little bit lower, towards the part of her where a curious ache was growing.

"It's fine," she said quietly.

"Good." He nestled further against her, and his breathing

slowed. "It was lovely seeing you blossom in front of our guests today," he said, evidently not ready for sleep yet.

"I would hardly call it blossoming," she said, wanting to wriggle her backside against him but not daring to. "I was simply doing as I've been instructed to do."

"Hmm." Armand adjusted the blankets over them. "It seems to me that you've had far too much instruction and far too little amusement in your life."

An ache in her heart joined the one growing in her core. "Perhaps."

Armand was silent for a moment, long enough for Lavinia to wonder if he'd fallen asleep, before surprising her by saying, "Are there things that you've wanted to do that your mother has forbidden?"

She could have laughed. "A great many things," she said, letting herself relax at last and soften against him.

"Such as?" he asked.

She thought for a moment as sleep tempted her once again. "I always wanted to ride a horse, but she would never let me. Never mind that some of the grandest ladies in England are accomplished equestrians, she believed it was too dangerous and that riding negatively effects a woman's ability to conceive."

As soon as the indelicate words were out of her mouth, Lavinia winced. Had she really brought up conception at a moment like that? It didn't help matters when she felt that part of Armand twitch against her. He cleared his throat and shifted as though looking for a more comfortable position, then went very still as that part of him continued to expand.

"It's settled then," he said, his voice slightly rough. "As soon as possible, once we're rested and the duties of the house had been taken care of, I'll take you down to the stables and teach you to ride." His body tensed in enticing ways. "A horse," he clarified. "I'll teach you to ride a horse.

Your mother would love that." He paused, then repeated, "Your mother," almost nonsensically.

For some reason, that eased the tension she could feel radiating from him. His member softened, and before too long, his breathing had steadied out into sleep. She, on the other hand, lay awake for a while longer, cursing her mother for reasons she couldn't quite put her finger on.

CHAPTER 10

A few days later, Armand awoke to the quiet sound of one of his maids setting the fire in the fireplace at the other end of the room. The knowledge that someone else was in the room while he lay in bed, Lavinia in his arms, was enough to knock the sleep right out of him. He lay as still as he could, sheltering Lavinia with his body and wondering if the presence of the maid bothered her. Anyone who had lived in any sort of fine home should be used to maids slipping in and out at all hours of the day and night to do their duties, but there was something intrusive about a third person bearing witness to what was undeniably a sensitive moment. Especially when the evening before had been spent in another awkward, unsatisfying attempt at love-making. Servants had a way of guessing exactly what was going on with their masters by the way the bedcovers were wrinkled.

But Lavinia slept on, and soon the maid was gone. Armand relaxed, and his thoughts turned to how perfect his lovely, young wife felt against him. He'd had such good intentions the night before. The days since returning to Broadclyft Hall had been busy and tiring as they both settled into their roles as lord and lady of the manor. He'd intended to make love to her far more enticingly than he had on their wedding night, but they'd both been exhausted, and while things had gone more smoothly than the first time, his performance had left much to be desired. Already, he was thinking forward to when he could try again.

His thoughts had a physical effect. They'd shifted during the night so that now he lay on his back with her snuggled against him. It was a blessing, because as the blood of arousal rushed to his groin, he wasn't poking her. Not that he wouldn't like to be poking her. Practice made perfect, after all, and they definitely needed practice.

A rush of giddiness at the thought had him shaking with repressed laughter. Few things could be more ridiculous than lying in his bed with a swiftly-growing erection while his beautiful, accidental wife snoozed softly against him. If they knew each other better, he would have nudged her to the side, swept off her nightgown and awakened her by making love to her tenderly. As things stood, he was fairly certain that if he tried that, she would probably wake up screaming. The maids would have something to say about that.

He attempted to relax. A few more minutes' sleep would do him a world of good. But neither sleep nor relaxation was in the cards. Lavinia stirred, her body undulating against his as she dreamed on. Her breasts pressed against him, only a few layers of cotton keeping him from touching her skin. His cock ached in response, begging him for relief. She was his wife, after all. It was only natural that the two of them should enjoy intimacy whenever the need struck.

He couldn't do that to her. He was next door to a stranger to her, one who had inadvertently implied he regretted being forced to marry her just a few days ago. He would be the blackest sort of villain to push himself on her now. So instead, he carefully slipped away from her, trying his best not to disturb her as he crept out of bed.

With his nightshirt tented in front of him, he hobbled across the room to the painted screen, behind which sat a convenient chamber pot. As soon as he was hidden from view of the bed, he bunched his nightshirt at his waist and took himself in hand. It was far better to quickly take care of things himself than to impose on Lavinia. And while a part of him felt guilty for closing his eyes and imagining her luscious body laid bare for him, her legs parted, revealing her glistening cunny, ready for him, her nipples taut, and her eyes beckoning as she licked her lips, the vision did the trick.

He swallowed the groan of pleasure that escaped from him and stroked himself feverishly, enjoying the act a little too much. He was as bad as a schoolboy playing with himself for the first time, but the Lavinia of his imagination was a siren that had him primed and ready to come. Someday soon, he prayed, they'd be close enough for him to feel her tightness around his cock instead of his hand, and to hear her pleasured moans mingled with his panting. Adding sound to his vision of her ignited the cannon of his climax.

"Armand?" Lavinia's soft question came just as he did. The heady relief of orgasm pulsed through him at the same time as the jolt of being caught. Of course, he hadn't exactly been caught, not yet.

"Just a moment," he said, his voice far too winded to be innocent. He leaned against the wall, letting his nightshirt fall back over his spent member. Sweat dripped down his back and dotted his forehead. He mopped it away with his sleeve, but the flush he was certain reddened his face wasn't going to go away as soon.

"I'm just going to pop down the hall to wash and dress for the day," Lavinia said.

Armand jerked straight at the sound of her climbing out

of bed and padding across the carpet. He stepped out from behind the screen and attempted to greet her with a calm, unsuspicious smile.

He failed.

Lavinia blinked when she saw him. "Is something the matter?" She changed directions to approach him, touching the back of her hand to his forehead. "You're flushed."

"I'm fine," he said, still not completely recovered. He took her hand away from his forehead and rested it over his heart—which wasn't the best thing to do.

"Your heart is racing," she said, her expression full of concern. "Are you certain you shouldn't call a doctor?"

"I am a doctor," he reminded her. "And I'm fine."

She bit her lip, studying him with concern. "Perhaps you should go back to bed for a while."

Images of her in bed with him, the two of them tangled and sweating, ignited the whole process he'd just embarrassed himself to complete minutes ago.

"There isn't time to go back to bed," he said, stepping away from her and heading to the window to throw it open. The burst of cold air did just what he needed it to do. "I'm going to teach you to ride today," he said, then quickly added. "A horse."

She watched him with puzzlement. "What else would I ride?"

Visions of her atop him, breasts bouncing as she impaled herself on him scattered Armand's thoughts. "Nothing," he said, feigning innocence. He needed to get his imagination under control, and he needed to do it soon. "Let me know if there's anything you need and I'll have Mrs. Ainsworth direct the maids to fetch it at once."

"All right." She smiled and started for the door, but turned back to him as she reached for the handle. "You would tell me if you were ill, wouldn't you? Or if there were anything I could do to make you feel better?"

She could strip off her nightgown and leap back into his bed, but he wasn't about to ask her for that.

"Of course I would," he said instead, managing a genuine smile for her kindness. "But for now, you'll want to pick out the most appropriate dress you've brought with you for riding."

"Yes, right away." Her smile grew excited and she opened the door, rushing out into the hall.

As soon as the door shut behind her, Armand sagged against the broad windowsill. He shook his head. He was shocked with himself for being so suddenly consumed with desire for his wife. Was it the fact that they'd escaped the meddling of Winterberry Park? The comfort of home? It wasn't as though he'd never had lovers, though it had been a while. Or was it simply that with every new surprise Lavinia had for him, every revelation of her character and her kindness, the impulse to make her his wife for genuine reasons and not just because a dozen other people had wanted it was taking over his body? Or was that his heart? He hadn't thought of India for days.

He stood with a sigh, heading to his washstand to clean himself up. Whatever the reasons, he owed it to Lavinia to be a steady, undemanding husband and not one consumed by lust. But that didn't stop him from hoping that there might come a time when she was consumed by lust for him as well.

HE WAS HIDING SOMETHING FROM HER. LAVINIA WAS absolutely certain that Armand was hiding something crucial from her. He couldn't have been more suspicious if he'd tried when she'd awakened that morning to find him using the chamber pot. Was he ill? Was that the reason he'd been so moody at Winterberry Park? Of course, anyone would be moody if they'd had a surprise marriage sprung upon them. But perhaps he'd been willing to go along with the marriage because he knew his health was delicate and he wouldn't be married long.

But no, that was ridiculous. Armand was as healthy as an ox. He hadn't had the air of a sick man at all. Quite the contrary. There'd been something alluring about him, something enticing and a bit naughty. It'd left her unsettled, but in a good way. She'd surprised herself by enjoying what they'd done the night before, although it had still been frustrating and inadequate somehow. And the teasing glimpses of his chest, arms, and legs through the gaps in his nightshirt just then, the way the cotton garment was almost thin enough for her to see through, had made her want to lift up the hem and—

His hand brushed hers as he swayed closer to her on their walk down to the stables, and she nearly stumbled. It was as though an electric shock had gone straight from her hand to her unmentionables.

"Are you all right?" Armand asked, reaching out to steady her.

"I must have stepped on a stone," she lied, sending him an apologetic smile.

"Yes, I imagine the ground is a bit uneven after those storms a few days ago," he said, offering his arm.

She took it, highly aware of the muscle beneath his coat. She'd learned that he was forty-eight, younger than his friends by a few years, but still much older than her. Thanks to their wedding night and the night before, she was aware he had the form of a much younger man, though. But then, a doctor would know how to keep himself healthy, and if he rode for exercise as much as he'd implied over breakfast, then he would be in good shape.

Perhaps it would be wise, for the sake of building healthy marital relations, if she were to become better acquainted with his form.

"Are you certain something isn't wrong?" he asked as they approached the stable. "You seem awfully quiet. And you're a bit flushed."

"I can't think of anything to say," she admitted, ignoring his observation of her color. He didn't need to know that what she really couldn't think of was a proper way to ask him what he was keeping from her.

Armand smiled, resting his free hand over hers. "It's a wise person who keeps quiet when they have nothing to say."

His comment put her at ease. "I'd hardly consider myself wise."

They crossed through the stable door and into a row of dim, straw-lined stalls, each occupied by a fine specimen of equestrian grace.

"You wouldn't?" he asked, then shrugged. "In the past week, I've come to the conclusion that you are very wise indeed."

Lavinia blushed at the compliment. "I'm not sure how I gave that impression."

"Good morning, my lord," the groom greeted them before Armand could answer her.

"Morning, Dashiell," Armand greeted the young man. "Do you have the horses ready?"

"Yes, my lord. Mozart for you and Kitty for her ladyship," Dashiell answered.

Any further inquiries into the mysteries of Armand were forgotten as he led Lavinia out into the yard, Dashiell bringing the horses behind them. Kitty had been outfitted with a side-saddle, and, with a minimal amount of confusion and fuss, Armand helped Lavinia to climb a mounting block and settle herself comfortably. Whereas Lavinia had been afraid she would feel nervous on top of a large, powerful animal, she was surprised to find she had no fear at all.

"She's a sweet horse," she said, leaning forward to stroke Kitty's neck as Armand mounted Mozart.

"Kitty has the steadiest temperament of any of Lord Helm's stable, my lady," Dashiell explained. "She's the best mare to learn on."

"Thank you, Mr. Dashiell." Lavinia smiled at the groom.

"We'll go slowly," Armand said, walking his horse over to hers and petting the mare's neck. "I'm sure you'll get the hang of it as we go."

Dashiell took a quick moment to explain the basic commands needed for a woman riding side-saddle. None of it seemed too complicated to master, though Lavinia had the feeling that Kitty knew far, far more than she did and moved on instinct more than because of any command she gave.

"She likes you, I can tell," Armand said as they rode out of the yard and onto a wide path that curved through a meadow down the hill from the main house. He cut a fine figure atop his horse. So much so that Lavinia went straight back to feeling a stir deep inside of her. The strength of his legs was particularly apparent as he rode. She remembered what the power of his thighs had felt like between hers.

"How does one tell if a horse likes them?" Lavinia asked, a slight catch in her voice, desperate to tame her thoughts. A ridiculous part of her wanted to ask how to tell if a man liked her, if *he* liked her.

"Her gait is smooth and easy," Armand answered. "She isn't pulling or shaking her head or showing any signs of distress."

A wry grin flittered across Lavinia's lips before she could stop herself. "Perhaps it's because I know how she feels a little too well."

"Do you?" he asked with an enticing half-smile.

Lavinia sighed. "It's surprising how much the strictures one's mother places on one can feel like being bridled and saddled and led about by the bit."

Armand hummed, his face pinching into a frown. "If there's one thing I'm finding I don't regret in this whole strange business that brought us together, it's that our marriage has managed to get you away from your mother."

Lavinia smiled, but her gut twisted at his words. She knew he had regrets, but she wished he'd stop saying as much. "It's a strange thing," she said instead. "Finding yourself in a life you never set out to live."

His sudden, ironic laugh, had both his horse and hers flinching. She tightened her hands on her reins and tensed to stay solidly in her seat.

"I know far too much about being thrust into a life I never set out to live," he said.

Her initial burst of guilt turned to sympathy as she realized he wasn't referring to their marriage, but to his title. Her heart seemed to swell with affection, a sensation she rather liked. "But surely inheriting a peerage is a useful thing," she said.

He glanced at her, his frown lightening. "Useful? I wouldn't have used that word to describe it."

Lavinia shrugged. "I can see that you regret being forced to give up medicine, though I still don't understand why a viscount couldn't also be a practicing physician."

"Gentlemen aren't expected to work," he answered. "And besides, as my friends continuously remind me, now that I have a seat in the House of Lords, my time must be better spent debating sanitation laws and international trade relations."

"But surely, serving your country could be seen as healing the nation, couldn't it?"

His brow rose as he glanced her way. "I'm surprised you care so much about the nation."

"Because I'm a woman?" she asked, challenging him by meeting his eyes with determination.

He grinned, and a burst of heat rushed through her. It ignited sparks of longing in noticeable places. The sensations were both exciting and unnerving, reminding her of how she'd felt the night before.

"I stand corrected," he said, his smile growing. "It shouldn't surprise me that you care about politics at all, considering the company you keep. I'm pleased to see that my friends and their wives have had a positive effect on you. For me, on the other hand, their interference has cost me a career I loved and thrust me into a position where I feel utterly out of my depth."

"Out of your depth?"

He rolled his shoulders uncomfortably. "Most men know when they're destined to become a peer. They grow up with their education tailored toward learning the law of the land, how our government works. Peter deVere, for example, studied law intensively at Oxford before joining the army because he knew he would someday serve in Her Majesty's government. I had no warning what would be required of me."

"So you studied medicine," Lavinia said.

"After the war, yes." Armand nodded. "Now all that studying, all that training, has gone for naught, and I'm left in a job I'm ill-suited and ill-prepared for."

He was bitter. Kitty could have figured that much out. "The nation is at a critical point right now," she argued. "Especially now that the Liberal Party has regained control of Parliament. The rights of women and the working class stand on the brink of being expanded. Ireland could win

Home Rule, as they've wanted for so long. Even the fates of the people of the colonies hang in the balance."

A flush of color painted his cheeks at her mention of the colonies. He stared forward, avoiding her gaze.

"Are the colonies important to you?" she asked, suddenly eager to learn more about what he cared about.

"I have some contacts in India," he began slowly. "A Dr. Maqsood, who works at a hospital in Lahore. I was thinking…."

An awkward silence fell between them. Lavinia stared at him, once again overcome with the feeling that he was hiding something from her.

He took a deep breath and glanced at her with a tense smile. "I was thinking that we could ride closer to the tenant farms on the other side of the estate," he said. "Broadclyft Hall has a quaint village on its grounds, complete with a well-maintained cricket pitch."

"Do you play cricket?" she asked, feeling as though he'd changed the subject deliberately. She wouldn't call him on it. If he had a reason for not wanting to talk about India, then she wouldn't press him.

"I did," he said. "I still do once in a while, when the village is short a man. Mr. Bondar is widely regarded as the finest umpire in Devon."

"Is he really?" Lavinia smiled, settling comfortably into her saddle once more. She liked it when she and Armand could talk about unimportant things as though they were friends. She wanted more of those moments, more closeness with him. Perhaps then he wouldn't regret the way they'd been thrown together.

"Devon is cricket-mad," he nodded, guiding them down a secondary path that cut through the meadow. "We have quite a few competitive teams that—"

The conversation ended abruptly as Kitty stepped on a

loose bit of ground that turned out to be a hive of wasps. In an instant, several zipped to protect their home, stinging Kitty's leg. Before Lavinia knew what had happened, Kitty cried out and leapt forward. It was all Lavinia could do to cling to her saddle as the poor horse tore into a frightened run. The speed with which Kitty bolted was enough to blow Lavinia's hat off.

"Lavinia!" She barely heard Armand's frantic cry behind her as Kitty galloped across the meadow. Her full focus was on the single task of holding on. Her muscles tensed and her hands locked around the reins and the saddle. There wasn't even room for fear, only tight, all-consuming focus.

The meadow tore past in a blur of green and brown. Ahead, Lavinia could make out the edge of a stretching woodland and a small, thatched cottage nestled between the trees and the field. Perhaps the sight of something so human and domestic would calm Kitty, and perhaps someone lived there who could help. Without knowing what she was doing, she willed the horse to turn toward the cottage and to calm down.

Surprisingly, it seemed as though her attempt at mind-control worked. That or Kitty recovered from the initial shock and pain of being stung and slowed on her own. She came out of her run, trotted for a few more paces, walked the last few steps, then stopped entirely. The only indication Lavinia had that she was still upset was the way she shook her head and stomped her stung leg.

Lavinia was in no hurry to go for another gallop, so as fast as she could, she unhooked her leg from the saddle, let go of the reins and attempted to dismount. The ground was farther away than she anticipated, though, and instead of alighting gracefully, she tumbled to the dirt, plopping into a messy ball of skirts and arms and legs. Her left ankle tweaked uncomfortably as she did.

"Lavinia!"

Armand's cry was closer than she expected it to be. He charged into the clearing beside the cottage where she'd fallen and dismounted so swiftly that she wasn't sure Mozart even stopped. The sudden arrival startled Kitty all over again, and she ran toward the woods, only stopping when Mozart trotted after her.

"Lavinia, are you hurt?" Armand flung himself to the ground beside her, scrambling to pull her into his arms and right her.

"Surprisingly, I'm not," she panted, shaking now that the ordeal was passed. Her breath came in sudden gasps, and she could feel sweat trickling down her back. But it was his proximity that kept her heart racing. All of her earlier thoughts swooped back in on her.

"Are you sure?" he asked, testing her arms and wrists, then lifting her skirt to handle her ankles and calves.

He was a doctor. She reminded herself of that as his probing hands tested her knees. But he was also her husband. Whether it was the fright of the wild ride or whether she was mad as a march hare for other reasons, she found herself wishing he'd touch her as intimately as the night before. His hands on her legs didn't feel medicinal at all.

"Nothing seems to be broken," he said. "You gave me such a fright. I shouldn't have taken you on a ride in such open territory until we'd practiced in the safety of the paddock for a while. Can you forgive me?" He glanced up to her, his eyes filled with genuine regret.

"I can," she panted. The breathless feeling of excitement wasn't going away. It loomed larger as he inched closer, placing his hands on her sides.

"Does anything hurt?" he asked as he squeezed her. "Anything at all?"

Her ankle was tender, but she was loath to switch his

focus away from the shrinking space between them, so she shook her head.

"Is there anything I can do?" he asked. "Anything to make you feel better?"

"Well," she said, still panting, "you could kiss me."

He froze, meeting her eyes with a look of surprise. It quickly heated to levels that had her trembling for entirely different reasons. He closed his arms around her, pulling her close, and captured her mouth with his own.

CHAPTER 11

His lips molded against hers with far more insistence than when he'd kissed her on their wedding night. His tongue raked against her bottom lip, and when she gasped at the sensation, he slipped it past her lips to tease hers. The sensation was captivating and left her aching to reciprocate the pleasure he was giving her. It left her aching in other ways too.

She reached for him, circling her arms around the broad expanse of his back as she did her best to return his kiss. A tiny voice at the back of her head worried that she was doing it all wrong and that he would think she was a ninny, but before she could do anything about those thoughts, he'd lowered her to her back in the soft, cool grass.

A whole new wave of desire washed over her as he stretched by her side, half atop her, and continued to kiss her, nibbling at her lip and trailing a quick burst of kisses to her neck before returning to her mouth. His hand stroked her side, rising to cradle her breast. His thumb brushed across her nipple, sending a jolt of need through her and making her curse corsets, restrictive bodices, and clothing in general. It seemed wildly strange that she should feel more of the heady sort of passion Elaine wrote about and Lady Stanhope had hinted at with both her and Armand fully clothed and lying in the grass than she had in bed.

Armand brushed a few heated kisses toward her neck, his hand gently squeezing her breast and his knee delving between her legs, but then he stopped suddenly.

"I'm sorry," he said, panting, and planted his hands on either side of her shoulders so he could hold himself above her. "I don't know what came over me."

"Don't stop," she begged him, clutching the lapels of his coat. "Please, please don't stop."

He blinked, his eyes going wide. "You don't want me to stop?"

He was maddening and endearing at the same time. As charming as the respect in his question was, much to Lavinia's surprise, she didn't want to be respected right then. Quite the contrary.

"You're my husband," she told him, deliciously breathless. "It doesn't matter for how long. You have every right to ravish me in the meadow if you wish." She was fully aware that her tone, and likely her expression, were begging him to do just that.

A wicked grin spread across his lips, making her heart beat faster and the maelstrom of need within her grow frenzied. "Don't tell me that the whole time, through these last few, difficult days, you've harbored fantasies of me having my way with you."

She shivered at the purr in his voice. "You're a handsome man," she said. "My friends are all mad for their husbands and the things they do. And after the little we've shared…." She paused, unable to resist smiling over his sudden, curious, embarrassed look. "That can't be it," she said. "I know there's more."

"There's so much more," he said, lowering himself enough to pull a long, tender kiss from her lips. "But I was worried you wouldn't want it, that you'd be frightened or put off. I didn't want to start this whole thing by terrifying you."

"I promise not to be terrified," she said, moving her hands down to unbutton his coat. "As long as you promise not to leave me in the dark about anything."

A brief, uncertainty flashed through his expression, and for a moment, the feeling that he was keeping something from her returned. But it was fleeting. As soon as he lowered himself so that their bodies came into full contact from chest to hips, and as soon as his mouth covered hers once more, kissing her with a need that left her shivering, all other thoughts were forgotten.

For a second time, he stopped at exactly the moment she didn't want him to, when her body was tingling with excitement. But when he rocked back, balancing on his knees and pulling her to sit with him, it was to say, "If I were twenty years younger, I'd take you right here in the grass. But the gamekeeper's cabin is right there, and I happen to know for a fact there's a bed inside."

"Will the gamekeeper mind?" Lavinia asked as he helped her to her feet.

"I suppose he would if I had one," Armand said, taking her hand and leading her to the cottage door. "I don't know what happened to the last one, and I haven't bothered to hire a new one."

"You really should," Lavinia said as he fetched a key from the top of the doorframe, then unlocked the door. "He would prevent your game from being poached and provide you with food for—"

Her advice was cut off as he pushed open the door, looped an arm around her waist, and swung her inside. The cottage was a bit musty and had a feeling of disuse, but that was all the assessment Lavinia had time for before Armand closed her in an ardent embrace and slanted his mouth over hers.

It was like being carried away by a whirlwind of instinct. Lavinia had never found herself in a situation of such sensual potency, and while her lack of experience should have made her confused and clumsy, the need to be as close to Armand as possible overrode everything else. She fumbled with the buttons of his waistcoat as he picked at the impossibly numerous buttons of her bodice. All the while, they stepped blindly through the front room of the cottage toward what she assumed was the bedroom, stopping for kisses every few feet. In the process, she nearly stumbled over a chair. She yelped in surprise, and Armand caught her, clutching her tight.

"We could do this the wild, romantic, and potentially accident-prone way and continue to undress each other blindly while kissing," he panted, humor lighting his eyes. "Or we could choose the far less exotic path of walking calmly into the bedroom, undressing without each other's help, and meeting in the bed already fully naked."

Lavinia shivered at the mere thought of being naked with Armand. She hadn't been naked with anyone since she was a child with a maid helping her bathe. Thus far, they'd made love in their nightclothes. "Which would be faster?" she asked, eyes wide with expectation.

"Probably undressing ourselves, since we're likely to get distracted if we try to undress each other," he said.

She glanced down at his unbuttoned coat and half-unbuttoned waistcoat, but it was the bulge in his trousers that caught her eye. She bit her lip, partially eager to explore that part of him, but partially certain she'd do something utterly ridiculous with him and ruin the delicious mood.

"We'll undress ourselves then," she said, glancing up to meet his eyes.

There was so much heat in his gaze that she almost rethought her decision, just so she could see his expression as he peeled off her clothes. "Good choice," he said. "But first…."

He pulled her into his arms, planting one more long, wet kiss on her mouth. By the time he let her go, Lavinia wasn't certain she would be capable of movement, let alone working open the myriad buttons that kept her constrained in her clothes. She wouldn't have moved at all if Armand hadn't stepped away first, taking her hand and leading her into the bedroom.

Like the rest of the cottage, the bedroom had a distinct feeling of abandonment. There was a bed, but it wasn't made, and a puff of dust swirled up from the mattress when Armand tested it with a firm pat. Lavinia continued with the process of climbing out of her clothes all the same, as certain that Armand would think of something as she was that it didn't matter what sort of surface they had available, as long as she could continue to feel the magnificent stirring inside of her. As it happened, Armand found a pile of neatly-folded and relatively clean blankets and quilts in the wardrobe. As Lavinia shrugged out of her bodice and set it aside, going to work on her skirts, he draped several layers of blankets over the mattress.

With that done, he undressed. Lavinia's pulse shot up as she watched the layers of his clothes come away out of the corner of her eye. She cursed her tendency to tremble when overcome with emotion as she loosened her skirts and stepped out of them in one go, leaving a pile on the floor.

She had just managed to unhook her corset and toss it aside when Armand stepped up behind her and circled his arms around her. She gasped as his hands spread across her stomach under her chemise, then broke out in tingles at the sensation of his completely naked body against her back. His staff was hard and stood upright as it pressed against the small of her back.

"I got impatient," he growled against her ear, sliding one hand up to cup her breast and the other down to pluck open the drawstring of her drawers. As soon as they were loose, his fingers delved into the curls between her legs.

"Dear heavens," she panted, reeling with the sensuality of the way he touched her.

"Please tell me this feels good," he said, kissing her neck and fondling her in more places than her over-sated senses could keep track of. "Because I intend to do this frequently if it does."

"It does," she echoed.

"I'm glad to hear it," he said, shifting his hands so that he could catch her chemise and lift it over her head.

Once that had been discarded, he smoothed his hands down over her hips, pushing her drawers and stockings down with them. It took a moment of completely unromantic wriggling to kick them aside, but once they were gone, he spun her in his arms until they were face to face, body to body. Lavinia let out a tremulous sigh as he pulled her into his arms, holding her back with one hand and cradling her backside with the other. There was nothing between them, nothing at all. His thick staff was hot against her belly, but she was afraid to peek at it.

He tilted her head up for a kiss, but as sweet as that was, when he leaned back to see what she thought, the only thing that burst from her mouth was, "We're naked."

He laughed, lines crinkling around his eyes and joy filling his expression. "We are," he said. "Fortunately, there are a lot of very enjoyable things we can do in this state."

"Oh?"

"Yes."

He bent to kiss her again, his tongue sliding along hers in a slow, heady rhythm that instantly brought other things to mind. Like the way he'd felt inside of her the night before. The memory had her body instantly begging to feel that invasion again.

For a moment, Lavinia thought she was going to get what she wanted. Armand picked her up, and she instinctively wrapped her legs around him. That brought the part of her that wanted attention right up against to the part of him she wanted attention from. She was on the verge of following impulse and wriggling against him when he walked two steps to the bed before setting her down in the nest of blankets.

"If I do anything you don't like," he said as he settled between her legs, tossing one blanket over top of them to block out the slight chill in the air, "let me know. I'll stop anything you don't want."

"And what if I want it all?" she asked, raking her hands up his sides and digging her fingertips into his back.

He laughed, the sound rumbling through her, and kissed her neck. "Darling," he said, "you don't know half the things that are possible, in spite of what your friends might have told you."

"I don't?" Her heart raced and every part of her wanted to encompass every part of him.

"No." He kissed his way to her collarbone, then lower. "But after a while, if you find you want to explore, I am perfectly willing to indulge any fancy that might take you."

Her mouth fell open at the underlying wickedness of his statement. Her mind couldn't even fathom what sort of naughty things he was implying, but the rebellious part of her wanted to find out.

Even those thoughts were cast aside when his mouth

reached her breast and closed over her nipple. She let out a long moan of pleasure as he licked and suckled her. At last, the implications of everything her friends had whispered about seemed fulfilled. His mouth was magical as it worked her nipple into a hard point. He teased her other breast with his hand, sending electric sensation soaring through her. Every touch and kiss increased the ache in her core and made her feel more and more as though she was at his mercy. Strangely enough, she loved the sensation, loved feeling as though she was his to play with.

"If I had known you would be so sweet," he murmured as he moved to treat her other breast to the same delicious sensations as the first, "I would have bedded you this way on our wedding night. I wanted to, you know."

"You did?" she managed to squeak out.

"Yes," he confessed, trailing his fingers over her belly and lower. "I wanted to do all sorts of things to you then, and last night, and this morning."

"Why didn't you?" she panted as his fingers delved into her curls once more.

"We hardly know each other, remember? We are mere acquaintances who were maneuvered into a loveless marriage by conniving friends and family."

He brushed over her clitoris as he finished, causing Lavinia to arch into his hand. At the same time, he closed his mouth over her breast, nipping at her nipple with his teeth, then sucking. The burst of pleasure sent Lavinia flying and brought her very close to what felt like an explosion. The only thing that stopped her from shattering was Armand's change of position. He inched down, disappearing under the blanket covering them.

"What are you doing?" she asked, laughing excitedly.

A moment later, his hands gripped her knees, pushing them far apart. She gasped at the sensation of being spread and gripped the blankets. He kissed her inner thigh, and she would have gasped again if she'd had any air left in her lungs. It was maddening to not be able to see him or what he was doing. All she could see was the mound of him under the blankets below her waist and her breasts, the nipples reddened and taut, where the blanket had been pulled low enough to expose them.

Then she felt his hands slide up her thighs and right into the heat between her legs. She cried out at the sensation as he traced her opening, then teased a finger inside of her. Her fists tensed in the blankets as he stroked her inner walls finding the most delicious spot inside of her and working it.

"Armand," she moaned, not sure if it was a plea or a prayer.

He answered with a throaty laugh that tilted her even closer to the edge. His fingers continued to play, to part her in delicious ways. He kissed her thighs higher and higher, making the most unnerving noises of pleasure, until his mouth reached the apex of her sex, and he groaned in delight.

He wasn't the only one. She let out a wanton moan as his tongue repeated what his fingers had done. The pleasure that had been building inside of her swelled to unbearable intensity. He had barely begun to stroke her clitoris with his tongue when she came apart with a powerful burst like sunlight that tipped into throbbing waves of pleasure. He groaned in victory and slipped two fingers inside of her, intensifying everything she was feeling.

He pushed the covers back as her body pulsed with pleasure, catching her with what she was sure was a contorted expression of ecstasy. "God Almighty," he growled, watching her as he moved his fingers inside of her, extending her climax. Her whole body was exposed to his view as she was overcome, and only as the sensation began to settle did it dawn on her he might enjoy the sight.

A feeling of utter bliss filled her as Armand withdrew his fingers and shifted above her. She sucked in a breath, her heavy-lidded eyes popping open as he thrust inside of her. There was no pain, only the amazing feeling of being stretched and filled by him. And unlike before, there was nothing careful or methodical about the way he thrust in her. He was just on the other side of control, moving with a measure of desperation inside of her. Part of her wondered if she should be frightened by his frenzy after all, but she wasn't. It felt so unbelievably good to be taken that way, in spite of how big he was, that she was crying out in time to his thrusts and speeding toward another release herself in no time.

At last, something switched within him. Lavinia could feel his body tense as his thrusts became even more urgent. He gripped her backside, lifting her off the bed and thrusting at a different angle. That was enough to send another wave of orgasm ripping through her. Her body clenched his, and within seconds, he groaned and tensed all over. From there, his thrusts slowed and softened until he had no energy at all. He flopped over top of her, his body still inside of hers, panting and hot.

"Yes," she gasped for breath along with him, closing her arms and legs around him to keep him joined with her as long as possible. "I believe that's what my friends were talking about."

His panting shifted to laughter—light, joyful laughter. He extracted himself from her, rolling to the side and collapsing onto his back. Lavinia snuggled against his side, ignoring how blazing hot she was and how sweaty they both were.

"So you don't hate me now?" he asked, stroking her back lightly.

"Hate you?" She propped herself on one arm to look down at him so she could gauge whether he was serious.

"For being a lustful, old roué and having my way with you."

Her brow rose. She couldn't tell if he was serious or not. "You're welcome to have your way with me any time you please," she said, laughing, then snuggling by his side once more.

"Good," Armand said, hugging her close and closing his eyes. "Then perhaps I shall find it in my heart to forgive your mother for her machinations after all."

Lavinia made a disgusted sound as she settled against her husband's side, fully intending to sleep for a bit. "Don't mention my mother at a time like this."

"Never," he agreed, then let out an exhausted breath.

Lavinia smiled in spite of the mention. Perhaps she would have to forgive mother as well.

Armand floated in and out of sleep, happy as a clam. A not-so-silly part of him mused that he might just be falling in love. He wasn't debauched enough to believe it was merely Lavinia's sensuality that attracted him. She'd driven him to new heights of pleasure, true, but it was the way she made him feel so accepted afterwards, the way she snuggled with him as they napped to recover from the exertion, that left him feeling as though he never wanted to leave the musty gamekeeper's cottage. No matter what course his life took, no matter what duties were thrust upon him or what changes his life was forced to undergo, she accepted him. Acceptance was a powerful aphrodisiac.

"Sweetheart," he whispered to her after they'd spent an hour dozing. "We'd better find the horses before they run back to the stable and set everyone to worrying."

Lavinia replied with a wordless grumble, then stretched her way out of sleep. She was simply gorgeous in every way imaginable. Whether it was the sweetness of her half-asleep smile as she nodded and pushed herself to sit, or the erotic beauty of the way she'd looked as she came earlier, Armand had a feeling he would never get tired of looking at her. He would never get tired of making love to her either, and if not for the nagging problem of the horses roaming free, he would have indulged a second time.

As it was, they tumbled out of bed and stretched the languidness away as they picked up their scattered clothing and got dressed. He would have preferred a long bath after love-making like that, or at least a wash with a sponge and jug of water. They could change as soon as they got back to the house, though. It wasn't as though they had guests or anything.

They walked out of the gamekeeper's cottage hand in hand. Armand made a note to ask Bondar to send someone down to clean the cottage and to keep it fresh, just in case he and Lavinia found themselves in need of a getaway some other time. Fortunately for them, both Mozart and Kitty were nearby, munching on fresh grass in the meadow. It didn't take long to call them over, but rather than helping Lavinia to mount Kitty, he had her ride with him atop Mozart while leading Kitty back to the stable.

But when they reached the stable, Armand was surprised to find Dashiell busy rubbing down three unfamiliar horses.

"What's all this?" he asked as he helped Lavinia dismount, then climbed down himself. He led Mozart and Kitty into the stable, where Dashiell's assistant came to get them.

"Guests, my lord," Dashiell said with a frown. "They arrived about an hour ago."

"Guests?" Lavinia asked. She glanced to him in question.

Armand shrugged and frowned. "Thank you, Dashiell."

He nodded to the groom, then took Lavinia's arm to escort her up to the house.

"We're in no condition for guests," she said as they walked at a brisk pace. "Are you expecting anyone?"

"No." Armand clenched his jaw and tried to imagine who would show up at Broadclyft Hall unannounced. It couldn't be Lady Prior or any of his friends. They were idiotic enough to coerce him into marriage, but they were also smart enough to know not to follow him home to cause more trouble. Besides, none of the three horses belonged to anyone he knew.

"Bondar, what's this about guests?" Armand asked as Bondar opened the door for them on their return.

"They're in the sitting room, my lord," Bondar began, his stern face even more foreboding than usual. "I thought to bar them from entering, but your cousin has a right—"

"Ah, Dr. Lord Pearson Helm," a sharp voice called out from the side of the main hall where the sitting room was located. "You're back from whatever romp in the woods you've been on."

Armand clutched Lavinia's arm tightly and turned to face the familiar voice. There, standing in his front hall, looking as smug as a badger, stood Theodore Shayles. Shayles's toady, and Armand's cousin, Lord Gatwick, stood to one side, hands behind his back, staring up at the artwork in the hall that might have been his with a blank expression. Worse still, none other than Dr. Miller stood on Shayles's other side, looking as though it were Christmas and he was about to be served pudding.

"Get out of my house, Shayles," Armand said, instantly furious. He stepped slightly in front of Lavinia, shielding her from the unwanted guests. "You're not wanted here."

"No?" Shayles asked, all false innocence. His cold, blue eyes practically glittered with malice, and his pale hair made him look as washed out as a menacing ghost. "Not even when we've come to return something you've lost?"

Armand scowled and opened his mouth to order Shayles to leave once more, but Shayles produced a thick envelope on pure white stationery edged with berry red, holding it up with an evil grin. Winterberry Park stationery. It was the letter his friends had sent to Gladstone.

CHAPTER 12

"Give that to me." Lavinia watched, heart in her throat, as Armand stepped forward, holding out his hand and glaring at the letter Lord Shayles held aloft.

"Ah-ah." Lord Shayles stepped away, keeping the letter out of Armand's reach. "Finders, keepers."

"That letter does not belong to you," Armand insisted, though he didn't try to snatch it away again. "Return it at once."

"Now why would I do that?" Lord Shayles asked in a falsely innocent voice. "It's a very interesting read." He lowered the envelope and smiled at it as though he could see the contents. "Everyone loves a good bit of political intrigue, especially when it has the whiff of corruption about it."

"Corruption?" Lavinia blurted before she could stop herself.

Lord Shayles seemed to notice her standing there. His smile grew wolfish. He took a step in her direction before Armand blocked him. "Corruption," he repeated, sniffing loudly. "Manipulation. Subverting Her Majesty's government so that a cabal of insiders can have their wicked way with Britannia. Can't you just smell it? Although, to be honest, it's something else that I scent." He sniffed again, a devilish light sparking in his eyes, and licked his lips. "Been having a bit of newlywed fun, have we?"

Heat rushed through Lavinia and she backed away, bristling with self-consciousness. The horrible man couldn't actually smell what she and Armand had been up to, could he? The way he stared at her, as though he could see through her clothes, made her feel dirty and cheap. He bit his lip, giving her the feeling he knew exactly how she felt and that he liked it.

"Don't look at my wife like that," Armand growled, stepping fully in front of her to block her from Shayles's sight. "If you want to cause trouble, cause it with me."

"Oh, I fully intend to cause trouble for everyone," Lord Shayles said. "Although one could argue that you've brought the trouble on yourself." He tapped the envelope against his lips, then bit the corner.

A shiver passed down Lavinia's spine. She couldn't stand to look at the man, so she peeked at his cohorts instead. Dr. Miller looked as though he were at the theater, enjoying every second of the show. Lord Gatwick was a different story. He stared at Lord Shayles with a look of intense disgust, so much so that Lavinia was momentarily stunned. As soon as Lord Gatwick realized she was watching him, his expression went carefully blank once more, and he returned to studying the artwork instead of paying any attention to what was taking place in the hall.

Lavinia was so confused by the brief exchange that it took her a moment to catch up to what her husband and Lord Shayles were saying.

"Why here?" Armand was asking. "Why not pester Alex

with your demands? He's the architect of that letter. It's on Winterberry Park stationery."

Lord Shayles shrugged, glancing around. "Broadclyft Hall is a much more comfortable house. And besides, I believe there is some question as to whether it should belong to you or your cousin." He turned toward Lord Gatwick.

Lavinia's mouth opened in an "O" of surprise and understanding. "Lord Gatwick is your cousin?"

Armand narrowed his eyes. "Yes. We don't speak, for obvious reasons."

Lord Gatwick met the comment with a look of utter indifference and returned to staring at the paintings

"Whether you speak or not," Lord Shayles said, "just think, this could all be his. It's a pity the courts chose the least beneficial path for everyone involved."

"Mark has his own estate and the title from his mother's brother," Armand said. "The decision was made years ago. Why are you here now?"

"I met Lord Tavistock at an inn the other day," Lord Shayles said. "He told me you'd fled Croydon's party with a new wife in tow. I just had to see for myself."

Armand shook his head. "More likely that you decided to engage in blackmail with that letter, but you're too much of a coward to face Alex, Malcolm, and the others."

Lord Shayles's mask of smug indifference vanished, revealing ugly fury. Lavinia clutched a hand to her stomach. Armand had hit the mark. Lord Shayles was too afraid to face the combined might of Armand's friends. "We should send word to Winterberry Park immediately, informing them of our guests," she whispered to Armand.

"You're right," Armand said with a firm nod. He turned back to Lord Shayles. "Winterberry Park is less than a day's journey from here. I'm sure my friends could be here by morning."

Lord Shayles's expression flickered in alarm for a split-second before smoothing out to an obsequious grin. "By all means," he said, feigning ease. "A house party sounds like a wonderful idea. The more the merrier." He paused, turning the envelope in his spindly hands. "That way we can all sit down together and discuss whether I should send the contents of this letter to *The Times*, *The Observer*, or *The Telegraph*. Perhaps all three and more."

"What would be the point?" Armand asked, though judging by the sudden roughness in his voice and the tension in his stance, Lavinia was certain he knew the point exactly.

"I'm sure all of England will want to know how their government is being manipulated even before Parliament returns," Lord Shayles said with a shrug. "Imagine the scandal when it is revealed that several of the Liberal Party's top ministers and peers have hatched a plan to maneuver the nation into accepting their reckless policies and ruining private businesses to boot."

"This is about your despicable club," Armand said, taking a half-step forward and glaring at Lord Shayles. "You don't care about Parliament. You know we intend to shut down the Black Strap Club for good, and you need its sickening money."

Lord Shayles laughed with condescension that made Lavinia's skin crawl. "My club will always have a place as long as there are men to patronize it. And there will always be men who patronize it. My finances are safe and sound." The corner of his mouth twitched as if to contradict his words.

A low, swooping feeling twisted Lavinia's stomach. She didn't know what Lord Shayles was talking about exactly, but it wasn't hard to draw conclusions. The Black Strap Club had a horrible reputation, but few people in her acquaintance were willing to speak about why. Even Lady Stanhope refused to tell Lavinia what it was all about, even though Lavinia had the impression her sophisticated friend knew much more than she was saying. Lord Shayles's financial troubles, on the other hand, had been mentioned more than a few times. Lavinia instantly concluded he'd come to Broadclyft Hall hoping to sell the letter to Armand.

"If you take that letter to the press, my friends will stop at nothing to ruin you," Armand said, appearing unaffected by Lord Shayles's statement. Lavinia wasn't sure he'd reached the same conclusion about the financial value of the letter either, but she stayed silent.

Lord Shayles laughed. "They've tried before without success. Why should I be intimidated now?"

Armand didn't have an answer. Lavinia hated watching the way he seethed, his hands clenched into fists at his sides, impotent with rage. She wracked her brain to think of some way to help him, even though she felt miles out of her depth. The only possibly useful thing that came to her mind was the old adage to keep your friends close and your enemies closer.

She cleared her throat and stepped forward. "Lord Shayles, will you and your friends be staying at Broadclyft Hall?" she asked, pulling on every lesson her mother had ever given her about being a polite hostess.

Lord Shayles turned a surprised, snake-like smile on her. "What a delightful invitation." He glanced at Armand. "Pearson, it seems you've married a gem of a woman."

"Leave my wife out of your machinations," Armand threatened him.

"Now, now, man," Lord Shayles said with a scolding shake of his head. "I'm only trying to compliment your *choice* of bride." The way he spoke made it clear he knew Armand hadn't chosen to marry her at all.

Armand countered by turning to Mr. Bondar, who, along with a few of the footmen, had appeared around the edges of the room and stood only a few yards away, watching the scene with a dark scowl. "Bondar, have one of the footmen take my fastest horse to Winterberry Park immediately to inform Alexander Croydon of our guests."

"Yes, my lord," Mr. Bondar said, glaring at Lord Shayles as though he'd been instructed to arm the troops and prepare for war. He turned toward Maxwell and nodded. The young man nodded and rushed off.

"A house party it is, then," Lord Shayles said, tucking the incriminating letter into a pocket inside his jacket. "We'll have such fun. There's no telling what sort of mischief might happen at a house party. Why, I may even find myself married off to the first unfortunate girl to find herself tangled in the gorse."

"You already have a wife," Armand growled, eyes narrowed.

"Well then," Lord Shayles wiped his hand across his mouth, "if I find a girl in distress, we could just pretend to marry." He stared at Lavinia with wicked intent.

"Bondar," Armand snapped, his glare never leaving Lord Shayles.

"Yes, my lord." Mr. Bondar stepped forward.

"I want this man watched at all times," Armand ordered.

"Yes, my lord." Mr. Bondar seemed only too glad to obey. He nodded to Les, who stepped forward, seemingly out of nowhere.

Lavinia peeked around. In fact, all of Broadclyft Hall's servants were just barely visible, peeking around corners or hiding in shadows. The maids looked terrified, and the footmen seemed ready to strangle Lord Shayles in his sleep. In an odd way, it set Lavinia at ease. She and Armand wouldn't have to face the current invasion alone.

"Mr. Bondar," she said, cursing the slight tremble in her voice. "Would you be so kind as to inform Mrs. Ainsworth of our guests and to see that they are given suitable accommodation?"

Armand glanced sideways at her in question, but he didn't contradict her command.

"Yes, my lady," Mr. Bondar said with only the slightest bit of hesitation.

"Gentlemen," Lavinia continued to address their foes. "Would you care to come through to the sitting room for tea?"

It would have been much more appropriate for Armand to invite them to some more manly pursuit, but tea was the ultimate balm to any awkward situation, or so she'd been taught.

"How gracious of you, Lady Helm," Lord Shayles said in a way that made Lavinia's skin crawl. It wasn't lost on her how she referred to Armand as "Dr. Pearson" but was willing to address her as "Lady Helm".

"Is that Grandpapa's Gainsborough?" Lord Gatwick asked as Lord Shayles, Dr. Miller, and Armand started to move toward the sitting room. His tone was so banal and his expression so utterly without tension that Lavinia wondered if he had heard any of the previous exchange.

She glanced up at the painting Lord Gatwick had been studying. "To be honest, Lord Gatwick, I have not been mistress of the house long enough to educate myself about its artwork."

Lord Gatwick tore his eyes away from the painting and stared at her. "It is, I'm sure it is," he said with absolute certainty. Something flashed deep behind his eyes, as if someone else's soul were trapped inside his body. "Quite valuable."

Lavinia blinked, an odd shiver swirling down her spine. "Oh?"

Lord Gatwick looked as though he would continue

talking about art, but before he could, Dr. Miller said in a loud voice, "Honestly, Pearson, I'm surprised you're home. I'd've thought you'd be halfway to India by now."

Lavinia snapped to stare at Dr. Miller. Dr. Miller wore a smug grin and looked from Armand to her. When he met her eyes, his smile widened.

"Miller," Armand said in a warning voice.

"What have I done?" Dr. Miller shrugged in a clumsy imitation of Lord Shayles. "Doesn't your new bride know that you are about to set out for India to take up a position as a physician there?"

Armand was leaving? Lavinia's gut suddenly felt hollow. He hadn't mentioned a thing about leaving to her. Worse still, when she glanced to him in question, he looked guilty.

"Are you leaving for India?" she asked, feeling suddenly unsteady. What had been the point of marrying her at all, manipulation or not, if he was planning to leave the country?

Armand cleared his throat, glaring at Dr. Miller. "Sir, why are you even here?" he asked.

"He's my employee," Lord Shayles answered, though he was already at the doorway to the sitting room. "My club needs a physician. There have been too many…mishaps of late."

A chill settled in Lavinia's stomach at the statement.

"The opportunities in London are endless," Dr. Miller said. "And Lord Shayles has offered me a unique set of benefits for providing services exclusively to his, um, other employees." A greedy flush painted the man's face.

Lavinia started to Armand's side as fast as she could, but halfway across the hall, she stopped. Armand bristled with anger. His face was red and his shoulders bunched. There was nothing soft or safe about him in that moment at all. After everything they'd shared that morning, he was suddenly a complete stranger to her again, frustrated and menacing. Panic welled up in her gut. She was out of her depth once again.

"Please do come through to the sitting room," she said to Lord Gatwick. Insane as it was, he suddenly seemed like the least threatening man in the hall.

Lord Gatwick had returned to perusing the paintings, but he nodded to her, then started toward the sitting room.

"You know," Dr. Miller murmured as she passed by his side. "Once your husband is gone, if you need a little company now and then, I still love a red-head." He was close enough to brush her arm with his fingers.

Lavinia cleared her throat and jumped ahead, making a bee-line to Mr. Bondar. "Please make sure our guests' rooms are nowhere near the private, family rooms," she said in a strangled voice.

"Of course, my lady. Have no fear."

Lavinia smiled, but fear was all she had. Fear that her guests were up to far more evil than what they laid claim to. Fear that her husband had lied to her about his intentions. Fear that her mother had landed her in a horrible situation that she wouldn't be able to get out of.

The last thing she wanted to do was to entertain a pack of villains in a house that was unfamiliar in spite of being her own, but she drew in a deep breath, stood as tall as she could, and prepared to do the impossible. Only, before she could step into the sitting room, Armand closed his hand around her arm and pulled her to the side.

"I'm sorry about all of this," he said, still rigid with anger.

"You're leaving." It wasn't what she'd wanted to say, but the words came out anyhow.

She prayed Armand would deny it, but he simply let out an irritated breath and lowered his shoulders. "I do have an offer to take up a position as a physician in India," he confessed.

"Then why did you go ahead and marry me?" she asked. "Did you intend to take me with you, away from my friends, family and everything I know, without any notice or preparation?"

"No, I wouldn't make you leave England like that unless you wanted to go," he said.

Lavinia's eyes widened. "So you intended to abandon me so soon after our marriage? Did you go through with Mama's plots because you needed a glorified housekeeper for your estate?"

"No, I never intended to marry you at all," he answered in a rush.

A moment later, he blinked and their eyes met. That was the heart of it, then. After everything that had passed between them in the last few days, he still didn't want her. The passion they'd shared that morning had been nothing more than carnal enjoyment. Lady Stanhope had always hinted that a man and a woman didn't have to be deeply in love to enjoy the pleasures of the flesh together. And Armand was old enough and sophisticated enough to know that. He'd probably had a dozen lovers before her and expected no more from her than he had from them. He wanted to be a doctor, not a husband, and it seemed he'd already laid plans to be just that.

"I see," she managed to say at last. "I'm sorry you didn't feel you could share your plans with me earlier." She turned away, spotting Mrs. Ainsworth across the hall and heading toward her.

"Lavinia," he called after her, careful not to raise his voice loud enough to draw attention from the sitting room. "Please come back. That's not what I meant at all. We need to talk this through."

Lavinia stopped, squeezing her eyes shut and blowing out a breath through her nose. She felt like a disobedient child throwing a tantrum, but regardless of how unjust those feelings might be, she'd been hurt. She turned back to Armand. "Yes, we do need to talk. But whether what you said is what you meant or not, we have dangerous guests to entertain. That should be our focus right now."

Armand rubbed a hand over his face, looking defeated. "You're right, of course. But we need to find time for us."

"Agreed," she said. "But not right now."

He nodded reluctantly, then looked toward the sitting room for a moment, before meeting her eyes again. "Be careful while these vipers are in the house," he said, his voice lowered. "I don't trust them."

"Neither do I," she admitted. The trouble was, she wasn't entirely sure she could trust her husband either.

CHAPTER 13

Shayles was a trial. He was a conniving, evil-hearted man who spent the rest of the day drinking Armand's finest spirits and making veiled threats and ribald jokes. But it was Miller whose neck Armand wanted to wring. Not only had the man blurted out his plans to take up the position in India to Lavinia before Armand had a chance to discuss it with her himself, the bastard watched Lavinia all through the afternoon and during supper as though he were a hawk sighting prey.

"You should relocate to London once your husband sails away for the Indian sub-continent, Lady Helm," he said with a drunken slur as Les and Carl served pudding at the end of supper. "That way you'd be closer to friends who could protect you." His words would have seemed kind if he hadn't delivered them with a lascivious grin while staring at Lavinia's breasts.

"Leave my wife out of whatever political games you're playing," Armand growled, regretting that the table was so blasted long and Lavinia was all the way at the other end. He wanted her by his side at all times so that he could shield her.

"Politics?" Miller jerked straight, swaying as he turned toward Armand. "Can't stand the stuff. Women, on the other hand." He laughed until he was cut short by a hiccup. "You should know all about women, Pearson, what with your *women's medicine*." He laughed harder, ending with a burp.

Armand scowled at him, well aware of how many doctors considered the new field of gynecology to be fluff medicine, unimportant, and slightly inappropriate. Which was the entire reason he'd been able to pursue it after being forced to give up what society thought of as serious medicine. "Women's health is as important as men's," he said, meeting Lavinia's eyes across the table. "Just as their rights are as important as ours."

It was as if someone had struck a match and lit a lamp. That was what his friends were fighting so hard for in Parliament. Women had every bit as much of a right to self-determination as they had to adequate healthcare in a way that focused on their unique physiology. And he was in a position to advance both notions.

But his moment of inspiration was dampened by the despondent droop of Lavinia's shoulders as she picked at her food yards away from him, at the other end of the table. She only barely met his eyes, and then only nodded out of courtesy. Armand wasn't sure she was listening to the conversation at all. Her lack of attention was an utter distraction to him, but it had a surprisingly positive effect.

When Shayles realized neither Armand nor Lavinia were paying attention to his pokes and prods, he grew silent and ultimately retired to bed early. The footman had to drag Miller out of his chair and practically carry him up to bed. And Gatwick wandered off to ask Bondar about Broadclyft Hall's artwork. That left Armand to escort Lavinia up to bed in relative silence.

The first thing she said after the awkward supper was,

"Lord Gatwick is an odd man." She'd bathed and changed into her nightgown in her dressing room, then settled into bed, leaving a gaping space between them. "I have a hard time believing the two of you are so closely related."

Armand stared at the empty space. So much for getting closer to her. Not that he would have had it in him to make love with Shayles under his roof, threatening him and his friends with ruin.

"Gatwick has always been odd," he said slipping between the covers and plumping the pillows restlessly.

"I was aware that everything could have been your cousin's if the courts had ruled differently, but why didn't you mention that Lord Gatwick was the cousin in question?"

Armand frowned and lay back, his back a field of knots. "We've never seen eye-to-eye. Mark has been Shayles's toad since university."

"Really? They've known each other that long?" Lavinia lay down, pulling the covers up to her chin.

"Yes," Armand answered, stretching to the side to blow out the lantern, throwing the room into darkness. "They're a few years younger than the rest of us, though Malcolm was in his final year when they both began. He entered university after a few years' gap when his father died."

"Lord Malcolm has known Lord Shayles for that long?" Lavinia's voice was quiet enough to seem miles away in the dark.

Armand laughed without humor. "Known him and hated him." He paused, wondering how much he could reveal without causing more trouble. "Malcolm's late wife, Tessa, was Shayles's first wife."

His revelation was met by a gasp of surprise. "But how," she started, then fell silent. "I suppose there was a divorce?"

"Yes." Armand settled onto his side facing her, longing to

reach out for her. But the wall between them was firmly in place.

"So how did Lord Shayles and Lord Gatwick become friends?" Lavinia asked.

Armand paused. "To be honest, I don't know."

Lavinia hummed, hesitated, then said, "Do you think Lord Shayles is here, Lord Gatwick with him, because he has his sights set on the Helm title and fortune?"

Armand blinked, completely taken by surprise at the comment. "Shayles has nothing to do with the Helms."

"Yes, but he's in dire financial straits, Lord Gatwick is a friend, and perhaps Lord Shayles believes there's a way to get money from his friend through his connection to the Helm title."

Armand stared straight up at the canopy above the bed, his mind spinning. The connection had never occurred to him. It seemed outlandish, in a way. "Shayles wants to bribe my friends," he said, thinking the problem through. "He's opposed them for years. He hates Malcolm. He'll do anything he can to destroy their credibility and bring down the new government. That's why he has the letter. He brought it here instead of Winterberry Park because he's a coward."

A long silence met his thoughts. "I'm sure you're right," Lavinia said at last in an unconvinced voice. She said nothing else.

A restless buzz stopped Armand from closing his eyes and attempting to sleep. Whatever Shayles's aim, it was the least of his problems. Even in the dark, he could feel the disappointment that rippled off his wife. She tossed and squirmed, unable to sleep as well.

"Lavinia, about India," he said once he realized neither of them was relaxed.

"If you want to go, I won't stop you," she said, rolling to lie with her back facing him.

Armand let out a breath of defeat. "I won't go."

"Please don't let me stand in the way of your dreams any more than I already am," she said, so quietly that he almost couldn't make out her words.

"It's not that." But in a way, it was. If not for his sudden marriage, he would have been packing his bags and putting his English affairs in order in preparation for a new life. He still hadn't had a response from Dr. Maqsood about delaying his departure, which meant there might still be a chance to... to what? "Lavinia—"

"Please, Armand." She twisted to speak over her shoulder, sadness lacing her voice. "I'm exhausted. It's been a trying day, and tomorrow will be more of the same. And I will be hosting even more guests in an unfamiliar house while still adjusting to my new position. Go where your heart longs to go, but leave me in peace to do what I must."

The snap of her words was like the slap of a schoolteacher's rod over his hands after he'd been caught misbehaving. "Very well, then. Good night." He rolled to his side, his back to hers, rubbing the stinging ache in his chest where his heart was supposed to be. The unreasonable part of him was sore that she wouldn't instantly forgive every misstep on his part and snuggle into his arms the way she had that afternoon. The older and wiser part of him knew she had every reason to feel hurt. And that he would have to work hard to regain her trust.

If only their situation were such that he had time to rebuild her trust in him. Unfortunately for them all—or fortunately, depending on how the situation was viewed—three carriages arrived just as breakfast was being served the next morning. Alex and Marigold Croydon, Malcolm, Katya, and her children, and, of all people, Lady Prior, landed at Broadclyft Hall simultaneously, throwing Lavinia into a frenzy of hostess duties. That would have been a challenge in and of itself, but of course Lady Prior was a nuisance right out of the gate.

"My, what a splendid house," she declared, stars in her eyes as she gazed greedily across Broadclyft's front hall. "I must speak to the housekeeper at once to get the lay of the land and to make certain she's running the house properly."

"Mama, Mrs. Ainsworth has been housekeeper here for decades. She knows her job and does it expertly," Lavinia told her.

Armand could see in an instant that Lady Prior had no intention of letting things go. But there were far larger problems at hand.

"Ah," Shayles said, strolling out from the corridor that led to the afternoon parlor as the bustling noise of the arrivals filled the hall. "And so our party begins in earnest." He eyed Katya's young daughters in a way that had Katya snarling.

"You have something that is mine," Alex marched straight up to Shayles after handing his coat off to Bondar, distracting Shayles from the Marlowe girls. "I want it now."

"I just bet you do," Shayles said with a vulgar twist of his lips. "What with that pretty, nubile wife of yours."

"My wife is off-limits," Alex growled. "This is serious business, not one of your filthy masquerades."

"Yes, it is serious." Shayles was instantly grave. "A new cabinet member manipulating the government before it's even returned to London is serious business indeed. How do you think the press will feel, knowing how deep corruption in Gladstone's new regime runs? Gladstone will be forced to boot you from his cabinet before you've attended a single meeting. Do you think they will lobby for another election? It would be a shame if all your quaint reforms were aborted before delivery, so to speak."

"Give me the letter," Alex hissed.

"He will," Malcolm said, stepping to Alex's side and

resting a steadying hand on his shoulder. "Especially if he turns up dead in his sleep tonight."

Instead of being cowed by Malcolm's threat—a threat Armand took seriously enough to be alarmed—Shayles laughed. "So you would add murder to the list of misfortunes your good friend, Dr. Pearson, has suffered? Marriage wasn't punishment enough for him?" He pivoted to face Armand, who was halfway across the hall, helping Katya remove her coat. "What charming friends you have, sir."

"That's 'my lord' to you," Katya said, glaring at Shayles.

"Yes, you would know, I'm sure," Shayles went on, looking as though he were having the best day of his life. "Is that what you called out in ecstasy when Dr. Pearson here was poking you through the back door? The two of you were close before that chit came along." He nodded to Lavinia.

"Filthy coward," Katya hissed, snapping away and refusing to look at Shayles.

Armand's face heated, with embarrassment as much as rage. He stole a glance to Lavinia, praying she hadn't taken Shayles's meaning. There was no telling whether Lavinia had even heard Shayles's accusation, though. She was busy directing the maids to take away coats and to show the Marlowe girls to their rooms. Although the bright pink of her cheeks and the miserable look on her face hinted that she'd not only heard Shayles, she'd come to understand more about his ancient past than she wanted to.

The mess was made worse as Miller wandered into the hall to see what all the noise was about.

"What is he doing here?" Alex seethed, staring daggers at Miller.

"Who, Dr. Miller?" Shayles said with a delighted smile. "He's my personal physician and an employee of my illustrious establishment."

"There's nothing illustrious about it," Rupert said, marching to join Alex and Malcolm.

"And how would you know, boy?" Shayles snapped at him, then broke into a leering smile. "Though if you want to find out, I am more than willing to give you a complimentary pass for one night."

"I wouldn't stoop so low," Rupert replied.

"Enough of this," Alex roared, silencing everyone in the hall. He faced Shayles, practically quivering with rage. "You will return our letter or you will leave this house in pieces."

"I say, Pearson," Shayles called cheerfully across the hall to Armand. "Do you let your friends speak to all your guests this way?" Before Armand could answer, he went on with, "I suppose you do, since you clearly don't know the first thing about being a gentleman. Why don't you just abdicate like a good boy and let Gatwick have it all?"

"Because he can't," Katya snapped. "And even if he could, he wouldn't."

"He could and he would," Shayles said in an undertone to Miller. "If he were dead."

Miller snorted with laughter. "Where'd old Gatwick go anyhow?"

"There's a cricket match on," Shayles said. "He probably went to ogle the players. Mark does love a man in whites."

"Really?" Miller's brow rose. "I could have sworn he wasn't…like that."

"I've had enough of this," Armand growled, crossing to stand with his friends against Shayles. "Why are you here and what do you want?"

"Ah, that's more like it." Shayles stepped away from Miller, smiling at the line of men opposing him. "Although I did enjoy our banter."

"What do you want?" Malcolm repeated Armand's question with his most intimidating glare.

Shayles barely flinched. "I want protection," he said. "I don't care about your efforts to extend the franchise to the pitiful working class or the rights of women, not that they deserve them," he added with an off-hand gesture.

"Get to your point," Alex said.

Shayles met his eyes and held them. "I want my club intact. I want any and all references to reform of sin laws stricken from the agenda. And I want the government to continue to turn a blind eye to my business dealings."

A sickening knot formed in Armand's stomach. Shayles's demands were as much an admission of what he'd suspected all along—that the activities of the Black Strap Club were every bit as illegal as they were reputed to be, that law enforcement had, so far, refused to investigate or report on them, and that Disraeli's government had somehow been complicit in keeping the whole thing under wraps. The truth shocked him, but neither Malcolm nor Alex looked the least bit surprised, leading Armand to wonder if their accusations that he needed to pay more attention were true.

"No," Malcolm answered unequivocally, crossing his arms.

"What a disappointing answer," Shayles said with a false sigh of regret. "It's a pity that something as easy to accomplish as looking the other way will bring down an entire government before it has a chance to take up the reins of power."

"Your club is an abomination and should be burned to the ground," Katya said, joining the men at last. "If I could light the torch myself, I would."

"Why?" Shayles blinked at her. "When I have offered you such amenable terms to become a part of the establishment."

Katya grunted in disgust, which only lit a fire in Shayles's eyes. His lust, in turn, had Malcolm turning red and looking ready to start a fistfight, or worse.

"You won't leave this house without handing over our letter," Alex said, swinging the conversation back to where it should be. "You made a mistake coming here to taunt us."

Shayles's smug grin faltered. It was the first sign of hope Armand had seen in the situation. Perhaps pride and arrogance truly had led the blackguard into making a critical error.

"What would it take for you to hand over that letter?" he said, praying negotiations would work.

Shayles blinked at him as though he were an idiot. "I just gave you my demands. Keep my club out of whatever machinations you are planning for November."

"And if we refuse to do that?" Armand asked, unable to shake the feeling Shayles wanted something more.

Shayles hummed. "A hundred thousand pounds might do it."

Alex and Malcolm hissed in derision. Katya snorted with wry laughter. Out of the corner of his eye, Armand caught Lavinia staring at him with a look that said, "See?" Armand narrowed his eyes and studied Shayles closer. Perhaps Lavinia was right about money being the man's sole aim after all.

Shayles shrugged before he could address it and said, "If you refuse to meet my terms, then your lovely wife will have a long and interesting house party on her hands. I do hope she is up to the task of providing entertainment that will suit my needs." He sent Lavinia a glance that made Armand want to strangle the life out of him.

Lavinia didn't hear the comment. She'd gone back to trying to keep her mother from lecturing Mrs. Ainsworth—who had appeared to assist the new guests. Armand had never been so grateful for Lady Prior's interference.

"Clearly, we aren't going to solve anything this moment," he said, scrambling to salvage the situation. "Alex, I advise that you make sure your wife is settled safely in your room. Katya, Rupert, I'm sure you can take care of yourselves and the girls. Malcolm, stay out of trouble. And Shayles." Armand wanted to order the man to leave his house and never return, but his friends had a point. As long as he was at Broadclyft Hall, he couldn't send the letter to the press and ruin them. At least, he couldn't if he was watched at all times. "Go back to drinking my whiskey and reading my books, or whatever you were doing."

"Am I being sent to my room without any supper?" Shayles asked, his lips twitching with mirth. "I'll go if Lady Helm promises to give me the spanking I deserve."

As much as Armand wanted to pummel the man, there were better ways to neutralize the threat he posed. "Bondar," he called to his butler, who glowered at the side of the room. "Please escort Lord Shayles and Dr. Miller back to wherever they were before and ensure that they are monitored."

"Yes, my lord," Bondar answered, looking devilishly pleased with the order.

"Our negotiations aren't over," Shayles said as though he'd been invited to tea. "In fact, they've only just begun. Good day, ladies," he called across the hall to Lavinia, Marigold, and Lady Prior.

"Oh? Good day, sir," Lady Prior replied as though she'd been addressed by the Prince of Wales.

Shayles chuckled, then motioned for Miller to accompany him away toward the afternoon parlor. Armand waited, watching to be sure they were truly gone, before turning to his friends.

"That ass will pay for everything he's putting us through," Malcolm said before Armand could speak. "He'll pay for everything."

"Yes, but if we're not careful, so will we," Alex said.

"Why did you dolts send your plans to Gladstone in writing?" Katya asked, shaking her head and crossing her arms. "Only a pack of fools leaves a trail of evidence."

"Thank you for your opinion, Lady Stanhope," Malcolm snapped at her. "But if you will recall, a highly-trusted, highly-competent man was entrusted to carry the letter and personally deliver it to Gladstone."

"Accidents always have a way of happening, no matter how clever and competent Mr. Phillips is," Katya shot back.

"Should we have sent you with the letter?" Malcolm went on, growing irate. "Would it have made you feel safer to transport the letter yourself, shoved up your—"

"Will the two of you stop it?" Alex cut him off. "This is no time for your flirting."

"You call this flirting?" Katya balked.

"Between you two? Yes," Alex grumbled.

"What are we going to do?" Armand asked. Across the room, he noticed Marigold stepping closer to Lavinia and whispering something in her ear. Lavinia bit her lip and cast a worried look in Armand's direction. "I know how important it is to keep Shayles under this roof until he gives us the letter, but I won't have Lavinia put in danger any longer than she has to be."

"Then don't let her out of your sight," Katya said. "That should be easy enough to do." Her teasing grin implied as much mischief as Shayles had suggested. Armand met her teasing with a sharp frown. "Is something wrong?" Katya asked, all too able to see through him.

"Never you mind that," he mumbled. He glanced to Malcolm and Alex. "Where is Peter? Didn't he come with you?"

Alex shook his head. "Peter took Mariah home to Starcross Castle. Since she's in a delicate condition, he didn't want her under this kind of stress."

Armand grunted. "I should send Lavinia to Starcross at once."

"Send me where?" Lavinia asked, a note of hurt in her voice.

Armand hadn't seen her and Marigold approaching. He winced. Timing never seemed to be on his side where his wife was concerned. "Shayles is dangerous," he said, caution in his voice and, he hoped, apology in his eyes. "It would be safer for you at Starcross Castle."

Lavinia blinked at him as though he'd embarrassed her in front of the entire contingent of their friends. "I am the mistress of Broadclyft Hall now," she said in a carefully controlled voice. "I have a duty to see to our guests, whether they be lions or lambs."

"We need her to help thwart Shayles anyhow," Katya said.

Armand sent her a flat look, which Katya met with a stare as though he was the idiot, not her. He sighed and rubbed a hand over his face. "Fine. What do we do to get the letter back?"

"Whatever we have to," Malcolm answered.

"Where is he keeping it?" Alex asked.

"I don't know for certain," Armand said with a shrug. "Either in his room or on his person."

"We won't have any luck stealing it if it's on his person," Katya said. "Not even I would be willing to touch that snake."

"You paint yourself in such a charming light, Lady Stanhope," Malcolm said, then sniffed. "Touching Shayles's snake."

Katya glared at him. "It wouldn't be the first time I used my *considerable* talents for a worthy cause," she snapped. Malcolm flushed deep red, his jaw clenched in anger. Katya turned back to the rest of them. "I certainly wouldn't ask any of your female staff to do the job for us. You'll have to try his room first."

"Which means we'll have to keep him out of his room for a length of time," Armand said, his mood souring on multiple levels.

"I can arrange it," Lavinia said, startling them all.

"No, Lavinia, I don't want you putting yourself in danger," Armand said.

"Let her speak." Katya stopped him before he could say more.

Lavinia glanced to Katya with far less openness than usual, proving that she had heard Shayles's suggestion that there had been something between Katya and Armand at one point. Lavinia cleared her throat, then said, "I am the hostess of this house party. I will come up with some sort of entertainment to keep Shayles and his friends occupied." She glanced hesitantly to Armand. "It's up to you to choose what to do with that time."

"I can help her," Marigold offered, taking Lavinia's hand. Lavinia sent her a grateful smile.

"What are you all doing over here?" Lady Prior joined their group at last, leaving a wary-looking Mrs. Ainsworth shaking her head at the other end of the hall.

Without missing a beat, Lavinia put on a bland smile and said, "We need to plan an activity for my guests for this afternoon, Mama."

"Oh, what a delight." Lady Prior clapped her hands and giggled. "I have ever so many ideas. We could play cards or charades or have a musical event."

"I was thinking of something out of doors," Lavinia said, sending a questioning glance to Armand. "Since Broadclyft Hall's gardens are so splendid."

"Yes, yes, of course," Lady Prior went on. "It may be September, but there is still plenty of sunshine, though it's a bit colder today than it has been. Perhaps a treasure hunt, or a game of sardines."

"An outdoor event it is, then," Katya said, stepping away from the men to form the ladies into a circle. "I'm sure we can think of something entertaining."

Lady Prior made a disgusted sound at the prospect of working with Katya.

"Thank you, Lady Stanhope," Lavinia said without looking Katya in the eye.

Armand writhed on his spot. The last thing he needed was yet another blow to his new and fragile marriage. At the rate things were going, he would have to get down on his knees with half the flowers in Devon and explain every year of his life in detail in order to make Lavinia see that he was not a lascivious coward who ran off to India when things didn't go his way. She began to walk away, Marigold on one side, her mother on the other, Katya keeping her distance, and he jogged after her.

CHAPTER 14

"Lavinia, wait!"

Lavinia stopped, squeezing her eyes shut and clenching her jaw at Armand's concerned shout. A headache was beginning to wrap around her temples like a tight band, and having her reluctant, experienced husband chase after her only made it worse.

"Please, go on ahead," she said to the others in a tired voice. "Mrs. Ainsworth, could you please provide my mother and friends with tea in the pink room?"

"Yes, my lady, though I thought your guests would like to see their rooms and freshen up first?" Mrs. Ainsworth asked with a compassionate look.

"Oh, no," Lavinia's mother snapped. "Planning for this afternoon is far more important. Do as you're told, woman."

Lavinia winced again, but there was no time to chastise her mother for ordering Mrs. Ainsworth around. Armand caught up to her, touching her elbow as he came to stand in front of her. The last thing Lavinia wanted to do was to air out her marital problems in the front hall when a wave of guests was shuffling about and almost all of the servants of the house were marching around them to prepare for the sudden house party.

"Lavinia, I'm—"

"I know." She cut Armand off before he could make yet another apology. She couldn't quite meet his eyes, though. "You're sorry. You're sorry you've allowed a dangerous man to stay in your house. You're sorry all of your friends have descended on me when I've barely begun to take up my role as the viscountess. You're sorry you have a past that involves other women, women of my acquaintance. You're sorry you never told me you are traveling half a world away so soon after marrying me, and you're sorry you married me. You're sorry, you're sorry, you're sorry."

She gulped for breath as her outburst ended, startled that she'd had the nerve to blurt it all out. Heart racing, she glanced up at Armand at last.

He stared at her, an odd look in his eyes. As if he'd never seen her before. At least he wasn't angry. Although anger would have been more recognizable than the blankness that stared back at her.

Her shoulders dropped as she let out a breath. "No, I'm sorry," she said, rubbing her throbbing temples. "I have duties to fulfill. A good wife does what is required of her without sullenness or complaint, Mama always says. At least I've made her happy."

Still, Armand said nothing. But his expression shifted from bewilderment to pain. Lavinia could only stand to look at it for a split-second before the hurt and disappointment of her life gaped too wide inside of her.

"Good luck finding the letter," she said, barely above a whisper, then turned to march off after her mother and friends. Her throat squeezed and her eyes stung with the temptation to weep, but there didn't seem to be any point. She'd never had any control of her own life, and it appeared that that hope was gone forever now. It was no use shedding tears over the independence she would never have, not when the entire house was sitting on a powder keg.

Before she entered the pink room—where she could already hear her mother and Lady Stanhope bickering—Lavinia took a deep, steadying breath. She could do this. She had one, key task ahead of her—find a distraction to get Shayles and his friends out of the house so that Armand and the others could search his room.

"Now then," she announced herself with feigned confidence as she strode into the room. "What activities would get everyone outside and keep them away from the windows?"

"I was thinking a treasure hunt," her mother answered immediately, her eyes bright. "Or a scavenger hunt. I hear that Lady Tavistock treated her house guests to the most amazing scavenger hunt last summer."

"Lavinia, dear, are you certain you're all right?" Lady Stanhope approached her with an expression of deep concern.

Lavinia stepped to the side to avoid her, marching across the room to open one of the windows. "What is involved in a scavenger hunt, Mama?" She glanced back over her shoulder in time to watch Lady Stanhope and Marigold exchange a wary look. Her stomach twisted. Her friends must have thought she was a baby. She was well aware they'd always considered her hopelessly unsophisticated, compared to them. And so she had been. But not anymore.

"Well," her mother said, dodging the antique furniture to reach her side, eyes bright with excitement. "A variety of unusual items are placed throughout the grounds and gardens of the house. The guests are given a list of those items. They must form pairs with other guests and traverse the grounds to collect them."

Lavinia didn't need the glimpse of Marigold and Lady

Stanhope's expressions to understand that the point of the game was the pairs and the secluded corners of the gardens, not the objects ostensibly being searched for, as her mother seemed to think. "Very well," she said. "Mama, I leave it to you to work with Mrs. Ainsworth and Mr. Bondar to choose items and locations for the objects. I will pair with Lord Shayles and—"

"No," Marigold and Lady Stanhope said at the same time. They rushed across the room to plead with her.

"That man is far too dangerous," Lady Stanhope said.

"So I've been told," Lavinia replied with a wry twist to her lips. She could barely look at Lady Stanhope without imagining her so-called friend entwined in a passionate embrace with Armand.

It was clear from the stolid frown that creased Lady Stanhope's brow that she could read Lavinia's thoughts. "What's in the past is in the past," she said, regardless of Lavinia's mother and Marigold standing on either side of them. "And if it makes you feel better, it was thirteen years ago. You were, I believe, twelve-years-old at the time?"

Lavinia bristled. "Mama," she snapped, "would you please find out what is holding up our tea?" Mrs. Ainsworth couldn't possibly have had time to make it so quickly, but giving her mother a reason to scold the servants was the best way to get rid of her.

"Yes, of course," her mother answered, taking the bait.

As soon as she was out of the room, Lavinia rounded on Lady Stanhope. "I have always looked to you as a role model, Lady Stanhope. I have admired your independence and your boldness. But I am beginning to question whether my mother has been right all along about your morals."

"Why?" Lady Stanhope asked, the widening of her eyes the only sign that Lavinia's words had offended her. "Because I've lived my life on my own terms? Because I made the best of a bad situation and refused to let the strictures of society stop me from enjoying myself? Isn't that exactly what you've always said you want for yourself?"

Lavinia jerked away from her, staring out the window and feeling as miserable as she ever had.

"This isn't helping," Marigold said, her voice calm. She stepped to Lavinia's side, nudging her to sit in the cushioned window seat and sitting beside her. "Men all have pasts, dearest," she went on, stroking Lavinia's hand. "Especially those who have lived longer than us. Fortunately, we rarely discover who was involved in those pasts. But you shouldn't hold it against Katya. The only reason we don't all have pasts of our own is because of the rules we've imposed on ourselves." Lavinia glanced up at her, biting her lip as she swallowed the truth. "I'm sure, if given half a chance, we'd all be as daring as Katya. But right now, that's not the point." She paused, taking Lavinia's hand and squeezing it. "What happened? You were upset when we arrived, long before that horrible man said the things he said. What did we miss?"

All at once, the tears Lavinia had struggled so hard to keep inside burst. "He doesn't want me," she wept, dropping her head onto Marigold's shoulder. "He's planning to leave me and go to India. He didn't even tell me until Dr. Miller mentioned it last night."

To Lavinia's surprise, Lady Stanhope huffed a laugh. "Armand has no more intention of running away to India than I have." She sat on the window seat on Lavinia's other side. "I doubt there even is a Dr. Maqsood."

"A who?" Lavinia asked.

"Dr. Maqsood, from Mayo Hospital in Lahore," Marigold said softly.

Lavinia's eyes went wide. "So there is an actual doctor making the offer?"

"Armand is bluffing to get under Malcolm's and the

others' skin," Lady Stanhope said. "I had my girls look, and there is no Dr. Maqsood at Mayo Hospital."

Lavinia barely heard her. "You knew all about this offer, and you never told me?"

"Because it doesn't exist," Lady Stanhope stressed.

"But you knew and I didn't." Lavinia sniffled, wiping her eyes and nose. "And that is the point."

Lady Stanhope shook her head, rubbing Lavinia's back. "The point is that men will never tell us anything without being prodded into it. They're as dense as Christmas pudding. If you want something from Armand, you have to stand up and demand it."

Lavinia stared at her, brow furrowed. She was still furious with Lady Stanhope, or at least she thought she was. "Am I supposed to stand up and demand that he love me?" she asked, trying to be as resolute as her mentor was, but feeling weak.

"Is that what you want?" Marigold asked. "For Armand to love you?"

Lavinia lowered her head, heat flooding her face. It seemed foolish to demand that a man she'd barely known up until a week ago love her. But the way things had been between them the morning before had been divine. Armand had made her feel free and cared for, and she'd never felt that way. It was like the bud of love had been nipped before it could bloom.

She sucked in a breath and lifted her head. "I don't want him to spend the rest of his life resenting our marriage," she said. "And I don't want him to continuously apologize, as if marriage were a bout of ague or a carriage wheel stuck in the mud."

"That's more like it," Lady Stanhope said, patting her back. "What else?"

"I don't want him to stay at Broadclyft Hall, moping like a

boy who has had his favorite toy taken from him. If he truly wants to go to India to practice medicine, then he should just go."

"And leave you here to run his estate in his place?" Lady Stanhope suggested, arching one brow.

"Yes." Lavinia nodded, although inwardly, her gut trembled at the overwhelming thought. "And as such, I have guests to entertain and a viper to subdue."

She stood. As luck would have it, her mother returned to the room, a maid with a tray full of tea things behind her.

"Lavinia, I need you to take me on a tour of your gardens immediately after tea," her mother said. "I have to know what sort of items to include on the scavenger hunt lists as well as where to hide them."

"Certainly, Mama," Lavinia said, crossing the room to pour tea for her friends. "We need to make this activity a true challenge for the gentlemen."

Her concerns and heartbreak weren't resolved, not by any stretch of the imagination, but Lavinia felt less like a wilting wallflower as she sipped her tea and listened to her mother prattle on about house parties she'd been to in her past. The important task of the afternoon was to enable Armand and the others to get their letter back. Her marriage would have to wait to be fixed. And as uncomfortable as she felt with her knowledge of Lady Stanhope's connection to Armand, it didn't take long for her to decide she didn't want to know a single further detail about whatever had been. She was determined to focus on Lady Stanhope's advice to ask for what she wanted instead. Just not yet.

"This is so exciting," her mother said a few hours later, as the entire house party gathered on Broadclyft Hall's back yard. "I've made up lists for all of you of things you will be able to find on the grounds of the estate." She nodded to the maid, Sophie, who glanced warily at Lord Shayles as though expecting him to assault her at any minute as she handed out lists. "Some of the objects can be found naturally in nature, but others are things from the house that have been specifically placed."

"And what does the winner of this scavenger hunt receive?" Lord Shayles asked, eyeing Lavinia with a wolfish grin.

"How about a certain letter?" Lord Malcolm growled.

"I'd be willing to part with the letter if, in exchange, I can have what I want, should I win," Lord Shayles replied, biting his lip at Lavinia.

"No." Armand stepped between Lavinia and Lord Shayles, blocking the man from Lavinia's sight.

Lord Shayles made a disappointed sound. "Come now, Dr. Pearson. If you want something valuable, you have to be willing to offer something valuable in return."

"Valuable," Armand said. "Not priceless."

A whisper of hope swirled around Lavinia's heart, but she pushed it away. She'd gotten her hopes up too many times in the last few days to indulge in hope now. Besides, they had a mission to accomplish.

She stepped around Armand, ignoring him as she addressed the others. "The winner of the scavenger hunt will have the privilege of walking into supper first this evening, regardless of order of precedence," she said.

"Ooh." Her mother clapped her hands together as though Lavinia had offered a pot of gold. "It makes me wish I was playing instead of organizing."

"Lord Shayles," Lavinia stepped closer to the man, fighting to hide the tremor in her hands. "Would you care to partner with me?"

"Lavinia, no," Armand hissed behind her.

"My lady, I advise against it," Mr. Croydon said in a grave voice.

Lord Malcolm glared at Lord Shayles as though it were his fault.

"Well, well." Lord Shayles sidled across the lawn toward Lavinia. "This is an interesting turn of events. Your wife is quite the hostess, Pearson."

"Dash it," Dr. Miller murmured to a distracted-looking Lord Gatwick behind him. "I was going to partner with Lady Helm, if you know what I mean." He elbowed Lord Gatwick, who jolted out of his thoughts and sneered at him.

"Lavinia, you shouldn't do this," Armand continued to protest.

"Oh, Armand," Lady Stanhope cut off what looked as though it would develop into a lecture. "Do let your wife play hostess as she should."

"But—" Armand gaped, gesturing from Lavinia to Lord Shayles.

"Makes you wonder why you bothered, eh, Pearson," Shayles laughed.

Lavinia held her ground, staring hard at Armand, demanding he trust her and get on with whatever he planned to do. Armand turned pleading eyes on her, but his expression morphed to a frown when he met her eyes. He glanced momentarily to Lady Stanhope, who also stared him down with a look that demanded complete trust. "Carl," Armand snapped at one of the footmen hovering by the scene. "I want you to accompany Lady Helm and Lord Shayles. Watch them at all times."

"Yes, my lord," young Carl answered, looking pleased to be entrusted with the task.

"Wonderful," Lavinia's mother said, suppressing a giggle. "We have our first pair. Now, who else will pair up?"

Within moments, Marigold had stepped up to Lord Gatwick's side and Lady Stanhope had gone to stand by Dr. Miller, looking thoroughly put out. Lord Malcolm strode to stand beside Natalia Marlowe, whispering something in her ear, and Rupert hooked arms with Bianca.

"I suppose the two of us will have to pair up," Mr. Croydon muttered to Armand.

"Yes, because that is entirely trustworthy," Lord Shayles said, dripping with sarcasm, as he offered an arm to Lavinia.

Unease prickled across Lavinia's skin. The game had yet to officially start, and she suspected that Lord Shayles knew exactly what they were up to. Her heart raced as she ran through their options in her head. The one thing she knew was that they couldn't call off now.

"Mama, if you will give the word for us to start," she said, pleased that her voice didn't quiver for a change.

"Yes, yes, my dear." Her mother cleared her throat. "Ladies and gentlemen, you may begin."

"Good luck," Lord Shayles said over his shoulder as he whisked Lavinia off toward the French garden. "And may the best man win."

Lavinia remained silent for the first few minutes, darting glances this way and that to make sure Carl was following them and to make sure that Armand and Mr. Croydon would go straight inside. Malcolm broke away from Natalia and snuck into the house after them. If Lord Shayles asked what she was looking at, she would tell him she was keeping an eye on her guests, making sure they got off to a good start. But he didn't ask. He merely grinned as though he were on a pleasant stroll and escorted Lavinia into the sculpted flower beds and hedges of the French garden.

"This list says that we need to find a shard of china," he said at last, looking at the small list he carried. "I say we will never be able to find anything with as perfect a porcelain texture as your lily-soft skin, my lady."

Lavinia cleared her throat, forcing her back straight. "I'm certain that's not what my mother meant by that item."

"No?" He led her around a corner and onto a walk that held rows of apple trees in full fruit. The cloying smell of cider filled the air. "I would have pegged your mother as the sort to steer you into precisely the situation that would prove the most advantageous for your social connections."

Lavinia stopped, letting go of his arm and turning to stare at him. Carl stood several yards away, looking ready to leap to her rescue, but she steadied him with a subtle shake of her head.

"If you are referring to the unusual nature of my marriage to Lord Helm, then I'm afraid you are mistaken, my lord," she told Lord Shayles, praying she could hold her own against him. "Lord Helm and I have been on friendly terms for over a year. The house party at Winterberry Park merely enabled us to clarify our intentions toward each other." She didn't know why she told the lie, but she couldn't stand the smug look on Lord Shayles's face.

"Certainly, my lady," he said, clearly not believing a word. "But we must remember, marriage is only one kind of intimate relationship." He brushed the back of his fingers along the row of buttons running down her bodice, raking her breast as he did. "Especially when the husband runs off to exotic lands."

Lavinia froze. Her heart raced, but she didn't move a muscle either to panic, push him away, or, God forbid, give in to him. She merely stared hard at Lord Shayles's cold, blue eyes, without flinching. Within seconds, what began as a fear reaction caught hold in her mind. She was suddenly reminded of the way Lord Shayles had abandoned supper when no one rose to the challenge of his prodding.

"Hmm." Lord Shayles took a half step back and studied her, head tilted to the side. "That wasn't what I was expecting," he said, hinting she might be right.

"And what did you expect, my lord?" she asked in as much

of a monotone as she could muster. Her mind raced. How much time did Armand need to search Lord Shayles's room? She couldn't keep up her current façade long.

Lord Shayles shrugged, then crossed his arms. "To be honest, I'm not certain. I figured there was an equal chance that you'd either scream rape and dissolve into a pitiful mess, or...."

He didn't continue, so Lavinia asked, "Or?"

A devilish smile pulled at his lips. "Or you'd fling yourself at me and beg me to show you all the things I'm certain your husband would never dare to."

Lavinia's heart sped up, but not because of the lewd suggestion. She'd stumbled across something, possibly Lord Shayles's weak spot. He needed a reaction. "What things are those, Lord Shayles?" she asked, terrified on the inside but desperate to keep her face as blank as possible.

The curiosity in Lord Shayles's eyes intensified. "I could tell you things that would make you shriek in horror," he said, his voice a seductive purr. "That is, if they didn't make you so wet your juices dripped down your thighs."

Lavinia blinked. Revulsion warred with a strange sense of power and arousal within her—not for Lord Shayles or his words, but because of the power she sensed she suddenly had in the situation—but she battled to maintain a mask of banality.

A frown creased Lord Shayles's brow and he shifted his weight to his other leg. "There is an exquisite amount of pleasure to be had in pain, my dear," he went on. "I could do things to you that would have you begging me for mercy in more ways than one."

Lavinia cocked her head to the side. "Oh? Such as?" Her stomach writhed with snakes, but she stood her ground.

"I could tie you up with rope so rough it would chafe your sweet skin, with knots pressed hard against your most delicate parts," he said, leaning forward and arching a brow at her. "I'd stimulate you until you were on the verge of coming, and then I'd deny you over and over and over."

The memory of the way Armand had touched her and the blissful relief she'd felt when her body responded flooded her. But they also left her wondering what it would have felt like if he'd stopped before she'd burst, leaving her suspended in that bittersweet agony of need. But her only outward reaction to Lord Shayles's fiendish suggestions was to blink once more. "And what would be the point of that?" she asked.

Lord Shayles inched back, studying her. "Perhaps there are other things that would tempt your fancy. I doubt your upright, doctor-viscount-husband would ever dream of smacking that sumptuous ass of yours until it glows pink, then spreading those cheeks and taking you in the most sinful of ways."

Lavinia simply stared at him. No one actually did that, did they? She kept her question buried as far inside as she could, betraying no emotion at all. No fear, no shock, no curiosity. She would give the horrible man nothing.

With a short, impatient breath, Lord Shayles changed his stance yet again. "All right, then. Perhaps you are more the sort that enjoys fucking two men at once, or more."

It took everything Lavinia had not to gasp at his use of such a foul word or his suggestion of something so wicked.

"It's possible," Lord Shayles went on. "Very possible. I've seen it." He leaned closer. "I've taken part in it," he whispered. "One man to fill your slippery little cunny, one up to his balls in your ass. I could even arrange a third to thrust his cock down your throat. It's quite a sight when all four participants come at once."

Her stomach churned in disgust, and she had to tense every muscle of her body to keep herself from shaking like a leaf in a storm. She focused every last ounce of her concentration on maintaining an expression of pure, absolute neutrality and disinterest.

Of all things, Lord Gatwick came to mind, the way he stared at artwork while Lord Shayles spewed the most hateful things, the way he seemed utterly nonplussed by the sewage he was mired in. A spark of genuine curiosity cut through her battle to hold back Lord Shayles's evil. Perhaps Lord Gatwick hated the man as much as she did and only feigned interest in art and such to keep his repulsion at bay. But why? Why would the man torture himself with Lord Shayles's company so frequently if he hated the man? Why would he—

"Bah!" Lord Shayles backed away from her, wiping his mouth as though he'd plucked one of the apples from the trees around them and bit into a worm. "I've never met such a cold fish in my life."

Lavinia drew in a slow breath, surprised that it wasn't a gasp of shock at being caught in her thoughts. "I'm sorry, my lord. It is my duty to make certain all of my guests are happy and at ease while under my husband's roof. Is there anything I could do to make your stay more enjoyable?"

Lord Shayles gaped at her, several vile emotions flickering across his face. He settled on condescension and snorted a laugh. "No, my dear. I don't believe you'd know how to make anything more enjoyable for me in any way. There's no point in seducing you after all. You'd probably just lay there like a limp squid while I buggered you senseless. You wouldn't even have the decency to scream when I hurt you." He tugged at his cuffs, licking his lips as if dispelling a bad taste, and glanced around. "At this rate, Pearson will abandon you for India without my help." He sniffed. "Which is the quickest way back to the house?"

"The house?" Lavinia asked, still clinging to her blankness, though, oddly enough, it was harder to keep up the ruse now that he wasn't interested in her. What did he mean about Armand abandoning her for India *without his help*?

"The house, yes, the house," Lord Shayles hissed with impatience. He stared at her, then rolled his eyes. "I'm not stupid, you know."

"I never said you were, my lord."

He ignored her, going on to say, "This whole stupid thing," he waved a hand, gesturing around the garden, "was just a ploy to allow your dear husband and his friends to search for their letter."

Lavinia tilted her head to the side, attempting a confused look.

Lord Shayles sneered at her. "Oh, give it up, sweetling. They're probably turning my room inside out at this very moment. But they won't find anything." He reached into his coat pocket, pulling an envelope far enough out for her to see. She knew the Winterberry Park stationery as well as her own. Marigold had sent her dozens of letters on the stuff. "I suppose we should head back to the house and catch them in the act," Lord Shayles went on as though bored out of his mind. He offered her his arm. "Shall we?"

Lavinia had to think fast. She cleared her throat. "If you don't mind, my lord, I feel I should check on my other guests first."

"Oh, very well," he said, rolling his eyes. "Go call for the cavalry. I'll race you to see who can catch the corrupt politicians first."

Without waiting, Lord Shayles turned and marched off toward the house. Only when he'd turned the corner did Lavinia let out the breath she felt like she'd been holding for the last ten minutes. She clutched her stomach, heaving for breath, then stumbled to the side and promptly cast up her lunch on the roots of one of the apple trees.

"My lady, are you all right?" Carl jumped into action, racing towards her.

"I'm fine." Lavinia gasped, shaking violently. "Go after him," she ordered. "And if you see Lady Stanhope or Mrs. Croydon on the way, don't prevaricate, just tell them what's happening."

"Yes, my lady." Carl nodded, then rushed off.

Lavinia darted off in the direction she thought she'd seen Lady Stanhope and Dr. Miller head in. The game was over, and if they weren't careful they'd lose.

CHAPTER 15

Armand burst into the room where Shayles was staying, Alex and Malcolm right behind him, Maxwell bringing up the rear.

"Now, if I were a disgusting shite of an excuse for a man that had crawled up out of Hell, where would I stash a letter?" Malcolm asked with a dark grumble. He headed straight for the wardrobe, throwing open the doors and yanking Shayles's clothes from the shelves.

"So much for subtlety," Alex said, sending Armand a wary look.

Armand returned the look with equal leeriness. Instead of helping Malcolm search the wardrobe or going with Alex to rifle through the bureau, he cut straight across the room and pulled aside the curtains to peer outside. Lavinia was out there somewhere in the company of a fiend. He should be by her side, protecting her, not upsetting Shayles's things to prove a point.

Not that he'd been much good at protecting her so far. He let out an impatient breath and leaned as far as he could to one side to get the best view of the part of the garden he'd seen Lavinia and Shayles head off into. In the short week of their marriage, Armand had disappointed his young wife more times than he cared to count, and there seemed to be no end in sight. A bride was supposed to glow with love, to float on air at the blessedness of her situation. Armand couldn't shake the heartbroken look Lavinia had given him earlier in the hall. Even when he was trying to do something right for her, it went all wrong.

"Don't just stand there, Armand," Malcolm called across the room as he upended a small purse and shook it, sending coins and bills scattering across the pile of clothes at his feet. "Help us."

Armand turned away from the window, anxiety gnawing at his gut. "I was keeping an eye out for Shayles," he half-lied.

"Is he out there?" Alex asked, glancing over his shoulder from the bureau.

"Somewhere." Armand rubbed a hand over his face, walking to the bed and pushing the covers back to check under the mattress.

"And your wife?" Alex asked on.

Armand frowned, thrusting his hand under the mattress. "She probably hates me at this point."

Malcolm huffed a humorless laugh and continued his search. Alex turned away from the bureau. "There's hardly been time for her to come to love or hate you," he said.

"No thanks to you lot," Armand muttered. Guilt instantly bit at him and he stood. "No, it wasn't your fault."

Alex fixed him with a flat look. "What did you do to that poor girl that puts you at fault?"

"I married her," Armand said. "She didn't want to marry at all, to anyone. She told me so. She wanted to live an independent life."

Alex crossed his arms. "It never would have happened. You've seen her mother. That woman was hell-bent on marrying her daughter off to a titled gentleman. Her father isn't much better. If it hadn't been you, it would have been someone else, someone worse."

There was a ring of truth to Alex's words. "Miller told her I was planning to go to India."

Malcolm snorted as he grabbed a pair of Shayles's shoes from the wardrobe and shook them before dropping them on the pile. "You were never going to India."

"The offer has been made, and it still stands," Armand said with a scowl. "And what are you doing with that mess? Shayles clearly doesn't have the letter in this room."

"I want him to know we mean business," Malcolm said. "Unlike you."

"I would have gone to India," Armand argued. "I want to keep practicing medicine."

"Then why aren't you?" Alex asked. "Other than helping Marigold last summer—for which we are endlessly grateful, by the way—and patching me up after I fell for Shayles's trap, you haven't so much as diagnosed a head cold or put a plaster on a cut."

"That's not true," Armand said, avoiding his friends' eyes. He marched back to the window, hoping to catch a glimpse of Lavinia. "Besides, you two and Peter have kept me up to my eyeballs in parliamentary papers and Liberal Party strategy sessions. When would I even have time to see patients?"

"You could have told us to bugger off at any time," Malcolm said, abandoning the mess he'd created in front of Shayles's wardrobe to join Armand and Alex by the window. "Not that we would have."

Armand sent him a peevish look. "Which proves my point." He leaned to the side, straining to see more of the garden through the window. "The worst part of it all is,

Lavinia said something to me yesterday that struck more of a chord than I wanted it to."

"What? That you're a sullen git who can't change direction when your path turns?" Malcolm asked.

Armand pushed away from the window, glaring at his friend. "You know, Malcolm, you have a mistaken idea of what it means to be a good friend."

"I speak the truth as I see it, when I see it," Malcolm said without the least hint of remorse. "The truth is hard, and so must I be. We have too much at stake. The women we love, and have loved, have too much at stake for you to waffle your way through this critical time. Basil saw the truth once I pounded it into him, and so should you."

"Malcolm, you need a woman in your bed," Alex said with a shake of his head.

"I do, but that's not up for discussion at the moment," Malcolm answered the jab without missing a beat.

"Besides which," Armand sighed. "He's right."

Malcolm broke into a lop-sided grin. "At last! A modicum of sense."

Armand pushed a hand through his hair. "As Lavinia sees it, by doing my duty as a peer, I could be healing the nation, even if I'm not treating individual patients."

"It sounds like your wife has a way with words," Alex said, smiling.

"I think my wife has a way with a lot of things that I've only begun to discover," Armand admitted. "Only now she thinks I'm on the verge of leaving her for India and the chance to continue to practice medicine."

"Are you leaving her?" Malcolm asked, one brow arched.

The answer wouldn't push past Armand's lips. The truth was staring him in the face, and he'd been resisting it with all his might. Not just in the past week, since Lavinia came into his life, but for the past five years, since the moment the court chose him over Mark Pearson, Lord Gatwick. He'd battled for years to escape the inescapable. He was Viscount Helm.

"No," he admitted at last, blowing out a breath, every muscle in his body loosening. "I'm not going anywhere. I have an estate to run, a seat in Parliament to take up, and a wife to make happy, if I can."

"Of course you can," Malcolm said, stepping close enough to slap him on the back a little harder than was necessary. "All you have to know about keeping a woman happy is how to say 'yes, dearest', how to open your purse-strings, and how to bring her to orgasm three times a night."

Armand stared at him. "Says the man who has been single for over fifteen years, and who can't coax Katya into so much as a tickle, despite the fact that the two of you have been in love for decades."

"Do you want a blackened eye, Pearson?" Malcolm growled at him. "Because I've worked up quite a bit of energy during this search, and I'm in the mood to break some bones."

"Then by all means, don't let me stop you."

Armand, Malcolm, and Alex all whipped to the door as Shayles spoke. Maxwell was nowhere in sight, which meant Shayles could saunter into the room without anyone stopping him. Gatwick stood just behind him, looking extremely put out.

"I'd ask what you three are doing in my guest room," Shayles went on with a casual wave of his hand and a brief frown for the pile of his clothes on the floor, "but even a child would know the reason for it."

A bitter sort of embarrassment sent heat rushing to Armand's face. Only fools got caught bickering while searching an enemy's room for something they knew probably wasn't there.

"You'll hand that letter over or you'll see worse," Malcolm said, taking a few threatening steps toward Shayles.

"My, my. You are ferocious for a man who is clearly in the wrong. Wouldn't you say so, Gatwick?" Shayles barely glanced over his shoulder at his friend.

"What a ridiculous mess," Gatwick said, glancing to the pile of clothes and sniffing.

"I'll say it is," Shayles went on. "Is this the sort of hospitality all your guests receive, Pearson?"

"Where is my wife?" Armand demanded, in no mood to play Shayles's games.

Shayles made a sour face. "You mean that unresponsive wad of soggy milquetoast in last year's fashion cast-offs?" The representation of Lavinia was so inaccurate that Armand blinked instead of answering. What had happened out in the garden to give Shayles that impression? "I'm surprised you haven't left for India already. You know you want to."

Only after Armand recovered from the initial discord of Shayles's words did he growl, "What did you do to her?"

"Nothing. Nothing at all." Shayles turned to Gatwick. "Who would want to do anything with a bland little nobody like that?"

"Enough of the insults," Alex snapped. "Where is the letter?"

Armand was grateful to his friend for redirecting the conversation, but he wanted nothing more than to barge past Shayles and Gatwick to go find Lavinia and make sure she was all right.

Shayles had other plans. "The letter is where it will stay." He reached into his coat and pulled the letter out of whatever concealed pocket it'd been in. "Really, gentlemen." He clicked his tongue. "Did you think I'd leave something this valuable unattended?"

"If you truly intended to bring down Gladstone's new government before this next session begins, you'd have already taken it to the press," Alex said.

"You are correct," Shayles said, tucking the letter away and strolling over to peek casually out the window. "So. How far are you willing to go to get this juicy morsel back?"

"We will not extend any sort of legal protection to your club," Malcolm answered for them all.

"It's a pity," Shayles sighed. "And here I was willing to negotiate."

The hair on the back of Armand's neck stood up. "Negotiate for what?" he asked.

"We don't negotiate with the devil," Malcolm snapped.

Shayles broke into a beaming smile. "I'm so pleased you think of me in such glowing terms, Malcolm. Perhaps our friendship could be salvaged after all."

"You are not now and never were my friend," Malcolm fumed.

"That's not how I remember it, eh Gatwick?" Shayles glanced over his shoulder to Gatwick, who merely hummed in reply.

"Games are getting us nowhere." Alex took charge once again. "We refuse to give your club any sort of immunity."

"Then I refuse to hand over the letter," Shayles said with a shrug. "And I refuse to sit by and let you pass a load of ridiculous laws that will give women ideas of rising above the place they're intended to be."

"You can't hold back the tide of progress forever," Alex said.

"No?" Shayles sent him a smug grin. "Watch me." Before any of them could argue or protest, Shayles hurried on. "I don't want to be stuck in this morass any more than you do. I want resolution, and I want it soon."

"Then give us the letter," Malcolm insisted.

Shayles sneered at him. "You're a bore. I'm not simply going to hand over the single greatest bargaining chip you lot have ever handed me. But," he raised a hand to stop anyone from interrupting, "I will give you a chance to win it back from me."

Armand instantly sensed a trap. His whole world had devolved into traps, it seemed. "What do you propose?" he asked in wary tones, rubbing a hand over his face.

Shayles shrugged and tapped a finger to his chin, pacing behind Armand and his friends like a lion circling his prey. "We could incorporate the letter into a scavenger hunt, like the one your charming mother-in-law organized for your wife's guests just now. Or I could risk it in a game of cards, provided you were willing to bet something of equal value."

Armand scowled. Shayles was toying with them by offering ridiculous suggestions. "We know what you're after, Shayles, and you're not getting it."

"You haven't heard all of my ideas yet," he said, pivoting to a stop next to the pile of his clothes.

"We have no interest in your ideas," Alex said. "Only in getting our letter back."

"We could go to the press first," Malcolm blurted, glancing from Alex to Armand. "We could circulate the idea that a counterfeit letter has been sent about, maligning the Liberal Party with false accusations of collusion."

Shayles's smug grin faltered. "They'd print the contents of this letter anyhow." He rested his hand over his chest. "Any whiff of corruption would damage your credibility, even if you sought a way to counter it."

"Not if we drag your name into print with it," Malcolm said. "You've already got a black mark because of your association with Turpin and Denbigh. Could you survive another?"

"Would your government survive a scandal?" Shayles

asked in return, then answered with, "No, we're gentlemen. We must resolve this like gentlemen, with a gentlemen's game."

"I'm not playing games with anything this important," Alex said. "Malcolm, draft a letter to *The Times* immediately."

"Or," Shayles said, stepping into Malcolm's path before he could take two steps, "Both sides could risk everything on one game."

Armand sighed, done with the whole thing. "Just tell us what you're thinking, Shayles."

For a moment, Armand had the impression that Shayles's mind was elsewhere, that his chief bargaining chip was his outstanding arrogance. Then the man's expression lit with inspiration. "We'll play for it," he said, "but not cards. No, something much grander is needed for a prize like this."

"Such as?" Alex asked.

Shayles glanced out the window and nodded. "Cricket. Devon is full of cricket pitches and cricket players. You form your team and I'll form mine. It will be like medieval contests where knights on both sides assembled to play for the honor of their lords."

"You would play a cricket match for the fate of a letter you value so much that you're keeping it tucked in your jacket pocket?" Alex asked with a flat stare.

"Why not?" Shayles grinned, but there was something desperate in the expression now. "It's a house party, after all. Fun and games are the natural order of things."

"He's only saying that now because he knows the letter will be worth nothing if we act," Malcolm said.

"And you would forgo the chance to best me in this or any sort of game on the odd chance that you can salvage your reputation with conflicting news stories?" Shayles asked.

"He has a point," Gatwick said. The fact that Shayles's

toady would speak at all shocked everyone in the room into silence. He shrugged, ignoring their stares, and went on. "Whether a second letter is drafted to counteract the effects of the first, a scandal will break. It may not bring down your new government, but it could erode public confidence. If you wish to avoid that, I suggest you take Shayles up on his offer. It's just cricket, after all."

Armand studied Gatwick with narrowed eyes, suddenly trying to recall what he knew about his cousin other than that he spent most of his time in Shayles's pocket. He was a peer thanks to a title that had come down from his mother's side, but rarely took up his seat in the House of Lords. As far as Armand knew, he cared more about art than politics. He had no reason to help Alex or Malcolm, or any of them, but Armand wasn't sure he cared as much as Shayles about destroying the Liberal Party.

"A cricket match," Armand said aloud, attempting to wrap his mind around the odd situation. "And the winning team gets the letter."

"Precisely," Shayles said.

"Who would play?" Alex asked.

"Whomever both sides could manage to recruit for the match by, say, tomorrow?" Shayles suggested.

"That doesn't leave us much time," Malcolm said.

"Which means it doesn't leave much time for cheating," Alex added, glaring at Shayles.

"How dare you suggest I would do such a thing?" Shayles said with false offense.

"Because we know you?" Malcolm offered.

"Do you?" The spark in Shayles's eyes said he'd rig the ball, stack the field, and command the weather if it would give him an advantage. He shook his head, brushing away the protest. "Is it settled then, gentlemen? Cricket, tomorrow, say, fifty overs?" Shayles asked.

"I know several men in the village who are quite good," Armand murmured to his friends.

"This is a ridiculous idea," Alex sighed. "I don't trust him at all." He stared hard at Shayles.

"How could I possibly twist this situation to my advantage with so little time to do so?" Shayles asked.

He had a point. Nothing about the situation seemed right, but as far as Armand could see, they could either continue to run around in circles, getting nothing done and damaging everyone's cause, or they could do the ridiculous, play cricket, and hope to get the letter away from Shayles without the press getting a hint of any inappropriate activity.

"I think we should do it," he said at last, turning to his friends. "We should at least try."

Malcolm and Alex remained silent, at least until Malcolm blew out a breath and threw his hands up. "Fine. Do whatever you want to do." He pivoted back to Shayles. "Actually, I'm looking forward to having a cricket bat in my hands around you."

"It sounds like you're decided, then," Shayles said, meeting Malcolm's threat with an oily smile.

"We are," Alex sighed at last. "Tomorrow, starting at ten in the morning, we play cricket for that damned letter."

CHAPTER 16

*B*y the time Lavinia fell into bed that night, she was too exhausted to wonder why she was still sleeping in Armand's bed instead of one of her own when it was becoming increasingly apparent he wasn't interested in her. As soon as she'd gathered her friends and headed into the house after her upsetting conversation with Lord Shayles, she'd been met with a wave of the incomprehensible. She'd expected to find Armand fuming and ready to hang Lord Shayles from the highest tree. What she'd discovered was a pack of men buzzing with plans for a cricket match that would be played the next day.

"Is this really the time for sports?" Lady Stanhope had asked precisely what Lavinia wanted to know as the men marched through the front hall, gathering their coats so that they could head down to the village to recruit players. "Aren't there more important things at stake?"

"This match will decide everything," Lord Malcolm informed her with a look as though he were heading into battle.

"But...but cricket?" Marigold asked.

"The winner of the match gets the letter," Mr. Croydon told her, planting a quick kiss on her lips as the men whisked out the front door. Lord Shayles and Lord Gatwick followed them without a glance for the ladies. Maxwell and Carl hopped into action, following on their heels like prison guards.

"Where are they going?" Dr. Miller—who had been loitering by the side of the hall, looking put out for being excluded—asked. "I want to come with you." He scurried after them like a puppy.

"Something stupid is going on," Lady Stanhope said as soon as the men were gone. She made a scoffing noise. "Playing a game to win a letter like that?"

"They could have at least paused to explain why they think a game will solve the whole thing," Marigold sighed.

"They're men," Lavinia said, barely loud enough to be heard. "They won't ever tell us anything."

Lady Stanhope sent her a sideways look full of unreadable emotion. Lavinia wasn't certain the woman had heard her statement. She took a breath and said, "As long as Shayles is gone, we should search high and low for that letter." She picked up her skirts and headed for the stairs.

"There's no point." Lavinia stopped her. "Lord Shayles is carrying the letter in his coat pocket."

Lady Stanhope let out an irritated breath and crossed her arms. "Well, we can't just stand here and do nothing while those fools attempt to solve their problems with cricket."

"Alex loves cricket," Marigold said, crossing her arms and chewing her lip as though trying to reason a way out of their predicament.

"Who came up with the idea anyhow? Lady Stanhope asked, pacing the hall. "If it was our men, then what were they thinking? If it was Shayles, then what is he up to?"

"And why hasn't he already sent the letter to the press, like he threatened to do?" Marigold added.

"I don't know," Lavinia sighed. She rubbed her head, which was still aching. "All I know is that I have guests to feed and now a cricket match to prepare for." When her friends glanced questioningly at her, she said, "Armand showed me the pitch the other day. It's on his property, which means I'll be responsible for providing tea tomorrow for eleven players on each side, two umpires, a scorekeeper, and who knows how many spectators?" She broke away from her friends and headed for the hallway that led downstairs.

"We'll help you as much as we can," Marigold said, rushing after her.

Marigold and Lady Stanhope were helpful, but that didn't stop Lavinia from practically expiring from exhaustion that night, or waking in the morning with her nerves already bristling. She hadn't heard Armand come in the night before. He'd stayed up late with his friends, planning for the match and whatever else they intended to do about Lord Shayles and the letter. He was still asleep when Lavinia rose and tiptoed from the room to head across the hall to her dressing room, or so she thought.

"Lavinia?" his soft question came just as she'd opened the door and started into the hall.

She paused, turning back to him. "Go back to sleep," she whispered. "You'll need to be rested for your match."

"No." He shifted in bed, rolling to face her and muscling himself to sit and rub the sleep from his eyes. "Come here."

Lavinia swallowed, dreading whatever reason he had to delay her. She shut the door and dutifully crossed to stand beside the bed, but once there, she couldn't think of anything to say.

Armand reached for her hand. "We'll win today, don't

worry," he said, looking as though he was still trying to wake up.

"I'm sure you will," she replied, not certain she believed it. Nothing about the situation seemed right.

"We need that letter," he went on, "but even if we lose and Shayles sends it to the press, Malcolm is convinced we can counteract whatever damage it would do with a second letter stating that ours is a fake."

"But it isn't a fake," Lavinia said, in spite of the fact that a few more pieces of the puzzle clicked into place in her mind. It was all a game of politics and pride, one side scoring points against the other in an effort to win the prize of power.

Armand sighed and pulled her closer. She sat on the side of the bed as he threaded his fingers through hers, his gaze focused on their hands. "I haven't been involved in what Alex, Malcolm, and Peter have been doing in Parliament up until this point. They're so determined to steer the government in the right direction. Determined enough to resort to a few underhanded tricks themselves."

"Isn't that what politics is about?" she said, staring at their hands as well. "I've been observing it for years now, and most of what I've seen is maneuvering and manipulation."

He huffed a humorless laugh. "Medicine is so much simpler. A patient presents with an illness, I heal them. If I can."

Lavinia pulled her hand out of his grasp and stood. "You should do what your heart tells you to do," she said, stepping away. "I need to get ready for what is bound to be another exhausting day." She started back toward the door.

"Lavinia," he called after her again. When she turned to glance at him over her shoulder, his mouth hung open for a moment and his face was lined with frustration before he said, "I'm sorry."

The words twisted her stomach as much as Lord Shayles's

filthy speech the day before. "Yes, Armand, I know," she said, then left the room before he could tell her yet again how he hadn't wanted to marry her and how he would soon be gone.

She didn't have time to dwell on the hollow ache that grew in her heart. She washed and dressed as fast as she could, then headed downstairs to see how the servants were doing with breakfast and preparations for the match. They were surprised to see her up as early as they were, but ultimately, Lavinia had the feeling they were grateful for her supervision and help.

And yet, as she assisted the servants in carrying food and supplies out to the wagons so that it would be transported to the cricket pitch, her thoughts refused to fully settle. Everything Armand had said whirled back into her mind whenever she tried to push it away. Lord Shayles hadn't sent the letter to the press yet, even though he kept insisting he would if Mr. Croydon and the rest didn't ensure his club was protected. Lord Malcolm said he knew how to foil Lord Shayles's plan to ruin the new Liberal government before it started by denying the letter. Was the letter truly that important, or was there some other, more sinister reason Lord Shayles was at Broadclyft Hall?

There wasn't time to dwell on the question. The match was set for ten in the morning, but Lord Shayles and his team arrived at the pitch well before nine to practice. Lavinia was already there, directing the servants to set up the table for the scorekeeper, and another table for refreshments. All it took was one glance at Lord Shayles's team as they arrived and began to toss the ball around for her to know something wasn't quite right. Over half of Lord Shayles's team was made up of dark-haired, brown-skinned men from India.

"Lady Helm," Lord Shayles greeted her with a lopsided grin as he and an Indian man in cricket whites ambled toward her. "I believe that's the most noticeable reaction I've seen from you yet."

Lavinia instantly schooled her features. "Lord Shayles," she greeted him with an even nod, glancing to the man with him.

"This is Dr. Tahir Maqsood," Lord Shayles introduced the man.

An electric jolt shot down Lavinia's spine. "How do you do, Dr. Maqsood?" she greeted the foreigner politely. Her heart beat double-time. Dr. Maqsood was the man who had offered Armand a position in India.

"Lady Helm," Dr. Maqsood greeted her with a respectful nod and a friendly smile. "It is a pleasure to meet you." His accent was crisp and genteel, hinting that he was educated and worldly.

"Dr. Maqsood is the captain of my cricket team," Lord Shayles said.

Lavinia couldn't stop herself from blinking, but instead of expressing shock that an Indian would captain a cricket team, she merely asked Lord Shayles, "You do not intend to captain it yourself?"

Lord Shayles made a dismissive noise. "It's all I can do to catch a ball without bruising my hands. I'll leave captaining to the experts."

Things still didn't add up. "I was unaware that you were acquainted with Dr. Maqsood," she said as blandly as she could with her mind racing over the connection.

"Oh, I don't know him at all," Lord Shayles said. "I only just met him yesterday. Your husband and his friends might have seen fit to recruit their team from the local sportsmen, but Gatwick, Miller, and I rushed down to Exeter as fast as our little feet would take us to see if we could find players of untapped skill. We were directed straight away to Dr.

Maqsood and some of the crew on the ship he is about to sail away on."

A fresh round of suspicion swept through Lavinia, but of all the things Lord Shayles said, the one that stuck with her was that Dr. Maqsood's ship was ready to sail.

"I was not aware cricket was played in India," she said to Dr. Maqsood with a pleasant smile.

"The game has been played by Englishmen in our homeland for over a century," Dr. Maqsood said. "But it is only recently that my countrymen have taken up an interest in the sport." He pivoted to glance over his shoulder. "The men on my team have honed their talents playing in coastal towns here in England when the ships they sail on are docked."

"I see," Lavinia said, studying the men spread across the field to practice. She didn't know much about cricket, but from what she could see, they were good. The entire match felt more and more like yet another trap with each passing second. "If you will excuse me, gentlemen, I still have much work to do."

"Of course, Lady Helm," Lord Shayles said. Instead of leaving as Lavinia turned back to the tables, he went on with, "It seems to me that when Dr. Lord Pearson Helm leaves with Dr. Maqsood in a few days, he'll be leaving his estate in good hands."

Lavinia froze, her spine going stiff. She turned back to Lord Shayles. "I am not privy to my husband's current thoughts on the position you have offered him, Dr. Maqsood," she said, hating the fact that she was forced to give away what she knew, "but I will do whatever duty is required of me."

"Is that so?" Lord Shayles said. "Perhaps you could put in a good word with your husband to give his cousin leave to administer his estate while he's gone."

Lavinia's heart hammered so hard in her chest that she

was certain any attempt on her part to pretend disinterest would fail. "I will," she said, figuring the fewer words she spoke the better. She nodded, then marched toward the table, determined not to let Lord Shayles side-track her again.

"I told you she was nothing interesting," she heard Lord Shayles say to Dr. Maqsood as they walked away.

As soon as Lavinia was certain they were gone, she let out a breath, hand pressed to her stomach. The pieces of the puzzle felt as though they were coming together, but she couldn't quite see the picture yet. Lord Shayles wanted Armand gone and Lord Gatwick in his place. She didn't believe for a second that he'd only just met Dr. Maqsood the night before. But that still didn't tell her what the letter had to do with anything, or why they were playing cricket with the letter as the prize. Unless the entire match and the letter itself were merely a way to distract everyone from Lord Shayles's true aim. But even if it were, what was Lord Shayles true aim?

"My lady, are you well?"

Lavinia gasped and glanced up at Mr. Bondar's question. The Broadclyft Hall butler was dressed in an umpire's uniform, but he still looked ready to serve her. Mr. Bondar, at least, was someone she could trust.

"Has Lord Shayles done or said anything that seems suspicious to you since his arrival, Mr. Bondar?" she asked, stepping to the side to speak to him quietly as more men in cricket whites and other observers began to arrive.

Mr. Bondar huffed a humorless laugh. "Everything the blackguard has said and done since arriving has been suspicious, my lady."

"Anything that stands out specifically?" she asked.

Mr. Bondar frowned. "He's been giving the staff a hard time, which is to be expected. I daren't go into the details of what he's said to some of the maids."

Lavinia blushed. "Thank you."

Mr. Bondar paused before saying, "I overheard him asking Lord Gatwick how much he thought the artwork was worth. That isn't suspicious in and of itself," he rushed to add, "but I have heard that Lord Shayles's financial situation isn't good."

"He's after money," Lavinia sighed, returning to the conclusion she'd entertained briefly from the start, before Armand had dismissed it. "And he thinks Lord Gatwick could somehow take Broadclyft Hall from Armand."

"Lord Gatwick has been well-behaved since arriving, my lady," Mr. Bondar said with a frown. "I've known him since he was a boy." Lavinia's brow shot up. "He's never struck me as the sort to cause trouble. He's always been very quiet and circumspect, even as a child. I don't know how he became so closely associated with the likes of Lord Shayles. When the courts awarded the title and estate to Lord Helm, Lord Gatwick accepted the decision without guile." Mr. Bondar paused, looking troubled. "It pains me to think Lord Shayles is using Lord Gatwick in some way."

Lavinia chewed on her lip as she mulled over Mr. Bondar's words. "Something isn't right here."

"No, my lady," Mr. Bondar agreed. "We must be vigilant during this match."

"I believe you're right," Lavinia said. Though it would have been far easier to be vigilant if she knew what to look for from Lord Shayles and his associates.

Armand was slow to roll out of bed to wash and dress for the cricket match after Lavinia left. More than games or letters or enemies, he wanted to find a way to make things right with her. He marched downstairs with the intention of seeking her out in the breakfast room, only to discover that she'd already gone down to the cricket pitch. His friends were helping themselves to breakfast, however, and before he could head down to the field himself, Alex caught him and dragged him into discussions of strategy.

"We managed to recruit several strong players for our side," Alex said, making a list of names on a card as Armand sat and helped himself to coffee. "I'm going to open the batting with Paul Green and Ernie Precious. They should be able to hold strong for a dozen overs at least. Then I'll come in at number three, followed by you at four, Jon Kennon at five, Chris Lawrence at six, then Malcolm, and—"

"Why aren't you letting Kennon open the batting?" Malcolm protested. "From what I watched yesterday, he's the best batsman on the local team."

"Yes, but he said he's a mid-order player," Alex said. He tried to go on with, "As for bowling, I want to get Mike Thomas in against their opening batsmen, and Ken Griffiths as—"

"Thomas is a slow-bowler," Malcolm argued. "That other chap, that young lascar, Kalim something. He was better."

Armand blew out a breath and stood. "To hear the two of you go on, you're more interested in the match itself than what we're playing for."

"We can't get what we're playing for without winning," Malcolm told him. "Sit down and finish your coffee and help us figure this out."

Armand sat, but only because the eggs and sausage on his plate were needed to get him through the match. He couldn't bring himself to listen to Alex and Malcolm's team maneuvering, though. Letter or no letter, nothing would be right in his life until he made things right with Lavinia. And the only way to do that was to foil whatever plot Shayles had in mind and to get him and everyone else out of the house. Maybe then he could explain his ever-changing and conflicted thoughts on India.

He was ready to put everything aside and focus on what had to be done as they headed down to the cricket pitch, but the moment he noticed the opposing team, the instant he saw Shayles standing at the edge of the pitch chatting with an Indian gentleman in whites, a knot formed in his stomach.

"Ah, Dr. Pearson." Shayles rushed to greet him as Armand, Alex, and Malcolm approached. "I believe you know the captain of my team, Dr. Tahir Maqsood."

Armand was instantly on guard. "Dr. Maqsood." He shook the man's offered hand as Alex and Malcolm looked on with varying degrees of alarm and suspicion. "I trust you received my letter?"

"About delaying your posting to our hospital? Yes." Dr. Maqsood smiled, though the expression didn't sit right with Armand. "To be honest, when I heard Lord Shayles was searching for cricket players for a match on your estate, I jumped at the opportunity. We should sit down and discuss the advantages of you sailing with us next week."

"You see?" Shayles said. "It appears this match of ours is more serendipitous than anyone could have thought."

Armand narrowed his eyes, searching for reasons why Shayles would seem so pleased by the notion. He was stopped from saying anything as Gatwick approached their group. He looked odd and uncomfortable dressed in cricket whites instead of his usual, finely-tailored suit.

"Mr. Bondar would like to do the toss now," he said, glancing from Armand to Alex.

"Very well," Alex said, heading off with Gatwick toward the wicket. Malcolm sent Shayles one final glare, then walked with Dr. Maqsood as though expecting him to draw a gun at any moment. Armand stayed where he was, searching the area for Lavinia. Unfortunately, Shayles stayed as well.

"Imagine my surprise when the man I stumbled across to captain my team turned out to be someone you are associated with," Shayles said.

"You stumbled across him?" Armand asked, not believing it for a second. At the same time, he didn't want to find any sort of connection between Shayles and Dr. Maqsood. If Maqsood was somehow one of Shayles's cronies, then India was out of the question. And if India was out of the question, where did that leave his future?

To his surprise, Shayles thumped him on the back and steered him to walk toward the scorer's table. "I envy your chance to stay true to your future and your training," Shayles said. "It was such bad luck when you became viscount, but now you have a chance to change all that."

Armand sent him a sideways look, unable to tell if the man was just rubbing it in or if he had an ulterior motive. "Why should you care what I do with my life?"

Shayles chuckled. "If you can't see that, you're far denser than I imagined. One less vote in Parliament means far less danger to my club."

"I'm not gone yet," Armand growled, shaking Shayles's hand off his shoulder. Only a fool revealed his motivations for mischief, and Shayles was no fool. There was something deeper to his seeming encouragement. "I might not go at all now," he said, testing the waters to see what more Shayles would reveal if given the right prompt.

Shayles shrugged. "Perfectly understandable, what with your pretty new wife, dull as she is. But I suppose she'll do to get an heir. Poor Gatwick. He'll be so disconsolate once your red-headed dishrag pops out a son."

"Lord Shayles," Dr. Maqsood called from across the pitch. "We've won the toss and elected to bat first. Come on."

For a moment, Shayles looked put out at being ordered to the other end of the field, where his team was assembling.

"Come on, Armand. We're in the field," Alex called, gesturing for Armand to hurry.

Armand let out an impatient breath and glanced to where Lavinia was standing with Katya and Marigold near the scorer's table. Bondar and the other umpire, a local man named Bruce, were conferring with a woman, of all things, who had a scorebook set out in front of her and an array of colored pencils lined up beside it.

"Such a pity," Shayles said with an irritated sneer. "I was so hoping to continue our conversation. I hear India is lovely this time of year, and they are so desperate for trained physicians."

"I'm not going," Armand told him, surprised to discover that he meant it. He glanced to Lavinia. She looked up from her conversation at that moment, and their eyes met. He smiled. She blushed and glanced away. "I'm staying right here," Armand went on, half wishing Lavinia could hear him.

"If that's the way things are," Shayles said, striding away to join his team, "then don't say I didn't warn you."

"Warn me of what?" Armand asked with a frown.

But Shayles had already broken into a jog.

"Armand," Alex shouted from the field. "Get your arse over to mid-off, now! They want to start."

With one final glance to Lavinia, Armand trotted out to the position where Alex wanted him. He'd never been less excited about cricket. If it wasn't for the fact that they needed to win the letter back from Shayles, he would have prayed for a quick loss just to get off the field. But as it was, he would have to tough it out through hours of playing. Hours in which anything could happen.

CHAPTER 17

"Oh!" A long, cringing chorus of disappointment rose from the spectators on the side of the cricket pitch, including Lavinia, Marigold, and Lady Stanhope. They raised hands to their foreheads and squinted as they followed yet another ball as it soared through the air, landing well outside of the boundary rope.

"That's another six," the scorekeeper, an odd, American woman by the name of Meredith Pennington called out.

"How much does that make all together?" Lavinia's mother asked from her seat in the chair Maxwell had brought down from the house for her.

Miss Pennington held up one hand to silence Lavinia's mother, marked the runs in her book, then proceeded to say, "Two hundred thirty-two in the forty-third over, two balls to come, two wickets down."

Lavinia winced. She'd never followed cricket, but she knew enough to know that the match was a rout. They only had seven overs to stop Shayles's team before their side would have to chase an impossible total.

"We've been had," Lady Stanhope growled, pacing in a

short line nearby. "I don't care if they are Indian, Shayles's team is remarkably good.

"What's the name of the batsman who's facing?" Marigold asked.

"Krish Pusuluri," Miss Pennington answered, even though Marigold hadn't addressed her directly. "The non-striker is Satish Prabhakar."

"I'm never going to be able to keep all these names straight," Marigold sighed.

Lavinia kept silent. Her suspicions had only mounted since Lord Shayles's team—or rather, Dr. Maqsood's team—had begun to bat. She'd only seen three of their players face the best bowlers Mr. Croydon had been able to find in the village, but it was plain to see that every one of the Indian sailors was good. Very good.

"It doesn't make sense," she murmured as Mr. Pusuluri smacked another ball out into the field. It hit the ground short of the boundary, but rolled swiftly over the rope before Rupert could chase after it.

"Four," Mr. Bondar called from the wicket, waving his arm in the gesture indicating the runs. Miss Pennington raised a hand to acknowledge the signal, then scribbled in her scorebook.

"What doesn't make sense?" Lady Stanhope asked, her face set in a scowl.

"How good they are," Lavinia answered. "How easily Lord Shayles was able to find such skilled players." And how Dr. Maqsood was involved.

"Cheating, that's how Shayles found them," Lady Stanhope grumbled. "Clearly he had this match in mind before he even showed up at Broadclyft Hall."

"That's what I'm afraid of," Lavinia whispered.

The final ball of the over was thrown with no runs, and Mr. Bondar called, "Over." The players on the field mulled around as a new bowler was selected and the umpires switched sides.

"No wonder Shayles was so confident about the game from the start," Marigold said with a sigh. "He's going to win."

"We have to do something before it's too late," Lady Stanhope said. "I'm going to find a way to steal that letter."

Marigold reached out a hand to stop her. "There's no point. Shayles has the letter with him."

"No, he doesn't," Lavinia said. She blinked as her thoughts began to spin. "He gave the letter to Miss Pennington for safe keeping before the match started." Lady Stanhope and Marigold stared at her. Lavinia nodded to the scorer's table. "See? It's sitting right out in the open, next to Miss Pennington's pencils."

They all turned to look. Sure enough, the incriminating letter sat near the corner of the table, the sunlight shining off the whiteness of the stationery.

Lady Stanhope hummed. "The best place to keep something you don't want to be stolen is in plain sight with a crowd of witnesses, I suppose."

"Shayles will notice if it's suddenly missing," Marigold agreed with a frown.

"Still, Bianca and Natalia keep pestering Miss Pennington about the score," Lady Stanhope went on. "I suppose I could have one of them snatch it."

"But Shayles would still notice it's missing," Marigold said. "And it's not as though there are many people around who would be motivated to take it."

The only sign that Lady Stanhope agreed with Marigold was her frustrated grunt. "What on earth possessed those men to write their sins in a letter that could be stolen?"

"Gladstone, if I remember correctly," Marigold said. "I wish I'd never penned the thing for them."

Lavinia's eyes popped open. She'd forgotten Marigold was the one who physically wrote the letter, but as her memory was jogged, an idea took hold in her. "I know how we can get the letter," she said, shocked that the plan forming in her brain was so simple.

Lady Stanhope and Marigold turned to her. "How?" Lady Stanhope asked.

Lavinia stopped herself from answering. There were too many people around for her to blurt out such a sensitive plan. It didn't help that part of her was still convinced the letter itself was just a decoy for something much bigger and more sinister.

"I have to run up to the house for a moment," she said, turning and starting off.

"Could I fetch something for you, my lady?" Les asked, stepping over to join her and proving that someone was listening to the entire conversation at the same time.

Lavinia nearly told the young man that she didn't need his help, but her sense that everything was wrong had grown too strong. "I'd appreciate someone to accompany me back to the house, since no one is there," she said in the end.

"Yes, my lady." Les nodded.

"Lavinia, what's this all about?" Marigold asked as Lavinia walked away.

"You'll see," she called over her shoulder.

As she hurried away from the cricket pitch, she spotted Armand watching her from the field. His look was full of questions, but there wasn't time for him to do anything about it. A ball came sailing his way, forcing him to concentrate on the game. It was all for the best. If he'd realized what she was about to do, he would probably have tried to stop her.

The minutes seemed to speed by, filling Lavinia with a

sense that she was moving too slowly, as she and Les hurried back to the house.

"Is there something I can get for you?" Les asked as he held the front door open for Lavinia to speed through.

"No, I just need to fetch something from my dressing room," she answered.

She picked up her skirts and bolted up the stairs. By the time she made it to her dressing room, she was flushed and winded with sweat trickling down her back, but she knew exactly what she needed. She rushed to the small writing desk that had been in her dressing room before the maids had unpacked her things. Tucked away in one of the slots was a letter she'd received from Marigold the day everyone had arrived at Broadclyft Hall. Marigold had written the letter the day Lavinia and Armand had left Winterberry Park, apologizing for the madness that had led to her marriage. But it wasn't the content of the letter that mattered, it was the stationery. It was exactly the same as what the incriminating letter was written on.

"Do you have what you need, my lady?" Les asked when Lavinia rushed back out into the hall.

"Yes, I think I do. We need to hurry back to the pitch," she answered.

Lavinia clasped Marigold's letter to her stomach, cursing the fact that she didn't have a pocket to hide it in. The jog back to the cricket pitch was ten times more stressful than the one up to the house, especially when they returned to the pitch only to find that the game had just broken for tea. Instead of having a field full of distracted men and all the spectators watching the game, everyone was milling about, helping themselves to the finger sandwiches she'd had Mrs. Piper make up. Worse still, a cluster of Shayles's players huddled around the scorer's table, glancing over Miss Pennington's shoulder to check the score.

"Wait for me to add everything up," Miss Pennington was in the middle of scolding them as Lavinia approached the table. "I can't do the arithmetic with you lot hanging over my shoulder. Back up, please."

Lavinia squeezed her way along the table to the corner where the incriminating letter was. Her hands shook around her own letter. She pretended to be interested in the scorebook while madly searching for a way to switch the two letters.

"I said back up, please," Miss Pennington said in an irritated voice. "Give me just a moment."

"Do you need assistance?"

At first, Lavinia thought the question was directed to Miss Pennington. But it was spoken in far too soft a tone and right by her side. She peeked to the side, then gasped and nearly jumped out of her skin when she found Lord Gatwick standing almost flush beside her. His eyes didn't hold the usual vacant look of disinterest he usually wore. Instead, he stared hard at her with deadly seriousness.

"I…um…I was just…." Lavinia's voice shook.

Without blinking, Lord Gatwick reached for the letter on the table, drawing it to the side. The letter slipped off the table and fell into the grass. "Oh, I do beg your pardon." He squatted, tugging Lavinia's skirt.

Working on instinct alone, Lavinia squatted with him. Her voluminous skirt and the crush of eager players hid them from view. Without words, Lord Gatwick plucked the letter from Lavinia's hands, opened the envelope to remove the contents, then did the same with the incriminating letter. He stuffed Marigold's letter of apology into the envelope addressed to Gladstone and Gladstone's letter into Marigold's envelope. Then he stood and placed the envelope addressed to Gladstone back on the table. Lavinia jerked straight along with him, her eyes wide.

"Please forgive my carelessness, cousin," he said once they were both standing straight, the switched letter sitting on the table exactly as it had been before. "We are cousins now, I believe?"

Lavinia was well beyond speech. She simply gaped at Lord Gatwick, desperate to figure out whose side he was on.

"Keep a close eye on your husband during the second innings," Lord Gatwick went on. "I hear Dr. Maqsood has some devilishly clever tactics he wishes to employ on the field. I've heard his fielding skills are as *sharp as a knife*, and attempting to score against them is *murder*."

Lavinia gasped, crushing Marigold's letter against her stomach.

"I should like to become better acquainted with you at some point, cousin," Lord Gatwick said, resuming his bored tone. "Though I have no wish to return to Broadclyft Hall *in any capacity* any time soon, no matter what my friends might want me to do."

In a flash, everything came together in Lavinia's mind. She'd been right all along. Lord Shayles didn't want the letter, he wanted Broadclyft Hall, or at least he wanted Lord Gatwick to inherit it. But the only way he could do that was if Armand was dead. And if her interpretation of Lord Gatwick's message was accurate, Dr. Maqsood could be involved not in a plot to take Armand away to India, but to murder him, something that would have been easy to do once Armand was on a ship bound for foreign shores.

"Thank you, Lord Gatwick," she whispered, her throat hoarse. "I must return to my friends now."

Lord Gatwick nodded once, then turned and marched toward the table where tea was being served. Lavinia darted instantly away from the table, looking for Lady Stanhope and Marigold. She stuffed Marigold's envelope with the letter to Gladstone into the waistband of her skirt, praying that would be enough to conceal it until she could destroy it. She looked for Armand as well. He had to be warned that Dr. Maqsood was in league with Lord Shayles and that his life was potentially in danger.

But she stopped short halfway to the benches where Armand's team was preparing for their innings at bat. Lord Malcolm sat on one bench, his face contorted into a grimace as Armand knelt in front of him, testing his knee. From where she stood, Lavinia could barely make out his question of, "Does that hurt?" as he manipulated Lord Malcolm's knee in a variety of ways.

"Like bloody hell," Lord Malcolm grumbled in reply. "I shouldn't have stretched for that catch."

"What catch?" Armand said. "As I recall, you dropped the ball."

Lord Malcolm muttered a string of expletives that had Lavinia's brows racing toward her hairline, but Armand merely laughed and said, "I'll bind this, but you'll have to have a runner when it's your turn at bat."

He reached for a small medical kit that Lavinia hadn't noticed sitting in the grass, took out a rolled bandage, and began to wrap it around Lord Malcolm's knee. The way Armand worked, with such care and expertise, left Lavinia's heart aching. India might have been a ruse on Lord Shayles's part to do away with Armand so that the Helm title would pass to Lord Gatwick, but that was irrelevant. Armand was a doctor. He was meant to practice medicine, no matter what.

"Lady Helm, can I help you?"

Lavinia snapped out of her thoughts as Mr. Croydon walked up beside her, a cup of tea in each hand. He was heading toward Armand and Lord Malcolm, so Lavinia walked with him.

"Yes, actually," she said, keeping her voice down and darting a glance from side to side to make sure they weren't overheard. "In fact, I believe I need your help desperately. Or at least Armand does."

They'd drawn close enough to Armand and Lord Malcolm that both men heard her statement. Armand finished with Lord Malcolm's bandage and stood. "Lavinia, what's wrong?" he asked.

Lavinia glanced back over her shoulder, looking for Lord Gatwick. He stood in a group with Lord Shayles, Dr. Maqsood, and a few others. They looked as though they were plotting strategy for the second half of the game, but Lavinia suspected they were planning much more. She turned her attention back to her husband and his friends.

"Armand, I believe your life is in danger," she said, keeping her voice low so as not to be overheard.

"In danger?" Armand shook his head. "If I've avoided injury while out on the field, I'll hardly be in danger while batting."

"No." Lavinia started to reach out, intending to lay a hand on his arm, but stopped. The confused frown on her husband's face said that he wouldn't believe what she had to say. Regardless, she pushed on. "I don't know how or why, exactly, but I have reason to believe Dr. Maqsood intends to kill you."

Lord Malcolm snorted and shook his head. "His team may clobber ours, but we've got far more to worry about where that letter is concerned."

"You don't understand," Lavinia said, her voice a desperate hiss. "He's working with Lord Shayles somehow. I…I think they've known each other longer than Lord Shayles told me they did."

"When did you speak to Shayles?" Armand asked, alarmed. "Were you alone with him? Did he try to hurt you?"

"I wouldn't put it past the bastard," Lord Malcolm growled.

"No, listen to me." Lavinia's exasperation was growing by the second. "Lord Gatwick hinted to me that Dr. Maqsood has murderous intent where you are concerned, Armand. He suggested that Lord Shayles wants you dead so that he will inherit Broadclyft Hall and presumably use it to finance Lord Shayles."

All three men exchanged doubtful glances. Mr. Croydon looked embarrassed by the situation, and Lord Malcolm was doing a poor job of hiding his condescension. Armand rubbed the back of his neck and said, "Lord Gatwick may be my cousin, but he's Shayles's friend. You can't believe a word he says."

"And you certainly can't believe anything Shayles says," Lord Malcolm added.

"Exactly." Lavinia was close to stomping her foot over the stubbornness of the men around her. "Which is why you can't believe him when he says he only met Dr. Maqsood last night."

"Lavinia," Armand sighed, his frown etched deep. "I don't doubt every word that has come out of Shayles's mouth since he got here is a lie. I would be willing to believe there is a connection between him and Dr. Maqsood as well, given the right evidence. But you can't simply murder someone at a cricket match and get away scot-free."

"You think I'm making this all up," she said, beyond hurt. Try though she did to find a way to hold her own and be close to her stranger of a husband at the same time, she was beginning to feel as though she would never succeed. He would always be a stranger to her.

"I don't think you're making it up, sweeting," he said, resting a hand on her arm. "But I do think you may have mistaken things. Gatwick can't be trusted any more than Shayles."

"Dr. Maqsood is trying to kill you, and he's involved with

Lord Shayles," Lavinia said, no longer caring how far-fetched the story sounded. Good sense told her she should bring up the letter and specifics of how Lord Gatwick had helped her, but simple, sharp hurt destroyed any faith she had that Armand would believe her. "You need to be on guard. If you won't listen to me, then at least be vigilant."

"Of course I will, but—"

Lavinia didn't stay to listen to his excuses. She turned and marched off. If Armand and his friends wouldn't heed her for their own good, then she had to find her friends. They, at least, would believe her. They would be up against impossible odds, as women and as mere spectators to the game, but they had to do something to foil Lord Shayles for good.

Armand watched Lavinia storm off, feeling worse than ever. Once again, he'd said all the wrong things and flubbed the situation beyond measure. At the same time, he couldn't shake the possibility that she might have been right. He turned away from where Lavinia was marching toward Katya and Marigold to look for Dr. Maqsood and Shayles. When he spotted them chatting away, not at all like strangers, he rubbed a hand over his face.

"Did you bring that for me?" Malcolm asked, taking the spare cup of tea Alex held.

"I brought it for Armand, actually, but by all means, help yourself," Alex grumbled. He, too, had turned to stare at Shayles, Maqsood, and Gatwick. "Do you think there could be any truth in what Lavinia said?" he asked.

Armand answered, "I don't see how it would be possible to kill someone during a cricket match with a crowd looking on."

Alex glanced sideways at him. "But that doesn't mean you don't believe her."

Armand didn't know how to answer. He kept an eye on Dr. Maqsood as Bondar announced that there were five minutes left for tea before the second innings would begin. Maqsood eventually noticed him staring, and as a result, stepped away from Shayles and Gatwick to make his way around the edge of the pitch.

Armand steadied himself, no idea what to make of Dr. Maqsood's approach. Was he the assassin Lavinia seemed to think he could be or was he a colleague intent on helping him pursue his dreams?

"Strange, isn't it?" Maqsood asked once he was close.

"Strange?" Armand asked, on his guard.

Maqsood was all smiles, completely at ease. Not at all like a murderer. "That the first time we meet in person, it should be on opposite sides."

Armand forced himself into a friendly laugh. "It is strange indeed." His mind went blank. There had to be something he could say, some way to assess Maqsood's true intent.

"Mayo Hospital is so looking forward to having you," Dr. Maqsood went on before Armand could think. "The situation in India is dire. Cholera and malaria do so much damage, and that's without the ravages of poverty. A man like you could do so much."

"That's the thing, sir," Armand began, rubbing the back of his neck. "It's been impressed upon me that I could do much here as well. And I'm newly married."

"Yes, I understand that was unexpected." Something hardened in Maqsood's expression. "But I'm sure your wife would be well looked after in your absence."

Armand searched for Lavinia, finding her in a huddle with Marigold and Katya. All three of them looked alarmed and determined to cause trouble. "Yes," he answered Dr. Maqsood slowly. "I'm not certain leaving my wife is such a good idea at this point."

The words felt wrong, in spite of being true. They were too casual, too clinical. What his heart wanted to say was that he had no interest in leaving Lavinia and every interest in staying with her to prove she was a blessing in his life and not a trial.

"Come on, gentlemen," Bondar shouted from the wicket as he and the other umpire gestured for the teams to take the field. "If the fielding team doesn't take the field in two minutes, I'll start assessing penalty runs."

Dr. Maqsood sent a dark frown across the pitch to Bondar. It was such a change from the even expression he'd worn while wooing Armand that a chill shot down Armand's spine. Perhaps Lavinia could be right after all.

"I'm needed on the field," Maqsood said as though the game were an unwanted distraction instead of the reason they were there. He turned to Armand, and his smile returned. "But we should speak later. Perhaps at the end of the match? Surely we can find a quiet corner of this vast estate where just the two of us could sit and discuss medicine and our mutual interests."

Armand hesitated before saying, "Yes, of course."

"One minute," Bondar shouted from the field.

"You'd better go," Armand said, nodding to the field.

"After the match, then," Dr. Maqsood said, jogging out to the field.

Armand watched him go, watched as he took up a place in the field from which he could direct his team to their positions. Shayles marched up to him and said something, but just as Armand was about to believe the two were somehow in league, Maqsood handed Shayles the ball so that he could open the bowling. The whole exchange left Armand wondering what game he was actually playing.

CHAPTER 18

"And he didn't listen to you at all?" Lady Stanhope asked, her eyes wide with incredulity.

"No," Lavinia admitted, her shoulders sagging. "Armand and the others are convinced that Lord Gatwick must be bad and Dr. Maqsood must be good, or at least not part of whatever plot Lord Shayles is hatching."

"But you're convinced it's the other way around?" Marigold asked, looking uncertain herself. She must have seen some degree of hurt in Lavinia's eyes, because she rushed on with, "It's just that we've all known Gatwick is Shayles's strongest supporter and has been for years."

"Then explain this." Lavinia drew the letter from the waistband of her skirt, opened the envelope, and pulled out the letter the men had sent to Gladstone.

Marigold and Lady Stanhope gasped. "You can't let anyone know you have that," Lady Stanhope said, gesturing for Lavinia to hand it over. As soon as she did, Lady Stanhope tucked the letter back in the envelope and thrust it into a hidden pocket within her skirts. "We need to get this letter as far away from Shayles as possible as quickly as possible."

"It should be destroyed," Marigold said.

"I agree," Lavinia added.

Lady Stanhope nodded. "I'll take it up to the house and burn it." She started to move.

"But what about the match?" Marigold asked.

"And whatever attempt on Armand's life that is about to be made?" Lavinia added.

Lady Stanhope glanced from Lavinia to Marigold and back again. "If the men won't listen to us, which they never do, we'll have to take things into our own hands. We don't have to worry about the letter anymore, but we do have to worry about reprisals when Shayles finds out we've outsmarted him."

"Why let him know he's been duped?" Marigold suggested. "Let him think he's won and get him out of here as fast as possible."

"Good thinking." Lady Stanhope nodded. "Which means we can't tell Malcolm and the others about switching the letters until after Shayles leaves. They'd gloat too much and give it away," she added with a smirk. "And they think we're the overly emotional ones. Lavinia," she went on, "if you truly believe Armand is in danger, see what you can do about pinpointing exactly what will happen. Marigold, keep an eye on Shayles to see if you can help her."

"I will." Marigold nodded. "What are you planning to do?"

Lady Stanhope's eyes narrowed. "After I burn this letter, I'm packing my things and heading to Starcross Castle to tell Peter and Mariah what's going on."

"Do you think Lord Dunsford could help?" Lavinia asked.

"If Armand is in as serious trouble as you think he is, yes, then I believe Peter can help. At the very least, he'll want to be involved in whatever the men choose to do next."

"Agreed," Marigold said.

With a final nod, Lady Stanhope marched away, heading

toward the house. Lavinia glanced across the field. The second innings were already underway, and from the look of things, Armand's team was having a hard time. Not more than two overs could have passed, but already, one of the opening batsmen had been bowled out. The Indian players were far more dangerous than they looked. But it was danger of a different kind that had Lavinia bristling with anxiety.

"I need to move closer to where Lord Shayles's team is sitting," she told Marigold as she searched for an inconspicuous path through the crowd. "That's the only way I'll be able to tell if what Lord Gatwick said to me was true. He mentioned a knife."

She started to leave, but Marigold caught the sleeve of her dress, holding her back. "Do you really believe Lord Gatwick?" she asked, her expression serious. "Or are you simply predisposed to think Dr. Maqsood is out to do your husband harm because of the hospital offer? I wouldn't put it past Gatwick to use that against you."

Lavinia shook her head. "I trust Lord Gatwick. I can't tell you why. He simply comes off as trustworthy to me." She paused, then said, "There's more to Lord Gatwick's story than meets the eye. I felt it from the moment he arrived at Broadclyft Hall the other day."

Marigold still looked wary, but she said, "All right. You follow your instincts and I'll see what I can do to keep Shayles under observation."

They parted, and Lavinia made her way through the crowd feeling far less confident than she wanted to. She was still several yards away from Shayles's team's kits and other bits and pieces, attempting to look like nothing more than a hostess ensuring her guests were enjoying themselves, when a groan swelled up from the crowd. She glanced toward the wicket to see Lord Malcolm walking off the field, swatting the grass with his bat, looking red-faced and furious. The majority of the Indian players had rushed to congratulate the bowler, but Lord Shayles and Dr. Maqsood stood chatting seriously several yards apart from the rest of the team. Lord Gatwick stood near the boundary with his arms crossed, looking unconcerned with the match.

That would have sparked Lavinia's curiosity enough on its own, but as Lord Malcolm reached the bench where the rest of his disheartened team sat, Armand walked out toward the wicket. Lavinia's heart beat faster. She'd been certain he wasn't supposed to bat until lower in the order, but Mr. Croydon must have sent him in sooner. It gave her no time at all.

She wedged her way through a few spectators to stand right on the edge of the boundary. Lord Shayles and Dr. Maqsood broke apart, and Dr. Maqsood called out a friendly greeting to Armand as he took his place on the wicket, facing the bowler.

Before the over could begin, Dr. Maqsood held out a hand, signaling for the bowler to wait. "Shariq, a word," he shouted and jogged up to the wicketkeeper.

The two had a brief exchange, then Dr. Maqsood jogged backwards to his place in the field. A slow, deadly smile spread across the wicketkeeper's face, and he adjusted his keeping gloves as Armand thumped the ground with his bat just a few yards away on the other side of the stumps.

As the bowler began his approach from the other end of the wicket, Lavinia could have sworn she saw a flash of something metallic in the wicketkeeper's glove. The ball hurdled toward Armand, he missed it, and the wicketkeeper caught it and leapt forward as though trying to stump Armand. Lavinia gasped as she saw what could happen. If the wicketkeeper had some sort of weapon, all it would take was a feinted stumping and he could stab Armand in the back of his legs where his pads didn't protect him with whatever he held. She may not have known much about anatomy, but she knew there were vital veins in the legs that, if cut, would cause a man to bleed to death within minutes. Pandemonium would break out, and the wicketkeeper would be hauled off to jail for murder, but if Shayles truly had planned the whole thing, chances were the murderer would be on a ship headed far away from England by day's end.

"He's bold, I'll give him that much," Lavinia murmured, praying that Armand could see what was going on.

But he had his back to the wicketkeeper as the bowler prepared for another delivery. Lavinia squinted hard to try to make out what the wicketkeeper was holding. The action on the wicket was too fast. Armand hit the ball, then ran for the other end.

Lavinia was so busy watching the wicketkeeper that she jumped when a howl of pain erupted from the field. She jerked her head to see what had happened, only to find Dr. Maqsood collapsed in the grass, clutching his leg. Lord Gatwick straightened beside him, throwing the ball toward the wicketkeeper. His expression was unreadable as he then bent to help Dr. Maqsood.

As soon as the play was over, Lord Shayles rushed to Dr. Maqsood and Lord Gatwick, along with several of the Indian players. Lavinia glanced back to the wicketkeeper, who was fiddling with his leg pads. She thought she saw whatever shiny thing the man had in his hand slip into one of the pads. Mr. Bondar and the other umpire didn't notice the action. They were too busy heading over to where Dr. Maqsood was still rolling on the ground, clutching his leg. The wicketkeeper stood, calling out something to the other umpire, who nodded, then jogged toward the boundary. On the field, Armand moved to join the rest of the men crowding around Dr. Maqsood, but he stopped as Alex, the other batsman, met him in the middle of the wicket.

"I've got it, I've got it," Dr. Miller called, looking winded as he trotted across the field to attend Dr. Maqsood. "I'm a doctor, I can handle this."

Lavinia didn't know where to look. On the one hand, with Lord Shayles, Lord Gatwick, and Dr. Miller huddled around Dr. Maqsood, anything could happen. On the other, the wicketkeeper reached his team bench only a few yards away from her. He said something rapid-fire in his own language and was met by a flurry of comments that Lavinia couldn't understand. He sat on the bench and unbuckled his pads.

"Wait." Lavinia took a step toward them. "Wait, you can't just cast those aside. You have a knife."

A few of the spare Indian players glanced in her direction, but it was unclear to Lavinia whether they understood what she'd said. One got up and held up his hands, attempting to keep her away from their area.

"But he has a weapon hidden in those pads," Lavinia insisted. A few of the English-speaking spectators were beginning to look at her strangely. "You can't just—"

It was too late. The wicketkeeper's pads were off, and in a rush of movement so fast that Lavinia couldn't fully see what happened, they were whisked away by other players and replaced with fresh pads.

"No," she shouted. "You can't."

"Watch out. Move out of the way."

Lavinia was forced to leap back as Dr. Maqsood was carried toward the remaining cluster of players and deposited on the ground in front of the bench.

"I've never seen a ball hit so hard that it fractured a man's ankle," Dr. Miller said in awe and delight as he squatted by the pale and groaning Dr. Maqsood's side. "Gatwick, you were standing right next to him. How did this happen?"

"He tried to stop the ball with his ankle," Lord Gatwick

said with a bored sniff. He spotted Lavinia hovering near the edge of the encroaching onlookers and stepped subtly in her direction.

"No," Dr. Maqsood moaned. "You did this."

"I may have failed to block the ball on my own," Lord Gatwick admitted. His mouth pinched in a look of extreme distaste. "Give the man some laudanum so he stops groaning."

"Yes, yes, I've got some right here," Dr. Miller said, gesturing for one of the Indian players to hand him a medical bag.

"No," Lord Shayles said, wedging his way between the others, wide-eyed, in an attempt to stop him. "You can't give him anything. I need him alert and functioning."

"You brought fifteen players, my lord," Mr. Bondar said from the side. "You'll have to take over captain duties, but it doesn't look like Dr. Maqsood will be able to play anymore. Two more minutes and we resume play."

"No," Lord Shayles growled, dropping to squat beside Dr. Maqsood. "Snap out of it, you filthy native. I need you."

"Excuse me, my lord." Dr. Miller wedged his way between Lord Shayles and Dr. Maqsood, holding a small vial to Dr. Maqsood's lips and urging him to drink it.

"What the devil?" Lord Shayles exclaimed as Dr. Maqsood drank the mixture and lay back in the grass. "Miller, you fool!"

"He's in pain," Dr. Miller defended himself, looking shocked at the force of Lord Shayles's ire.

"I'll flay you alive," Lord Shayles growled. He pushed back, standing. "Where's Khan?" He spotted the wicketkeeper and marched toward him.

Lavinia swayed into action, ready to follow in an attempt to catch Lord Shayles red-handed. But the wicketkeeper was nowhere in sight. And before she could take a step, a hand on her arm stopped her.

"This isn't a scene for a lady," Lord Gatwick said, just inches behind her.

Lavinia whipped to face him. "Why are you helping us?" she demanded in a whisper.

"I'm not helping you," Lord Gatwick said, his expression blank but his eyes flashing with emotion. "I'm helping myself. It just so happens that, at the moment, helping you helps me."

There wasn't time to untangle the motivations behind his words. Mr. Bondar was calling for the match to resume, Dr. Miller was carrying on about taking Dr. Maqsood to the village physician's house, and Lord Shayles was tearing through the confused Indian players, looking for the vanished wicketkeeper.

"Is Armand safe now?" Lavinia asked, grabbing Lord Gatwick's arm in case he tried to bolt.

"For now, yes. The wicketkeeper knows he was almost caught, and Dr. Maqsood will be in no condition to carry out what he was planning for after the match."

"Did you break his ankle?" Lavinia blinked.

Lord Gatwick blinked right back. "How would I be able to do that?" he said, though his eyes told a different story.

"Get Lord Shayles away from Broadclyft Hall as soon as you can after the game," Lavinia whispered, letting Lord Gatwick in on part of their plan. "It's essential for what my friends have planned."

Lord Gatwick nodded and started to walk off. He paused and turned back to her. "Someday, my lady, I do hope we can become better acquainted."

In spite of everything, Lavinia smiled. "I think I'd like that, even if my friends think I'm mad for trusting you."

"You are mad for trusting me," he said, then nodded and

walked back onto the pitch, resuming his position in the field as though nothing had happened.

Lavinia let out a breath and wove her way through the dispersing crowd around Dr. Maqsood as fast as possible. She spotted Marigold coming toward her with a curious and panicked expression and switched direction to meet her.

"We're out of danger," she told her friend as soon as they met.

Marigold grabbed her hands and squeezed them in relief, but Lavinia felt as though she'd told a lie. Armand's life might have been safe for now, and the incriminating letter destroyed, but with those external impediments out of the way, all she had left to concentrate on was the raw hurt Armand had inflicted on her by pushing her away.

Armand was bowled out within five balls of the match resuming. His focus was no longer on the game. Dr. Maqsood had been carried off the field in pain, and from his vantage point on the wicket with Alex, it looked like he wouldn't be coming back any time soon. In fact, as Bondar resumed the match, Armand caught sight of Dr. Miller accompanying the men who hoisted Dr. Maqsood on their shoulders and carried him off toward the village.

All that aside, the letter was still at stake, and Shayles's players were still far, far better than the Broadclyft men. No more than five minutes after Armand was bowled out, Alex was caught out.

"This is a disaster," Alex grumbled as he marched off the field and threw his bat aside.

"We're not going to get that letter back," Armand said, wracking his brain to think of an alternative plan on the fly.

"If Shayles wins this," Malcolm began, but was unable to finish. His face was a mask of rage, and Armand was afraid the man would burst a blood vessel in his temple. Rupert took one look at him and scooted farther down the bench.

Two more of their batsmen got out within three overs, leaving them at the very bottom of their order. Armand paced restlessly in front of his team's bench. There had to be a way they could salvage the situation. It wasn't too late to simply steal the letter from the scorer's table and rip it to shreds. The blasted thing was still sitting there, the red edges of the envelope as bright as blood, mocking them.

His gaze traveled beyond the table to the sloping lawn that led up to the house, and his heart dropped to his feet as he spotted Lavinia walking away from the pitch. Without a moment's hesitation, he took off after her.

"Armand, where are you going?" Alex called out. "The match isn't finished yet."

"Yes, it is," Armand called back. He dodged around a few people until he was free of the crowd, then broke into a run.

He was halfway across the lawn by the time he caught up to Lavinia. "Lavinia, wait!"

She turned with a startled expression that quickly dampened to the same sort of weary disappointment with which she'd looked at him for the past few days. "Armand, what are you doing? The match isn't over."

"We don't have a chance of winning now," he said, moving to stand between her and the house. "Malcolm is fit to be tied, and Alex isn't much better. We've lost the letter, which means our problems are just beginning."

To Armand's surprise, Lavinia glanced down, her cheeks going pink, but not in alarm or panic. "I suppose you'll want to go off with your friends to make things right, then," she said instead.

"Of course," he said. "We'll need to put Malcolm's plan into motion by writing another letter and sending it to the press. We may all have to return to London earlier than anticipated."

Lavinia glanced up at him, her expression pinched. "India. London. Where to next? Peru?"

Inwardly, Armand winced. "I mean for you to come to London with me, of course. I need you to find a suitable place for us to live."

She nodded, but he had the distinct impression his words hadn't actually made anything better. "I'm sure Mama already has half a dozen places in mind."

"I'm sure." Armand attempted to grin, but instead of turning into a moment they could share, Lavinia glanced off over the cricket pitch.

"It appears as though the match has ended," she said with a sigh, then met his eyes. "You'd better go back to your friends."

"Lavinia." He took a step closer to her, reaching for her hands. "It feels like whatever I say is the wrong thing and whatever I do only makes a bigger muddle of things. Please, tell me what I can do to make things right between us."

She glanced up at him, a spark of hope in her beautiful eyes. He squeezed her hands harder, praying that she would say something that he could act on. He was ready to abandon everything else but her if she told him to.

"I need to know that you're committed to—"

"My lord, Mr. Croydon needs you immediately," Maxwell called as he dashed across the lawn toward them.

Armand cursed under his breath, cursed his title and position as a peer, cursed Parliament and its machinations, and cursed the blasted day he befriended Malcolm, Alex, and Peter as they'd all lain in their cots in the Crimean battlefield hospital.

"You need to go," Lavinia said, slipping her hands out of his. "And so do I."

A chill passed down his spine, making him wonder what she meant. "As soon as this is taken care of, I'll come find you so we can talk."

She lowered her eyes and nodded, then turned and headed on to the house.

Everything within Armand wanted to go with her. He wavered on his spot for a moment, debating telling Alex and Malcolm what they could do with their stupid letter.

"My lord?" Maxwell prompted him.

Armand growled and turned away from the house, jogging with Maxwell by his side back to the cricket pitch. As much as he hated it, in that moment, affairs of state needed his attention more than his marriage. The spectators were already leaving and the Indian players were packing up their kits when he arrived.

"I believe this is the prize, gentlemen," Miss Pennington said, standing from her seat behind the scorer's table and handing the letter to Shayles.

"Bad luck, lads," Shayles laughed as he took the letter. "Looks like Gladstone is going to have a tempest on his hands come November. Sooner than that, really."

"That letter will get you nowhere," Malcolm snarled at him, the picture of fury. "We'll have the press believing that letter is a fake in no time."

"Your plot will fail," Alex added. "Your club's days are numbered."

Shayles continued to laugh. "My club will still be alive and kicking years from now, though I can't say the same for all of you." He sent Armand a pointed glance.

It could have been another of Shayles's baseless, bold threats. The man liked to hear himself talk, especially when he could frighten others by doing it. But Lavinia's cautions hung in the back of Armand's mind. Though with Dr.

Maqsood away receiving medical treatment, it didn't seem likely that he was in danger.

"We should leave," Gatwick said from his standard place by Shayles's side. "All this country air disagrees with me."

"You're right," Shayles said, still looking at Armand instead of Gatwick. "I trust you'll allow us to exit your estate without impediment?"

"Over my dead—" Malcolm started.

"Yes, of course," Armand grumbled. The sooner all of them left Broadclyft Hall, left him and Lavinia alone, the better.

"Come along, then, Gatwick," Shayles said. "We'll collect Miller on our way through the village." There was a menacing note in his tone that made Armand glad he wasn't Dr. Miller.

"Should we warn Miller that Shayles isn't in a good mood?" Armand asked a few minutes later as he and his friends and Rupert cleaned up the last of their team's things.

"Let's leave them to sort it out amongst themselves," Alex answered, his eyes narrowed.

It took them half an hour more to set everything to right on the cricket pitch and to direct the servants to take down the tables and chairs that had been brought from the house. By the time Armand started up the hill to the house, Malcolm and Alex walking in silence with him, the sun was already low in the sky.

"We need to get a new letter sent tomorrow," Alex said as they made their final approach to the front door of Broadclyft Hall. "We need to act faster than Shayles can act."

Armand surprised his friends by saying, "I want you all out of my house by tomorrow." When they glanced to him, stupefied, he said, "My marriage has suffered enough already. I need to be alone with Lavinia for a while."

"I'll gladly be out of your hair tonight if you tell me this means there will be no India," Alex said.

Armand sighed. "There was never going to be an India." He could see that now. Whether by Dr. Maqsood's alleged alliance with Shayles or simply because he would rather spend his time with Lavinia than patients, India was out of the question.

He was on the verge of explaining as much to his friends when the front door opened. Katya stepped out, carrying her own suitcase and dressed for travel. But to Armand's distress, Lavinia stepped out after her with a bag of her own, her traveling coat buttoned up tight.

"Lavinia? What are you doing?" he asked rushing ahead of his friends and up the stairs.

"I told you," she said, her face a mask of misery. "I need to go."

CHAPTER 19

Armand rushed up the steps to stand face to face with Lavinia, resting his hands on her arms. "You don't have to leave," he said, more passion in his voice than he was used to. "That's not what I meant at all."

"No, Armand," she contradicted him in a quiet voice, her eyes downcast. "I do have to leave. This whole thing was a mistake." She glanced up at him, an inner strength in her eyes that took him by surprise.

He took a step back. "Mistakes can be corrected," he said. "I can do better."

She shook her head. "I thought I could cope with a loveless marriage, but I was wrong."

Armand's heart sank and misery tightened every muscle in his body.

"If it was simply a matter of waiting for time to work its wonders and for the two of us to find some degree of love, I could have been patient," she went on. "But we both know that's not it. You are a physician, Armand. You will always want to be a physician. I saw the way you treated Lord

Malcolm's knee on the field just now. You loved it. That part of you will always be missing, and I can't fix it."

"I don't—"

"The least I can do is to give you the freedom to pursue the life you want," she cut him off before he could protest. She attempted to smile. "And this way, I can have the life that I want as well."

Armand let out a breath, his shoulders drooping in defeat. "You want to be an independent woman," he said. It's what she had told him before their lives careened so wildly off track.

She nodded, blinking rapidly as her eyes grew watery. "And thanks to you, in a way, I'll be far better situated to have that independence as Vicountess Helm than I would have as Lady Lavinia. I'll start my new life at Starcross Castle, and we will both be able to have what we wanted."

Except that, as she spoke, the gnawing feeling that the picture she was painting wasn't the life he wanted at all consumed him. He wasn't sure what he wanted anymore, only that he didn't want to continue the way things were.

"Mama, what are you doing with that suitcase?" Bianca Marlowe's question cut through the miserable tension on the stairs. Bianca and Natalia approached Broadclyft Hall's front entrance looking exhausted and put out as they accompanied their dejected brother up from the cricket pitch. Katya had moved down the stairs and had her head together with Marigold, but she glanced up from the intense tête-à-tête at Bianca's question.

"Lady Helm and I are leaving for Starcross Castle," Katya told them. "I've instructed Mrs. Ainsworth to have your things packed and to send you along tomorrow."

Immediately, the two young women broke into sharp protest. "I like Broadclyft Hall," Natalia whined.

"I want to stay here." Bianca followed suit.

"Do you need me to travel with you, Mama?" Rupert asked. "Give me half an hour and I can wash and change and have a bag packed."

Katya looked hesitant for a moment before saying, "All right." Rupert dashed into the house as she turned to her daughters. "I've left the two of you on a long leash for more than long enough. You'll do as your told and prepare to leave tomorrow. Malcolm can bring you out to Cornwall."

"Oh no." Malcolm stepped forward with a wry laugh, limping slightly. "I'm not letting you out of my sight. Besides, if you're going to Starcross Castle, then I'm coming with you so I can tell Peter all about what just happened here."

Katya crossed her arms, stepping into Malcolm's path when he tried to enter the house. She had a mischievous glint in her eyes that increased Armand's sense of having lost control of the situation. "I think I know a damn sight more about what just went on here than you do," she said.

"Do you think so?" Malcolm snapped back at her. "We just lost the match with Shayles. He has our letter, and he's leaving for London immediately."

"That's quite right, I am," Shayles himself said as he stepped out of the house, Gatwick behind him, Carl bringing up the rear with their baggage. Rage joined with the misery tearing through Armand, making him feel even more impotent. "Do forgive us if we fail to stay around for lengthy goodbyes," Shayles went on, passing them all with barely a side glance as he rushed to the carriage waiting in the drive. "We've places to go and people to blackmail. I mean, see."

It was a sign of just how defeated Armand and his friends were that none of them tried to stop Shayles as he bolted into the carriage. Gatwick climbed in behind him without so much as a word of goodbye. He did send a quick glance to Lavinia, though, if Armand was right. Armand peeked at his wife out of the corner of his eye to find her waving to

Gatwick with a weak smile. A sudden burst of jealousy filled Armand. Had something developed between his wife and his cousin in the last few days? Had he been so busy worrying what sort of corrupting influence Shayles would be on Lavinia that he had failed to see the threat Gatwick might pose?

That didn't feel right either. He tamped down his errant assumptions, reminding himself that he was distraught about too many things and likely seeing things that weren't there. Although Lavinia had defended his cousin at the cricket match. She'd insisted Mark was the one who warned her of the threat to his life.

As soon as Carl had the baggage secured, Shayles's carriage rocked into motion, pulling away from the front door. No sooner had they rounded the corner of the drive to the straightaway leading to the road than the horses switched to a run. Shayles was in a hurry to leave. The dust from his departure hadn't settled when a second carriage, one of the ones that had brought everyone down from Winterberry Park, pulled up.

"This one is ours," Katya said, nodding to Carl as he jogged over to take her bag. Katya turned to Lavinia. "Are you ready?"

Lavinia drew in a long, shuddering breath. With clear reluctance, she turned to face Armand. "Everything will be better once I'm gone," she told him. "Your life will return to normal. And while the offer to practice medicine in India might have been false, I'm sure you have the will and the resources to find a way to be the man you want to be regardless."

"This doesn't feel right," Armand said, stepping closer to her and cursing the fact that they still had a full audience of their friends. "I wish you would—"

"What is going on here?"

Armand swayed back and rolled his eyes so hard that he was surprised he didn't fall over as Lady Prior stormed out of the house. Medicine, female independence, and the trials of Shayles be damned. The real reason he and Lavinia struggled so much to make things work was because of the tsunami of interference they'd been plagued with every second of their married life.

"Lavinia, I demand you go back into the house and change out of that ridiculous traveling costume at once," Lady Prior demanded.

"Mama, no," Lavinia said, rubbing her temples and looking as aggravated as Armand felt.

"Don't you 'no' me, girl," Lady Prior went on, marching up to Lavinia and shaking a finger in her face. "Where do you think you're going?"

"To Starcross Castle," Katya answered for Lavinia.

"And I suppose this is your doing?" Lady Prior shrieked, looking like an avenging fiend. "A woman's place is with her husband," she snapped at Lavinia before taking on Katya once more. "I never should have let her associate with you in the first place. I was wooed by your lofty title and what I thought it might be able to do for my daughter, but I was wrong. You are the worst possible influence my daughter could have." She turned back to Lavinia. "Get into the house at once."

"No, Mama," Lavinia said with a strength born from being at her wits' end. "I'm going to Starcross Castle."

"Have you ever heard anything so ridiculous?" Lady Prior turned to Armand. "Stop her at once. She's your wife."

"Yes, she is," Armand said, frowning. He offered his arm to Lavinia. "May I escort you to the carriage?"

Lavinia burst into a grateful smile. "Yes, please."

She took his arm, and Armand led her down the stairs to where Katya's driver held the carriage door open. "You'll still have to wait a bit for Rupert and Malcolm," he said, "but something tells me you'll find more peace waiting in here."

Lavinia nodded and stepped up into the carriage. Behind Armand, Katya and Lady Prior were still bickering, but that gave the two of them a moment of peace. "I'm sorry about all this," Lavinia said.

Armand huffed a laugh. "It seems we've done nothing but apologize to each other in the entirety of our short marriage. I wish we'd had time to truly get to know each other instead." He lifted her hand to kiss her knuckles before he let it go.

For a moment, Lavinia glanced at him with desperate, pleading eyes. It was enough to make him want to yank her from the carriage and into his arms so that he could hold her and kiss her and promise her that he would never leave her, that things would be different. But how could they be different? Their friends would always crowd around them. His duties to the nation would take him away from her as surely as a ship traveling to a hospital in India. There simply wasn't an easy way for them to be together.

"Thank you, Armand." Katya's tap on his shoulder shook Armand out of any second thoughts he was tempted to have. "I've told Carl to let Malcolm and Rupert know that we're going on ahead now and that we'll wait for them tonight at an inn in St. Austell."

"Very well." Armand gave Lavinia's hand one final squeeze before stepping back and making way for Katya to climb into the carriage.

Before she did, she reached for his hand. "Everything will work out for the best, you'll see," she said. With a glimmer in her eyes, she leaned in and whispered, "Hope may not be as lost as you think it is."

She backed away from him and climbed into the carriage, leaving Armand puzzled over what she could mean. As far as he could see, there was no hope. He'd lost the letter, he'd lost any chance to defeat Shayles, and he's lost his wife. And most of it was his own fault.

"Drive on," he called to the driver once Katya was seated inside.

"What are you doing?" Lady Prior shouted as the carriage rolled away. She rushed down the steps as though she would strike Armand, preventing him from watching as the carriage drove off. "You wretched man! You can't just let her leave."

Armand turned to her, pinching the aching spot between his eyes. "Lavinia is not a child. She is a grown woman who has a right to make up her own mind."

"No, she isn't," Lady Prior insisted. "She's a woman. We never have a right to make up our own minds. That right belongs to our fathers and our husbands."

"Then who makes up your mind, Lady Prior?" he asked, perhaps harsher than he should have.

Lady Prior jerked back. "Why, I act on full authority of my husband," she insisted.

"Really? Then where is he, madam?" Armand asked.

"He's in London," Lady Prior fumbled. "He doesn't like the countryside. He has chosen me as his envoy in all things concerning our daughter."

"Or have you chosen yourself?" Armand said. Lady Prior began to protest, but he shook his head and walked away, heading into the house.

"What are you going to do?" Alex asked, falling into step beside him, Marigold on their heels, as they crossed through the front hall and toward the grand staircase.

"I'm going to have a bath," Armand grumbled. "Then I'm going to change clothes. After that, who knows?" He let out a heavy breath.

"We have to decide what to do about Shayles, now that he has the letter," Alex went on, following Armand as he began to mount the stairs. "If we could just—"

"Alex, let him be," Marigold said, grabbing her husband's sleeve. As Armand turned the corner on the staircase, he noted that Marigold had the same glint of mischievous confidence in her eyes that Katya had.

Alex writhed with impatience, seemingly caught between his wife and pursuing Armand. "We can't just sit back and let Shayles destroy Gladstone's new government before it gets started."

"It will be all right," Marigold insisted. "Go to our room, change out of your cricket things, and come down to the dining room. Mrs. Ainsworth said that supper will be ready soon, regardless of everything else."

"But—" Alex continued to protest.

"Trust me," Marigold said.

Armand paused near the top of the stairs to watch his friend writhe. In the end, Alex let out a frustrated breath, stepped down to kiss his wife quickly, then continued up until he was by Armand's side. "The ladies are up to something," he muttered as he and Armand strode down the hall toward their rooms.

"Aren't the ladies always up to something?" Armand asked.

Alex let out a humorless laugh. It seemed appropriate. As far as Armand could see, there was nothing funny in their situation.

"STOP HERE," SHAYLES SHOUTED UP TO HIS DRIVER.

It was well after dark. They'd been speeding through the countryside for hours after picking Miller up in the village. The idiot had dosed Maqsood with laudanum, then proudly seen that the man was handed over to the care of his shipmates. Maqsood had been whisked off to Exeter before Shayles could catch up with him and slice his throat to get him to keep quiet. The whole, carefully-laid plot had fallen apart spectacularly, and all because of an errant cricket ball and Dr. Miller's ham-fisted stupidity.

"Why are we stopping?" Miller asked as the carriage rocked to a halt. "I thought we were headed for Weymouth. This looks like a moor."

"It's just a quick stop," Shayles said, scooting toward the door. He nudged Gatwick to wake him as he did. "Come on."

Like the useless, confused puppy he was, Miller followed him out of the carriage. His driver had chosen their route well. Silent darkness stretched out in every direction. Gatwick stumbled out of the carriage behind him, rubbing his bleary eyes.

"What reason do you have to stop in the middle of nowhere like this?" Miller asked. Immediately, he answered his own question with, "Ah. Nature calls, I presume. There seem to be some amenable trees over that way."

"Gatwick," Shayles said with barely a hint of concern. "My blade."

Wordlessly, Gatwick leaned back into the carriage and brought out a long-handled, razor-sharp knife. It was a small miracle that he'd been able to retrieve it from Maqsood's wicketkeeper's pads. Khan had been just as incompetent at the task given to him as Miller was at, well, everything he did. It would have been simple to puncture Pearson's femoral arteries, as Miller had instructed him, so that the idiot viscount would bleed to death. Khan should have trusted his betters to get him out of the murder charge, not that Shayles had actually intended to help the fool once the police apprehended him. Pearson would have been dead, though, Gatwick would have inherited the Helm land, title, and money, and his financial woes would be alleviated.

Gatwick handed the knife over with a disinterested cough. At least the man was taking the failure to secure the Helm title in stride. But then, Shayles could count on one hand the number of times his friend had displayed emotion, and he'd have fingers left over.

"Henshaw, light a lamp, would you?" Shayles called up to his driver. "I need to see what I'm doing."

"Very good, my lord," Henshaw replied. A moment later, a match struck, then a lamp illuminated the darkness around the carriage.

"Oh, I say." Miller turned toward the lamp, shielding his eyes from the sudden light.

"No," Shayles said, "You don't say anything. And you never will."

"What are you talking about?" Miller asked with a confused frown.

Shayles toyed with his knife, testing the tip. "How long do you suppose it would take a man to bleed to death once his neck had been slit?"

Miller shrugged. "It depends on how deep the cut and whether the jugular veins on both sides were cut or only—" He stopped with a strangled cry as Shayles twisted to grab him from behind and sliced his neck as deeply as he could. When he let go, Miller fell to the ground, sputtering, blood oozing everywhere.

"You fool," Shayles sneered over him. "Maqsood will talk, now that you allowed him to go free. There's no telling who he'll share my plan with."

"Maqsood won't darken England's doorstep again, I think," Gatwick said, watching Miller gurgle and bleed to death with an expressionless face. "Even if he did, who would believe a lascar would pose as a doctor with the sole purpose of luring a peer aboard a ship and disposing of him at sea?"

Shayles hummed, watching with growing excitement as Miller's life drained away. "I suppose."

Miller's eyes slowly rolled back in his head. Apparently bleeding to death happened in no time at all. A grin spread across Shayles's face. His cock was growing hard as fast as Miller's life left him. Watching people die was the best aphrodisiac he'd yet to discover. They'd have to stop and find an amenable brothel before reaching Weymouth, or, failing that, a farm with a suitably young daughter for him to fuck as a victory celebration.

"Henshaw," he shouted. "Get down here and figure out a way to make this look like highwaymen."

"Yes, my lord. I know just the thing." The driver hopped down from the carriage, took the bloody knife from Shayles, and crossed to scoop Miller's body up by the arms, dragging him to the side of the road.

Shayles let out a satisfied sigh and leaned his back against the carriage. "The whole thing could have gone better, but at least I got to kill an idiot." He reached for the bulge in his trousers, contemplating giving himself relief while Henshaw did his job. Instead, he slid his hand into the inner pocket of his jacket to take out the letter from Winterberry Park. "At least we have this." He chuckled as he turned the letter over in his hands.

"Well done," Gatwick said, leaning against the carriage on the other side of the open door and yawning. "I still think you should charge more than you quoted to *The Observer* for a look at that," he added, closing his eyes.

"Perhaps I will," Shayles chuckled. "Perhaps I—"

He stopped. Something wasn't right with the envelope. It had partially resealed itself after spending so much time against the heat and moisture of his chest, but the flap was completely open now. He pushed away from the carriage, walking until he stood directly under the lantern, and yanked the letter out of the envelope.

"Something wrong?" Gatwick asked, one, bored eye open.

Shayles unfolded the letter and read. *"Dearest Lavinia. Can you ever forgive me for the situation I have had a part in thrusting on you?"* The rest of the pages held more of the same drivel.

Shayles growled in fury, which quickly turned into a shout. "Those filthy bitches." He ripped the letter, tearing it to shreds and dropping it to the ground to stomp on it.

"Is there a problem?" Gatwick asked, as if asking whether the fish at a banquet was to his liking.

"Those bloody bitches," Shayles continued to rage. "They switched the letters."

"You're joking." Gatwick pushed away from the carriage at last, looking startled. "When? How?"

"I have no idea," Shayles raged. "It had to have been at the cricket match. I knew it was a mistake asking Miller to guard the blasted thing." He marched off to the side of the road, where Henshaw was removing Miller's purse, coat, and anything that would have been considered valuable to a thief from his body, and kicked him. "You fucking idiot," he shouted, kicking Miller over and over.

"Calm down," Gatwick called from behind him, sounding more put out than enraged over the debacle. "What's done is done. Miller is dead anyhow."

"I'll climb down to Hell and murder him again if I have to," Shayles growled, stalking his way back to the carriage. His blood boiled, and he clenched and unclenched his hands, desperate for someone to strangle. "This is all Malcolm Campbell's fault."

"How do you figure?" Gatwick asked.

"It's always Malcolm's fault. He put that whore Marlowe woman up to pestering me. He's had it in for me since he stole Tessa from me." His breath came in heavy, hot gulps, and everything in his vision was red. "He won't get away with this. I'll see him dead if it's the last thing I ever do." Still seething, he leapt back into the carriage.

"Are we going back to Broadclyft Hall, then?" Gatwick asked.

"No," Shayles muttered, fighting to keep his breathing even and his temper in check. He would be better able to plot revenge if he controlled his emotions. "We're still going on to London. But Malcolm had better watch his back the moment he sets foot in town again. Katya Marlowe too. I'll see the two of them broken, humiliated, and dead if it's the last thing I ever do."

CHAPTER 20

*E*very muscle in Lavinia's body was in agony by the time the carriage stopped at the Seven Stars Inn in St. Austell. It was close to midnight, and though she'd managed to doze for a while as the carriage rattled over Cornish roads, her head ached and she felt as dull as mourning crape.

"We can rest the horses here for a while," Lord Malcolm said as he opened the door and helped Lady Stanhope, then Lavinia down. "And a bite of something to eat wouldn't be amiss."

Lavinia nodded to Lord Malcolm, then let Rupert escort her into the inn. The two gentlemen had caught up to them only a few miles away from Broadclyft Hall, though they'd continued to ride instead of joining Lavinia and Lady Stanhope in the carriage. All four of them looked the worse for wear as the startled innkeeper showed them to a quiet table, away from the inn's other late-night revelers.

"It shouldn't take long," Lord Malcolm reassured them as a sleepy barmaid brought a tray with tea, bread, and even a few bowls of stew. "Unless you'd prefer to get a room for the night."

"No," Lavinia said, helping herself to tea. She took one look at the stew, but even the smell turned her stomach. "I'd rather reach Starcross Castle as soon as possible."

"Understandable," Lady Stanhope said, patting her arm, then pouring tea for herself once Lavinia had hers.

"It's been a trying day," Rupert agreed with a sigh, taking one of the bowls of stew and digging into it.

"A trying fortnight for our Lavinia, I think," Lady Stanhope went on. "We all played a part in that."

Lavinia was surprised enough by the admission and by the unusual weariness in Lady Stanhope's voice that she turned to stare at her friend. The lines around Lady Stanhope's eyes and mouth made her appear older, for a change, instead of simply wiser and worldly. She sat back in her chair, sipping her tea and brooding.

"I suppose this is what comes of allowing a joke to go too far," Lord Malcolm said, tearing off the heel of the bread and munching on it sullenly.

"So you consider your friend's happiness a joke?" Lady Stanhope challenged him.

Lord Malcolm shrugged. He and Lady Stanhope must have been exhausted. Under normal circumstances, Lavinia was certain they'd be having a go at each other over an exchange like that.

"I honestly believed," Lord Malcolm went on, sparing a weak smile for the barmaid when she delivered pints for him and Rupert, "that marriage to Lady Lavinia would bring Armand the kind of happiness he didn't even know he needed in his life."

"And did you bother to ask whether marriage would benefit Lavinia?" Lady Stanhope asked, some of the light of challenge coming back into her eyes.

"No," Lord Malcolm admitted, taking a swig from his pint.

"But it did benefit me," Lavinia said, dragging herself out of the haze of exhaustion and thought that threatened to box her in. The others glanced at her with curious looks. "It did benefit me," Lavinia went on. "The life I would have been able to live as a single woman was more limited than I first thought," she said, mostly speaking her thoughts aloud without concern for who was listening. "I would have spent my entire life living at the mercy of my friends."

"We would have supported you in anything you wanted to do," Lady Stanhope said, resting a hand on her arm again.

"But I would have forever remained legally under the control of my parents," Lavinia went on. "Even though my marriage has been a dismal failure thus far, at least as Lady Helm I can command more respect. And," she continued with a wince, disliking the mercenary nature of everything she was about to say, "I suppose I'm due some sort of allowance from Armand that I could live off of."

"He'll gladly give you anything you desire," Lord Malcolm said.

"I don't think it will come to that," Lady Stanhope said, taking another sip of tea and reaching for the bread.

"You don't?" Lord Malcolm asked.

"No," Lady Stanhope said confidently. "I fully believe that Lavinia and Armand will work things out in the end." She turned to Lavinia. "The two of you will be reunited, and soon, if my instincts are correct."

Maybe it was the weariness of everything she'd been through, but Lavinia was instantly close to the brink of tears. She wanted everything to work out. She wanted to be happy, and for Armand to be happy too. In the pitifully few moments that the two of them had been together, by themselves, without interference from friends, family, and foes, they had enjoyed each other's company. The morning they'd shared together in the gamekeeper's cottage had been the stuff of dreams.

In an instant, Lavinia ached to feel Armand's arms around her again, to be swept away by the ardor of his kisses, no matter how frustrated she'd been with him hours before. What would have happened between them if Shayles and Gatwick hadn't shown up and if their friends hadn't come tumbling down on them a day later?

Her yearning thoughts were cut short as Rupert handed a bowl of stew to Lord Malcolm and said, "You'd better eat up, sir. Once we deliver the ladies to Starcross Castle and inform Lord Dunsford of the situation with the letter, I'm sure we'll have to turn right around and head back to Broadclyft Hall, or even London, to deal with the disaster."

"You're right," Lord Malcolm said with a sigh, reaching for the stew. "This whole thing is exactly the kind of bloody mess we didn't need to deal with."

"Only eat that if you want to," Lady Stanhope said with a wry grin. One glance and Lavinia could tell her friend was about to thoroughly enjoy revealing everything that had happened while the men were playing cricket.

Lord Malcolm must have sensed something as well. "What do you mean?" he asked.

"Only that once we arrive at Starcross Castle, we won't have to go anywhere if we don't want to," Lady Stanhope said, sitting back in her chair and arching a flirty eyebrow at Lord Malcolm as she took a sip of tea.

"Are you mad, woman?" Lord Malcolm said. "I mean, madder than usual. Shayles won't sit on that letter for long."

"Shayles doesn't have the letter," Lavinia said.

Lord Malcolm looked at her with the doubtful expression most men used when looking at her, as if she were no more than a child and couldn't possibly know anything about anything. "Lady Lavinia, we saw Shayles pocket the letter after the match."

"You saw Shayles pocket *a* letter," Lady Stanhope told him, her grin widening.

Lord Malcolm's frown popped into a look of surprise. "You didn't," he told Lady Stanhope.

"You are correct. *I* didn't." Lady Stanhope nodded to Lavinia. "Lavinia did."

"If Shayles doesn't have our letter to Gladstone," Rupert said, "then what does he have?"

If she'd been a lesser person or in a cheerier mood, Lavinia might have been tempted to gloat. As it was, the victory of the letter paled in comparison to the loss of her chance to have a loving marriage. So with a flat tone, she said, "I switched the contents of the envelope with a letter Marigold had written to me shortly after I arrived at Broadclyft Hall. Lord Gatwick helped me. I believe Lady Stanhope burned your letter to Gladstone."

"Hold up," Lord Malcolm said, setting down his pint and leaning across the table to Lavinia. "Lord Gatwick helped you?"

Lavinia nodded. "He created an adequate distraction and assisted me in stuffing Marigold's letter into the envelope addressed to Gladstone."

"Shayles might not discover he's been duped until he reaches London, and by then it will be too late," Lady Stanhope said.

Lord Malcolm glanced from Lavinia to Lady Stanhope and back again, his mouth hanging open. "You managed to get our letter away from Shayles without him being any the wiser, and without any of us knowing you were doing it?" He glanced to Lady Stanhope again.

"Don't look at me," she said. "It was entirely Lavinia's idea. I only found out about it after it was done."

Lord Malcolm turned back to Lavinia with a whole new light of respect in his eyes. "Shayles would have eaten you alive if you'd been caught."

"She wasn't caught," Lady Stanhope said. "And she may have discovered an unlikely ally in her efforts."

Lord Malcolm sat back, finally closing his mouth and shaking his head. "I refuse to believe that Gatwick is our ally, though I might be willing to concede that he isn't as much of a friend to Shayles as we thought."

"You didn't believe me when I said as much during the match," Lavinia said, suddenly angry. "You didn't believe me when I shared the information Lord Gatwick gave me about Armand being in trouble. You ignored everything I said."

Looking sheepish, Lord Malcolm said, "But Armand wasn't in trouble. He was fine. Nothing happened to him."

Lady Stanhope's eyes went wide. "You didn't see the knife that the wicketkeeper had at the ready while Armand was batting? Marigold told me it was as obvious as the nose on your face." She narrowed her eyes at Lord Malcolm, who touched his nose.

Lavinia could have wept in relief. She hadn't imagined it. Marigold had seen the flash of metal as well and had been confident enough about what she saw to tell Lady Stanhope.

"I...well...no," Lord Malcolm said.

Rupert shook his head as well. "We were focused on the match."

"Of course you were," Lady Stanhope said. "And you didn't think it at all suspicious that, after Dr. Maqsood's injury, the wicketkeeper disappeared? Marigold said that was obvious too."

"I was more concerned with winning the match and keeping the letter away from Shayles," Lord Malcolm grumbled.

"The letter which Lavinia had already taken care of," Lady Stanhope said.

Lord Malcolm flopped back in his chair and took a swig from his pint. "Point taken. Nothing can be done about it now."

"Because Lavinia did everything that needed to be done. Quietly, efficiently, and effectively." Lady Stanhope huffed and shook her head. "Will you men never see the value of the women who make your lives possible?"

"We do see your value," Lord Malcolm protested. "We just like to feel as though we're the ones looking out for you. Otherwise, what are we?"

"Useless clods?" Lady Stanhope suggested.

"It doesn't matter," Lavinia stopped them, rubbing her throbbing temples. "What's done is done. Shayles has nothing to blackmail you with, and you can continue to push the new government in whatever direction you'd like. Everyone will return to London, and Armand will find a way to go back to being a doctor, even if it's not in India."

As soon as it was over, Lavinia was embarrassed by her outburst. She fully expected Lord Malcolm to scold her, and was surprised when he smirked and said, "Armand was never going to go to India."

"He was," Lavinia insisted. "He's a physician. He wants to practice medicine again. And he won't stop until he's found a way."

"Armand's life took a turn that he didn't expect, yes," Lord Malcolm said, glancing across the table to her with a new frankness, the kind he used with his friends but had never used with her. "He loves medicine, it's true. But I've been friends with the man for twenty years and more now. He knows where he's needed, and right now he's needed in Parliament."

"But he wants to heal," Lavinia argued. "It's what he

trained for. He told me that he doesn't know anything about politics or government."

"But you do." Lord Malcolm nodded. Lavinia blinked at the surety of his statement. "You know more about politics and the government than most men in this country," he went on. "I've seen you by Katya's side these last few years. I've noted you attending parliamentary sessions and holding your own, when you're brave enough to speak, at political events. You'd make a better minister than the rest of us combined."

"I...." Lavinia shook her head. "I don't think so."

"Who was it who barged in on the rest of us at Winterberry Park not a fortnight ago and spelled out exactly the strategy we should employ to secure the extension of the franchise to working-class men before attempting to enact reform to the rights of women?" Lord Malcolm asked. "As if it were the most obvious thing in the world." He lifted his glass. "If you ask me, Armand only feels out of his depth because he has had no one by his side to guide and educate him. But that's all different now."

Lavinia swallowed, overcome by the exceptional compliment Lord Malcolm had just paid her. It had never dawned on her that she might be able to play a more active role in government, that she might be able to do more than sit through sessions and share ideas with her friends.

A second idea grabbed hold of her. Armand needed her. She realized it with a suddenness that took her breath away. Not only did he need her to run his estate, as her mother had suggested from the beginning, or to guide him through politics, like Lord Malcolm was telling her, he needed her to ground him, to help him make sense of the changes in his life. Medicine had been everything to him, just as the duties of a peer were supposed to be everything to him now. But the only time she'd seen him smile in the past two weeks was when the two of them were alone together, in each other's arms.

"Oh, no," she said, pushing her teacup away and gripping the edges of the table.

"What is it, dear?" Lady Stanhope asked.

Lavinia gaped in silence for a few moments as her thoughts settled. "I think I've made a terrible mistake," she said at last.

A wise and knowing grin spread across Lady Stanhope's face, and even though Lavinia was sure she knew the answer, she asked, "What mistake is that?"

"I shouldn't have left," Lavinia said, sitting straighter, ready to push her chair back from the table. "I should have thrown the lot of you out instead, but I shouldn't have left Armand like that."

Lady Stanhope merely smiled, as if she'd known Lavinia would reach that conclusion all along.

"This whole time," Lavinia went on, "I've been convinced that Armand and I were strangers and that we'd never be able to connect. I've told myself that he didn't want me, that he wanted something else, another life. But that isn't it at all." She stood, bracing her hands on the table to stop them from shaking. "The problem isn't the two of us, the problem is all of you. You threw us together, but then you wouldn't leave us alone."

"Technically, that's not entirely our fault," Lord Malcolm began. "Shayles was—"

"Shut up, Malcolm," Lady Stanhope silenced him, standing along with Lavinia.

"I love him," Lavinia said, the words billowing up like the warm light of sunrise on a summer's day. "Or at least, I think I could very easily love him if the lot of you would give us two seconds alone together. Even earlier, as I was preparing to leave." She took a breath and pressed a hand to her stomach as the realization of what had actually happened hit her. "Armand was on the verge of saying something to me. I think he was about to beg me not to go. But Mama blustered along and stopped him. It was as if he helped me into the carriage to prove she couldn't order me, or him, about."

She blinked, then looked around at her friends. "How dare you?" she demanded, though without as much anger as she'd felt just moments ago. There were more important things to focus on now. "How dare you interfere with my life and my marriage? And how dare you just sit there, drinking beer and eating stew, when I have to get back to Broadclyft Hall as quickly as possible?"

"That's the spirit," Lady Stanhope said, her grin spreading. "Rupert, tell the innkeeper to have a carriage prepared for Lady Helm immediately."

"Yes, Mama," Rupert said jumping to his feet.

"We may have to rent fresh horses to get you back to Armand, but it's a small price to pay," Lady Stanhope went on.

Rupert dashed off, but it was Malcolm's turn to stand with a frown. "We can't just trundle on back to Broadclyft Hall," he said. "We have to get to Starcross Castle to tell Peter what's happened. Now more than ever."

"I can go alone," Lavinia said. "You two head on to Starcross."

Lady Stanhope considered, then said, "Rupert can accompany you. Better safe than sorry."

"All right," Lavinia conceded. She was willing to put up with anything if it would get her home to Armand as soon as possible.

ARMAND PACED IN FRONT OF THE LARGE FIREPLACE IN THE library, wide awake, even though it was late at night. In a flagrant heedlessness of the rules of society, Marigold and the Marlowe girls had joined him and Alex for cigars and brandy after supper. Katya would probably murder him if she knew he'd allowed Bianca and Natalia to experiment with tobacco—something that had the two of them coughing and groaning in the corner while Marigold watched them with a disapproving, eagle eye…as she sipped a large glass of brandy. Then again, murder wasn't something he wanted to think about. There was a fair chance he'd come close to it earlier in the day without even knowing.

"She can't have been wrong," he said, knowing his comment would have come out of the blue to his friends.

"About what?" Alex asked, seemingly without the need to ask who.

"Shayles and Dr. Maqsood. Whatever plot they were hatching. Gatwick's involvement." He rattled off the things Lavinia had tried to tell them at the cricket match. "She's not prone to flights of fancy that way, and she certainly isn't a liar."

"No one ever said she was," Alex agreed.

Marigold blinked at the two of them in surprise. "Don't tell me that after all that, after Lavinia's warning and everything, you didn't see how close you came to being killed this afternoon."

Armand and Alex turned to her, both of them startled.

"What are you talking about, love?" Alex asked.

Marigold pursed her lips. "The knife?" Armand blinked and shook his head. "The one that the wicketkeeper had concealed in his pads?"

Armand exchanged a glance with Alex. "What knife?" Alex asked.

Marigold grunted in frustration. "The knife that the wicketkeeper almost drew on you while you were batting?" Armand stared blankly at her. Marigold clucked and shook her head. "Honestly. How could you not notice you were about to be attacked?"

"I was at bat," Armand said, feeling like a fool as he did.

"The only reason you weren't stuck like a pig at slaughter was because Dr. Maqsood was injured when you hit the ball."

"No, he wasn't," Natalia said from across the room, coughing up a storm. Armand and the others turned to her. She handed the cigar over to Bianca, who grimaced and set it in the ashtray. "The ball didn't hit Dr. Maqsood's ankle. Lord Gatwick kicked him."

"What?" Armand and Alex asked at the same time.

"You didn't notice?" Bianca sat straighter, a proud look in her eyes, like she knew something the others didn't. "I'm certain it *looked* like the ball hit his ankle, but right before it got there, Lord Gatwick kicked him square in his anklebone."

"Hard," Natalia agreed. "Or so it looked from where I was sitting."

"Can you kick someone hard enough to break their ankle?" Marigold asked.

"It depends on the angle of impact and what sort of shoes the one doing the kicking was wearing," Armand said, rubbing a hand over his face. "But it's possible." And if it were true, it meant that Lavinia had been right about everything. Gatwick had helped her prevent a disaster.

"Bloody hell," Alex muttered.

Marigold cleared her throat and nodded to the Marlowe girls.

"Oh, don't mind us," Natalie said. "Mama says much worse things all the time."

Armand would have chuckled at the odd dynamics of Katya's family, but a deeper truth hit him. Lavinia had been right all along. She had tried to warn him, tried to advise him, and he'd chosen to share his friends' doubts rather than believing his wife's truths.

"I've let her down," he said, sinking onto the sofa across from where Marigold and Alex sat. "I've been a terrible husband right from the start, a horrific disappointment."

"Yes, you have been." The comment came from none other than Lady Prior as she stepped into the door to the library. Judging by the look of exhausted fury on her pinched face, she'd been there longer than any of them had noticed. "You're a bitter disappointment as a husband to my girl, Lord Helm," she said, stomping into the room and over to Armand's sofa. "If I'd known you would be so inadequate, I would have looked elsewhere for my Lavinia."

Armand squeezed his eyes shut, rubbing his temples. "But you didn't look elsewhere, Lady Prior. You shackled your daughter to a man she didn't know, a man far older than her and utterly unequipped to be the husband she deserved, and why?" He was too weary to stand, but he stared hard at Lavinia's mother. She gaped and blinked rapidly, so he answered his own question. "Because of your own social-climbing ambitions, that's why."

"It's not true," Lady Prior said, turning pink and wringing her hands. "I did it for my dear girl's sake, to give her a chance to be somebody in this world."

"She was already somebody," Armand insisted. "She was and is a beautiful, intelligent woman. She is graceful and accomplished. She saw the truth of the situation we were faced with here far before the rest of us, and she tried to warn us all of the trap we were walking into, and we didn't listen to her. And now she's gone." His chest squeezed with agony far more potent than he wanted it to be as guilt wracked him. "I let her go," he said, shaking his head. "I let her step up into that carriage just to prove that you couldn't push me around."

"I told you not to do it," Lady Prior said in the same

scolding tone that would be used with a disobedient child. "I told you that a wife's place was with her husband."

"Yes, her husband," he said, anger finally propelling him to stand. Lady Prior took a step back, her eyes going wide. "Not her mother, and not her meddling friends." He glanced around at the others. "This all could have been prevented if the lot of you had left us alone."

"Technically, it's Shayles's fault," Alex said. The moment Armand twisted to glare at him, he put his hands up in surrender, looking contrite for making a joke at such a time.

"If we had left you alone," Lady Prior argued, squirming as she did, "the two of you never would have married. I think you owe every one of us a sincere apology." She tilted her chin up.

Armand had never come so close to wanting to strike a woman. He took a step away from Lady Prior for Lavinia's sake. "I would lay the blame for Lavinia leaving me at your feet, except that I know I am the one ultimately at fault. I never should have let any of you darken my doorstep. I should have turned Shayles away, regardless of what blackmail he carried and in spite of the fact that Gatwick is technically family. This is all my fault."

"Well," Lady Prior started. "I'm glad you see that now."

"Don't," Marigold stopped her from going on. "Don't say another word, Lady Prior."

For a moment, Lavinia's mother looked like she would chastise Marigold for speaking to her that way, but, miraculously, she kept her mouth shut.

"It's my fault," Armand repeated, swaying into motion, "and I'm going to do something about it."

"What are you going to do?" Alex called after him.

Armand paused in the door and turned back. "I'm going after them. All the way to Starcross Castle, if I don't catch them sooner. I'm going to get down on my knees and beg

Lavinia's forgiveness. I'm going to tell her that she's the most important thing in my life, that she matters more to me than politics or peerages or medicine. And then I'm going to spend the rest of my life doing whatever it takes to make up these last two weeks to her."

"Wait," Marigold called after him. "There's something else you should know."

Armand ignored her, marching on regardless of what his friends thought, although he heard Katya's daughters explode with cheers and coughs as he left. The iron had entered his soul, and he was going to do whatever it took to live up to the words he'd just said.

"Bondar," he called out to his butler as he crossed the front hall. "Have Dashiell prepare one of my fastest horses. And I'll need to pack a saddlebag with a change of clothes."

"My lord?" Bondar asked, following him as Armand began to climb the stairs.

"I'm heading to Starcross Castle to find my wife and bring her back," he said.

Bondar smiled. "Excellent, my lord."

The minutes seemed to take forever as Armand changed into attire suitable for tearing across the countryside on horseback at night. Maxwell came in with a saddlebag as he dressed and packed everything Armand would need. It wasn't a job for a footman per se, which had Armand thinking that perhaps the time had come for him to elevate Maxwell to the position of valet. He would need a valet, at last, if he went through with what his heart was telling him to do. He was a gentleman now, like it or lump it. He had a responsibility to his country, but more than that, to his wife and whatever family they would have together. Shayles was every bit the villain his friends had always told him he was, and the time had come for Armand to take up arms and fight alongside his friends once again.

He didn't bother to check whether the others had gone to bed or stayed up in the library as he marched back through the house and out the front door. His horse was waiting in the drive, and in spite of the dark and the chill in the air, Armand mounted and was on his way within minutes.

The road from Broadclyft Hall to St. Austell was straight and well-maintained, and at the speed Armand rode, he was certain he would be there in no time. Katya had said they would wait for Malcolm and Rupert at an inn there, and if they had any sense, they would stay the night. The only traffic Armand encountered on the road that late at night was a single carriage racing in the other direction, but he didn't give it any thought. His focus was on Lavinia and Lavinia alone. He had so much to say to her, so much to promise her.

It was well after midnight when he reached the inn. Thankfully a few sleepy souls were still awake, cleaning up.

"I'm looking for a woman," he told the man he assumed was the innkeeper as soon as he marched into the public room. "Lady Helm. She's traveling with an older woman, and possibly two men."

The innkeeper stared at him, looking as though he were wavering between showing Armand the respect he was due or telling him off for arriving so late. At last, he said, "There's been lots of folk through here tonight. There was two men and two women, but their party split up. One couple headed west and one east."

Armand shook his head. "I'm looking for at least two women, possibly a party of four, who headed west."

Again, the innkeeper shook his head. "Just the pair going west and the pair going east."

Armand let out a grunt of frustration. He'd missed them. And now he'd have to wait a bit for his horse to recover enough to ride the final stretch to Starcross Castle.

CHAPTER 21

*D*awn was just beginning to break over the dew-kissed meadows surrounding Broadclyft Hall when Lavinia's carriage rolled onto the gravel drive. The crunching sound roused her from her fitful slumber, the way it had less than two weeks ago—two weeks that felt like a lifetime—when she'd arrived for the first time with Armand. Unlike that journey, this time, a sense of dread at the confrontation that was bound to happen filled her.

Would Armand feel the same way she did? Would she be able to summon the courage to confess her love for him and to apologize for leaving? Or would he be cold and unforgiving? And did she truly want to eat humble pie for him? Perhaps it would be better if she marched back into Broadclyft Hall as though she owned the place and demanded that Armand see sense at last.

The very idea of acting so boldly sent a shiver down Lavinia's spine and started her hands shaking. But she stilled her tremors by gripping handfuls of her worn and wrinkled traveling dress. She was through with trembling in the face of adversity. She might have spent her whole life so far as a wallflower under her mother's sway, but she was a married woman now, a viscountess. Every bit of the independence she had longed for had slipped its way into her life while she was distracted. She would make the most of it now.

The carriage pulled around to the broad steps leading up to Broadclyft Hall's front door, but there was no footman to greet them, only the morning mist rising up from the greenery.

"Let me help you down," Rupert said, his kind voice laced with exhaustion as he opened the door and stepped down himself.

"Thank you, Rupert." Lavinia smiled wearily as she alighted. It dawned on her that, considering Rupert was an earl, even though he was younger than her by five years, it would only have been a matter of time before her mother would have attempted to match the two of them. Rupert was kind, gallant, and handsome, but with a flutter in her heart, Lavinia realized she would have chosen Armand, age, experience, and all, over someone as unformed as Rupert.

They'd made it halfway up the steps when the door opened and a surprised and puzzled Mr. Bondar stepped out to greet them.

"My lady," he said with a nod, eyes wide. "What are you doing here?"

Lavinia ignored the slight breach of propriety to answer, "I've come home, Mr. Bondar. I made it to St. Austell before realizing I shouldn't have left in the first place. I need to make my stand."

"Yes, my lady," Mr. Bondar stammered as he led her and Rupert into the main hall.

As grand as the front hall of Broadclyft Hall was, to Lavinia, it felt like home. In a short time, she had come to feel an affinity for the portraits of ancestors and others lining the walls. She caught sight of young Cherry, who carried a coal scuttle and appeared to be on her way back from lighting fires, and smiled at the girl as though she were a little sister. Cherry took one look at her and nearly tripped over herself. She burst into a grin before running on and out of sight. No doubt everyone downstairs would know within five minutes that the mistress of the house had returned.

"Is Armand still in bed?" Lavinia asked Mr. Bondar as Rupert helped her out of her traveling coat.

The anxious look Mr. Bondar gave her sent butterflies swooping in Lavinia's stomach. "Lord Helm isn't here, my lady," he said.

Lavinia froze, the butterflies wilting. "He's gone?" she asked, sounding young and pitiful. "Has he gone back to London already?" She'd told him to pursue the life he wanted, but she'd never dreamed he would abandon Broadclyft Hall so quickly.

Her thoughts came fast and hard, but they were stopped with equal speed when Mr. Bondar shook his head and said, "No, my lady. Lord Helm left to pursue you."

A different, far more excitable set of butterflies filled not just Lavinia's stomach, but her whole body. "He did?" she asked, hardly able to believe it.

"He left shortly before midnight, my lady," Mr. Bondar said with a hint of a smile. "He was headed for the inn in St. Austell, where he believed you might take rest, and his plans were to continue to Starcross Castle from there if he didn't catch you."

"Oh." Lavinia's shoulders dropped. She'd turned around and started home just after midnight, which meant Armand had probably passed her on the road. And Lady Stanhope and Lord Malcolm had indicated they would travel on to Starcross Castle immediately. Armand would miss both of them until he reached Starcross. Cornwall had never felt so far away.

Every muscle in her body ached, and she was so worn out she could barely keep her eyes open, but she knew what she had to do.

"Mr. Bondar, can you have Mr. Dashiell change out the horses on the carriage outside? I must depart for Starcross Castle without delay," she said.

Rupert and Mr. Bondar began to speak simultaneously, but Mr. Bondar deferred to Rupert. "My lady, you can't possibly leave so soon after coming home," he said. "I worry for your health, not to mention the distinct possibility that, once Lord Helm discovers you are neither at the Seven Stars Inn nor Starcross Castle, he may very well attempt to return here. You could cross on the road again."

It was a distinct possibility, one Lavinia hadn't thought of. She opened her mouth to agree, but before so much as a word could come out, her mother appeared at the top of the stairs and called out, "Lavinia? What are you doing here, girl?"

Lavinia turned to watch her mother rush down the stairs in a morning dress. She looked as well-rested as ever and hell-bent on throwing her weight around. Both facts raised anger in Lavinia's gut, but her mother seemed oblivious to it.

"What is this nonsense?" her mother continued as she descended the stairs and crossed the hall to join Lavinia. "You shouldn't be here, you should be at Starcross Castle with your husband. Though I don't think the man deserves you after the way he's behaved," she added with a sniff, turning up her nose. "His character is entirely questionable."

"Questionable?" Lavinia snapped, facing her mother as furious heat filled her. "You now believe that the man you manipulated me into marrying has a questionable character?"

"Yes," her mother answered, blinking as if surprised by Lavinia's frustration. "He should have rushed to put an announcement of your marriage in *The Times*. He should have concerned himself with purchasing a town home and scheduling social events, not—"

"Not working with his friends to develop a strategy for the new government to be a success?" Lavinia demanded, taking a step closer to her mother. Her mother backed up, but Lavinia kept at her. "Not attempting to thwart the plans of a notorious villain who was intent on blackmailing him and worse?"

"Well, possibly." Her mother shrugged. "But the man has his priorities all wrong."

"Because he puts the fate of our nation ahead of your vanity and social ambition?" Lavinia demanded.

Her mother stopped backing up, but she wrung her hands and flushed. Her gaze darted around, looking for a way out of the confrontation. She was lucky that Marigold and Mr. Croydon arrived on the stairs, on their way down to breakfast, at that moment.

"Mrs. Croydon." Her mother darted away, meeting Marigold at the bottom of the stairs. "Tell my daughter how important social standing and prominence is for anyone of a political bent."

Marigold might have answered her if she hadn't spotted Lavinia and broken into a pleased but bewildered smile. "What are you doing here, dear?" she asked, leaving her husband to hurry across the hall to Lavinia's side.

"I made a terrible mistake in leaving," Lavinia confessed, surprised at how badly she needed her friend by her side in that moment, especially when Marigold hugged her, in spite of the people looking on. "I should have held my ground and demanded Armand talk to me. And now, as I understand it, he's tried to go after me."

"He did," Marigold confirmed. "He was so distraught last night after you left." Marigold bit her lip, grabbing Lavinia's hands. "We've all made so many mistakes in this matter," she admitted. "But perhaps the biggest mistake is that none of us have given the two of you the space you need to find your own way."

Lavinia laughed in spite of the ache in her heart. "A month ago, I might have insisted that wasn't true, that you all know better than I do. But not now. I want my husband, and I want him to myself." Her burst of strength withered. "But he's gone now, and there's nothing I can do about it but wait."

"He'll be back before the end of the day," Marigold predicted. "The moment he realizes you're here instead of there, he'll rush home."

"Yes," her mother insisted, her eyes wild with desperation. "And you'll need to make sure that he has a grand welcome home. You must wash and dress in your finest gown. I'll have Mrs. Ainsworth prepare all his favorite foods, whatever they are, and—"

"No," Lavinia said, close to shouting. She broke away from Marigold and marched up to her mother. "You will do nothing, Mama. I want you gone from this house immediately."

"What did you say?" her mother asked, pressing a hand to her heart.

"I said that I want you to leave, Mama," Lavinia repeated, standing taller, shoulders squared. "You've meddled in my life quite enough, and I'm through with it. You played your hand and you lost. I want you away from Broadclyft Hall before noon. Furthermore, you will not return unless and until you are specifically invited."

"I don't think that's quite fair," her mother stammered.

"It's more than fair," Lavinia said. "Go home to Papa. Find someone else's life to meddle in. You will not set foot in my household again—either here at Broadclyft Hall or in whatever town home Armand and I purchase—without a written invitation."

"But…but you are my daughter. I've given everything to make sure you have a good life," her mother argued.

"You've done everything to use me to advance your own social ambitions," Lavinia corrected her. "I am through with being a tool for your vanity, Mama. I love you, I always will, but until I have recovered from the scars you have inflicted on me, I can't see you."

"But, Lavinia—"

"I'm sorry, Mama, but this is what I wish. Mr. Bondar," she turned to the butler in spite of her mother's wordless, whimpering pleas, "would you be so kind as to find one of the maids to help my mother pack. And when she is done, would you ask one of the footmen to accompany her to the train station and see that a ticket is purchased to take her wherever she wants to go?"

"Yes, my lady," Mr. Bondar said, his face an implacable mask, but his eyes dancing with pride and relief.

"Lavinia—" her mother tried one last time.

Lavinia stepped away without acknowledging her. It was rude and it hurt her heart, but they'd long passed the point where her mother could be swayed away from her machinations with kind words and entreaties. Without a backward glance, Lavinia crossed to Marigold.

"There's no need to say it," Marigold said before Lavinia could open her mouth. "Alex and I will be gone before noon as well. We'll take Bianca and Natalia with us when we go."

"I think it's time this house party relocate to Starcross Castle," Mr. Croydon added as he joined Marigold. "And, Lady Helm, I hope you can find it in your heart to forgive me for the part I played in all of this."

"I will," Lavinia reassured him with a smile. "And once I'm

finished forgiving you, it's entirely likely that I'll thank you from the bottom of my heart for everything."

"I look forward to it." Mr. Croydon bowed to her. "As I look forward to your continued input in matters of state." He glanced to Marigold, who rewarded him with a proud grin.

At last, Lavinia turned to Mr. Bondar. "Could you have one of the maids send breakfast up to my room?" she asked, the weariness of the last day seeping in and making her body heavy. "I think the best way to wait for my husband's return is to go to bed at once."

"Yes, my lady," Mr. Bondar said with a fatherly nod.

"Thank you." Lavinia smiled at him, gave Marigold's hand a squeeze goodbye, then marched for the staircase, head held high, feeling every bit the mistress not only of the grand house, but of her own life.

Starcross Castle was every bit as bleak and romantic as a novel set amongst the rugged landscape of Cornwall. The sky was just beginning to turn pink with dawn as Armand rode up to the front door. He was so weary from his journey and the weights that bore down on him that he nearly fell off his horse at the front door instead of dismounting gracefully. He had to knock for a while to rouse a footman to open the door, but it was worth the effort if it would bring him to Lavinia.

"Is Lady Helm here?" he asked Peter's butler, Mr. Snyder, as soon as the man greeted him.

"I'm afraid, my lord, that Lord Malcolm and Lady Stanhope arrived alone just a few hours ago," Snyder answered.

"Alone?" Armand's heart shuddered.

"Lady Stanhope informed me of the reason for their sudden, oddly-timed arrival, my lord. I must confess, I overheard her tell Lord Dunsford that Lady Helm and her son had been with them, but that they turned back from St. Austell, intent on returning to Broadclyft Hall."

A burst of relief washed through Armand that Lavinia had a protector, but that protector should have been him. "I have to go back at once," he said, turning to the door.

"If I might, my lord," Snyder stopped him. "The return journey to Broadclyft Hall would be much faster if you wait for the train, which will depart Truro Station at half nine. I would be so bold as to add that this would give you the opportunity to rest and eat before leaving."

Waiting for a train was the last thing Armand wanted to do, but he had to admit that a steam engine was far faster than a worn-out horse. "Very well, Snyder. I'll rest."

Resting involved an inadequate nap on the sofa in one of Peter's sitting rooms as the servants prepared and set out breakfast. Armand didn't realize how hungry he was until Snyder roused him to let him know the meal was ready, and when the scent of bacon, sausage, and butter lured him into piling a plate high with food. He'd barely seated himself at the table before Katya wandered into the breakfast room.

She took one, startled look at Armand, then said, "You're not supposed to be here."

"It seems Lavinia and I crossed on the road," Armand replied, in no mood to rehash the entire saga. "I'm waiting for the nine-thirty train to go home."

"What a surprise," Katya said, her usual, clever expression forming as she walked to the sideboard to help herself to breakfast. "A modicum of sense at last."

"Don't start with me this morning, Katya," Armand grumbled before taking a bite of sausage.

"I'm not starting anything," Katya pretended innocence. "Not this time."

The conversation lulled as she brought her breakfast to the table and poured coffee for herself. Katya never had been much for conversation before coffee. But Malcolm had a big mouth no matter what the circumstances, and the moment he bounded into the breakfast room a few minutes later, he opened that mouth.

"Well done, Armand," he laughed, heading straight to the sideboard and piling sausages on a plate. "I can only assume you're here for Lavinia, which shows that you're not a complete pillock."

"She turned back to Broadclyft Hall, I know," Armand grumbled, resenting the bright-eyed, grinning look Malcolm sent him. "I should have stayed put and waited for her."

"You were absolutely right to play the hero by chasing after her," Malcolm said, making a mountain of eggs beside his sausage and filling in the gaps with beans and mushrooms before joining Armand and Katya at the table.

He sent a cheery smile to Katya, who made a disgusted sound and said, "I hate you in the mornings."

"That's not what you used to say," he replied with a wink.

Armand arched a brow. If he didn't know better, he'd say things were thawing in the war his two friends had waged for years.

"Did you tell him about the letter?" Malcolm asked Katya.

"I didn't have a chance yet," Katya replied. "Some fat, old ray of sunshine burst into the room before the topic came up."

Armand winced. In his desperation to get Lavinia back, he'd completely forgotten about the deeper hot water he and his friends had landed in. "I'll join in whatever efforts you need me to if it counteracts Shayles's treachery," he said. "I can see now how important it is to fight for change, and how fortunate I am to have the privilege of a voice in Parliament." Lavinia had helped him to see that. Governing wasn't what he wanted to do or what he felt competent doing, but she was right about him having the chance to heal the nation.

And plenty of men began all new lives as the years turned. Peter was one of them, a fact which impressed itself on Armand just as Peter and Mariah walked into the breakfast room, Peter with his young son in his arms.

"Aren't you supposed to leave babies in the nursery with their nursemaids?" Malcolm asked, his mouth full of sausage.

"Armand, what are you doing here?" Peter asked, ignoring Malcolm.

"Give that sweet baby to me." Katya reached for little Peter, who was handed over as his father moved to fix his breakfast.

As peaceful and domestic as the scene was, Armand felt closed in by the crush of people. He loved his friends, but he wanted to be home with Lavinia, perhaps getting started on their own brood of babies. If Peter could be a father late in life, then so could he.

"I chased after Lavinia," he said, irritated to tell the story yet again. "Apparently, I missed her. I'm catching the nine-thirty train home. But more importantly, I want to know what you all plan to do about the letter Shayles has."

His statement was met by a flurry of exchanged looks.

"Nobody told him?" Mariah asked as she seated herself at the foot of the table. Peter brought her a breakfast plate before heading back to the sideboard to fix one of his own.

"What's going on?" Armand asked, suddenly suspicious. His friends all seemed far too happy for a group whose fate had been sealed by their own foolishness.

"The letter has been destroyed," Malcolm said at last, grinning from ear to ear. "Your charming wife was completely responsible."

"I'm sorry, what?" Armand shook his head.

"It's a very long story," Katya said to baby Peter, as though telling a fairy tale. "You'd best ask your wife for all the details, but the heart of it is that Lavinia was cleverer than any of us. She swapped out the letter to Gladstone with one Marigold wrote to her on similar stationery. What's more, Gatwick helped her switch the innocuous letter for the incriminating one. I burned your letter," she added.

Armand's mouth dropped open, and he glanced around at his friends. "Lavinia did all that?"

"Lavinia saved our bacon," Peter added as he sat, taking up a piece of bacon and biting it for emphasis.

"Lavinia," Armand repeated her name, his heart swelling with admiration and love. Of course she would find a way to save them all from their own stupidity. He'd long since figured out that her timidity was only surface-deep. She'd been brave enough to take on Shayles alone while he, Malcolm, and Alex had searched for the letter. She'd seen to it that his household was in top working order within minutes of arriving at Broadclyft Hall as Lady Helm. She'd helped him to see that his life could be more than he imagined it would in the wake of losing his ability to practice medicine, just as she'd hinted that he could still find a way to be a doctor if he wanted to. She was quiet grace and confidence, wisdom and will. His life with her could be perfect, wonderful, if she could only find it in her heart to forgive him.

"I have to go," he said, standing and tossing his napkin to the table. "I have to go back to her."

"Sit down," Peter told him with a compassionate smirk. "It's barely eight o'clock. You have a full hour until you need to leave for the train station."

Armand sat, but he wasn't happy about it. "This is torture," he grumbled for anyone who would listen. "I shouldn't be here, I should be with her."

"None of us are going to argue with that," Malcolm said with a laugh.

Instead of wanting to throttle his friend, Armand found

himself reluctantly grinning along with him. His friends were a trial, but without them, he wouldn't have Lavinia in the first place. Without them, he wouldn't have learned half the things he now knew made Lavinia so amazing. Perhaps, once the dust had settled and life had assumed its new normal, he would invite them all back to Broadclyft Hall. But at the moment, all he could think was that he wanted to be at home, alone with this wife.

CHAPTER 22

As much as a relief as it was to throw everybody out of her house—and she was determined now to claim Broadclyft Hall as *her* house, no matter what happened between her and Armand—Lavinia was convinced she would never be able to fall asleep.

"I'll just rest for an hour or so, then I'll come back downstairs and speak with Mrs. Ainsworth," she told Sophie as the maid helped her undress and climb between the covers of Armand's bed.

The last thing she remembered before closing her eyes was Sophie's amused, doubtful look and her demure, "Yes, my lady."

One deep breath of sheets and pillows that still carried Armand's scent was enough to send consciousness fleeing. Lavinia fell into a deep, heavy sleep. Her only dreams were vague notions of peace and silence, with an occasional flash of Armand's smile from the morning they'd spent in the gamekeeper's cottage, the way the sunlight had made the grey in his hair shine, the way the lines around his eyes had spoken of good humor and kindness. Her mind might have been in a wretched state over the whole debacle, but her heart clung to what few sweet memories she had.

Those memories took a turn for the ardent when the Armand of her dreams closed his arms around her and stole a long, lingering kiss. Only the dream suddenly felt too real, the heat of Armand's body too close and encompassing. In fact, it wasn't a dream at all.

Lavinia awoke with a gasp to find Armand in bed with her, resting on his side, gazing down at her with a smile. He brushed his fingers through her hair and stroked the side of her face. He was the picture of affection, but worry lines pinched around his eyes and mouth, and there was something anxious and expectant about the way he nestled so close without fully touching her.

"You're awake," he said in a deep, rich voice.

"You're home," she echoed, her heart fluttering. She wanted to curse the wave of longing that swept through her and the impulse she had to snuggle with him. She should be angry with him for everything that had happened and for the way he'd doubted her. But she was the one who had left him, and it was easy to argue that the rest of it hadn't been his fault. And it felt so unbelievably good to have him in bed with her.

"I couldn't stay away," he said, flexing and stretching as though he wanted to pull her into his arms, but didn't quite think he had the right. "I realized that this is where I belong."

"Broadclyft Hall?" Lavinia asked.

He shook his head, hesitated for a fraction of a second, then dipped down to plant a light kiss on her lips. "With you."

Lavinia opened her mouth to ask what he meant, but he answered with a deeper kiss, a sensual, probing kiss, that took her breath away. She abandoned whatever feeble resistance the restless part of her wanted to put up and rolled into his arms. Her body rejoiced as it came into contact with his. Only when her hand spread across his naked back did she realize that he wasn't wearing anything at all.

She pulled back from his kiss. "Did you climb into bed with me naked?" she asked, half tempted to laugh.

Armand grinned like a devil. "I took a chance." He kissed her again, running his hand down her side and lifting her leg over his hip. His hardening staff pressed against her belly, leaving Lavinia to curse the thin nightgown she wore.

"That was awfully bold of you," she said, attempting to sound like she was scolding him but certain she sounded eager instead.

"It's a sign of my contrition," he said, cradling her backside and kissing her lightly. "I've been wrong in so many ways. I've cruelly underestimated your brilliance. I've behaved abominably toward you. So now I've come to you, stripped bare, to beg for your forgiveness."

She shouldn't feel so excited by his contriteness, but a shiver of purely carnal anticipation swirled through her, causing her to ache with the need for him. But she was no longer content to lie passively while he took control. She pushed him to his back, rising to straddle his hips and to stare down at him. The flash of pleasure in his eyes at her daring filled her with a sense of power.

"I shouldn't have left," she voiced her own regrets. "It was a cowardly thing to do."

He shook his head. "You were under extreme stress. It was a trying day. I made it worse by not listening to you when I should have. And your mother—"

"Is gone," she said, laying a finger over his lips. A grin spread across her face. "I kicked her out, told her she was not welcome in any house of ours without my written invitation."

His eyes lit with surprise and pride, but rather than

saying anything, he captured her finger, sucking it into his mouth and licking his tongue across her fingertip. The gesture had her gasping and aching, and she was acutely aware of the heat of his member trapped between her straddling legs, but kept apart from her by a layer of cotton.

"That's a wicked thing to do," she said, breathless, as he let her finger go.

"I haven't begun to do wicked things to you," he said in a low purr, his hands burrowing under the hem of her nightgown and sliding their way up her thighs. "I've set myself a penance for my part in the misery of these early days of our marriage."

The way he said "our marriage", combined with what his hands were doing to hike up her nightgown and remove that barrier between them, left Lavinia giddy with desire. "What penance?" She gasped as his hands reached her bare backside.

"I am more than just your husband now, I am your slave," he said, kneading her backside and spreading heat through her. "I will do whatever you tell me to, take your advice on all matters." He paused, and for a moment, the heat of his ardor dimmed to practicality. "It has been brought to my attention that you are far more capable in the political realm than I am, and that I would be a fool not to take your advice on all things once I take up my seat in the House of Lords this November."

Lavinia blinked, a smile forming in spite of her instinct to care for his pride. "So you aren't going to find a way to practice medicine again?"

Armand let out a long sigh. "I'll always be interested in the medical field. I won't cancel my subscriptions to medical journals any time soon. But everyone who has insisted I've been called to a higher purpose is correct."

"But you love medicine," Lavinia insisted.

"I love you," he said. The statement took Lavinia's breath. She stared down at him with a swirl of emotion that had her heart thundering in her chest and her core aching to join with him. "I love you, Lavinia," he repeated. "But more than that, you are the thing that has been missing in my life. You are the rudder that my ship has been missing for these past few years. You are the compass I've needed to get me out of the woods of confusion I've been lost in."

"I'm hardly all that," she said, heat rising to her cheeks.

"You are," Armand insisted. His hands slid from her backside to her sides, pulling the cotton of her nightgown out from between the two of them as they did. The heat of his staff pressed freely against the heart of her. "You give me purpose and direction," he said, his voice gruff. "I was an idiot not to see that until I nearly lost you, but I won't be an idiot again."

"Of course you will," Lavinia said with a laugh that turned into a gasp as she twitched against him. "We're all fools from time to time. Especially when we let the outside world interfere with what should be our own."

"Never again," Armand insisted. "Never, ever again."

He gathered handfuls of her nightgown and tugged it up. Lavinia was as eager as he was to dispose of the garment and grabbed it from him, lifting it over her head and tossing it aside. The resulting motion left her naked astride him, her sleep-messed hair cascading over her shoulders and down her back. For a moment, Armand just looked at her, a growling moan of pleasure escaping from him.

"My God, you're amazing," he said, reaching to cradle her breasts. He swirled his thumbs around her nipples until they were hard nubs standing out against her pale skin. His penis jerked where it was trapped between them.

The restlessness growing inside of Lavinia was too much, the ache too potent. She wriggled her hips over him, trying in her inexpert way to sheath him inside of her. She didn't pause for a moment to consider if it was inappropriate of her to crave her husband's thickness inside of her or to work for that aim. Her mother would have told her a wife's duty was to lay still while her husband did all the work, and that she shouldn't enjoy it, but as she leaned forward and finally found the right angle to impale herself on Armand's staff, she groaned in victory.

Armand sucked in a breath and thrust deep within her with a moan. His hands raked her sides before returning to knead her breasts, but he seemed in no hurry to race toward completion.

"Yes, my love," he growled. "Whatever you need to find pleasure. I'm yours to command."

"This," she gasped, moving inexpertly against him and creating just enough friction inside of her to heighten every sensation. "This feels so good."

"If you like my cock in your pussy, then I promise you can have it there whenever you want," he purred, meeting her movements with small, deep thrusts.

A shiver passed down Lavinia's spine. "I like it when you talk to me like that too," she gasped, her face hot as a fire to admit it.

Armand's brow rose over passion-hazy eyes. "If you want me to say naughty things to you, I can do that too. Like how right now I want to watch you ride my cock until you come, and then I'll spend my seed inside you so hard we'll have triplets."

Lavinia didn't know whether to laugh or moan at what she was certain was the mildest naughty talk a man could come up with. It was beyond mild compared to the foul things Lord Shayles had said to her. But it was perfect in its way. Armand was perfect.

"I think I'm doing something wrong," she whispered a

moment later as her movements failed to do more than make her feel aroused and bothered without bringing release.

Armand laughed, low and seductive. "You're not doing anything wrong, love," he murmured, muscling himself to sit while still planted deep inside of her. "You're learning, and it's beautiful."

Lavinia gasped at the shift in sensation and at the press of her body against Armand's. He stroked her back, kissing her cheek and her neck and shoulder. It felt so good just to be with him that way, her body alive and pleasured, her heart increasingly free of worry and stress.

"I hear we have you to thank for defeating Shayles," he said as he kissed her. The comment would have befitted a drawing room conversation, but there they were, in bed and intimately joined, his hands and mouth doing amazing things to her.

"Yes," was all she could manage. Because of their position, he was starting to slide out of her, and her mind was more focused on keeping him inside.

"I plan to reward you for that," he said, rolling her to the side and laying her on her back.

They came apart, but that disappointment was momentary as he bent to draw one of her breasts into his mouth. Lavinia gasped and threaded her hands through his hair as he flicked with his tongue and suckled her. It was heavenly, and the ache in her core pulsed with more insistence.

"You're better at this than I am," she gasped as he kissed his way down her belly, spreading his hands across her thighs.

"I've had more practice, that's all," he said. "Practice that prepared me to give you everything you deserve." He kissed lower and lower until Lavinia was tempted to beg him for release. "I may be a terrible husband, but I can be an excellent lover," he said, parting her wet folds with his fingers and teasing her with feather-light strokes. "You are a brilliant wife," he went on as the tell-tale signs of orgasm began to mount within her. "You teach me to be a good husband and I'll teach you to be an amazing lover."

"Yes," she gasped, heart-racing. "Whatever you want."

"No, darling," he said in a mischievous growl. "Whatever you want, whenever you want it, and for however long."

He underlined his words by closing his mouth over her and flicking his tongue across her clitoris. The sensation was so pleasurable that Lavinia moaned like a wanton, digging her fingers into his scalp. It took no time at all for her to burst apart, throbbing with release. The pleasure went on and on as her imagination conjured up images of him doing this to her whenever she wanted.

She was only just beginning to float back down from the heights of heaven when Armand muscled himself up her sweat-slick body and thrust inside of her. It felt so good to be joined with him again that she cried out. There was nothing slow or leisurely in the way he claimed her this time. His thrusts were hard and deep, and his breath was ragged. She wrapped her arms and legs around him, urging him on, eager for the moment when he would spend himself inside of her. Hints of all the things that could be between them, all the ways they could make love, had her body on fire, and when Armand finally gasped as he came inside of her, she tipped over the edge into a second, powerful orgasm.

They collapsed into exhaustion together, arms and legs entwined, Armand still inside of her. They were messy, sweaty, and inelegant, but Lavinia couldn't remember being happier.

"I love you too, you know," she panted as he rested his head against hers, his breath heavy and ragged.

"You do?" He found the strength to prop himself up enough to look down at her.

Lavinia nodded, a broad smile spreading across her overheated face. "I think that's why it hurt so much when you ignored me."

"I'll never ignore you again, my love," he said, kissing her in spite of the fact that he hadn't yet caught his breath. "Please let me start over. Let me prove to you that you're all that matters to me."

"I hope I'm not all," she said, cradling his face with both hands. "I should very much like you to care about your household and the nation and everyone who depends on you as well."

"But you first," he said, kissing her again. "Always you first."

"I can accept that," Lavinia said, then giggled as he kissed her once more.

He slumped to her side at last, drawing her into his arms with her back against his chest. "I am in serious need of sleep," he said in a weary voice. "But as soon as I recover, I'm going to make love to you again and again and again. In every room of our deliciously empty home."

Lavinia giggled. "I think Mr. Bondar and Mrs. Ainsworth would take issue with that."

"All right, then," he sighed. "We'll just never leave this bedroom again, then."

"Silly man," Lavinia sighed, bursting with contentment, and hugged his arms as they circled around her.

She felt his body relax into sleep in record time and reveled in the feeling. More than that, her heartfelt peace at last. Rocky starts were nothing. She had a feeling the lessons they'd learned in the first two weeks would strengthen their marriage rather than ruin it. And as ridiculous as the truth was, she was absolutely certain that she couldn't have found a more perfect husband if she'd picked him out herself.

EPILOGUE

The November chill that swirled through the streets of London brought with it a sense of excitement and the dawning of a new era. Gladstone's new parliament had been in session for a fortnight, but for Lavinia, the excitement of the new came more from the vast, echoing rooms of the townhouse she and Armand had bought less than a month before.

"It still needs a lot of work," Lavinia told Marigold as they sipped tea in the front parlor. "And Armand doesn't have much time to help me. Besides Parliament, he has his new position as a consultant at the New Hospital for Women to attend to."

"I heard about that," Marigold said with a bright smile. "You must be so proud of him."

"I am," Lavinia beamed. "Although it means I've had to call on Mama to help with this house after all."

"But that's a good thing, isn't it? To reconcile with your mother so quickly?" Marigold sent her a cautious smile.

"It is," Lavinia admitted. "But who would have thought

that Mama would dither so much over wallpaper. I thought she already had designs for fifty rooms."

"She's probably drawing the process out so that she can spend as much time as possible in the house of a viscount," Lady Stanhope said, arching a brow as she glanced across the parlor to Lavinia's mother.

Lavinia turned to look as well. Her mother was deep in conversation with Lord Dunsford's friend, Captain Tennant, and his wife, Domenica. It came as a surprise to Lavinia that her mother would behave herself so well at the informal gathering, but she hadn't caused a single scene since Lavinia and Armand had arrived in town for the opening of Parliament.

"I think she's learned her lesson," Lavinia said with a thoughtful look. "She was telling the truth when she said she only had my best interests at heart all these years."

"She certainly had a strange way of showing it," Lady Stanhope drawled.

Lavinia laughed. She couldn't help it. She was too happy not to laugh. "We all have strange ways of showing those we love that we care, wouldn't you agree, Katya?" Lavinia arched a brow of her own and shot a sideways glance to where Armand, Alex Croydon, and Lord Malcolm were chuckling over something a member of the opposition had been reported to have said at an event the night before. Since returning to London, Lavinia had felt bold enough to begin calling Armand's friends, her friends, by their given names, even though her mother would faint at the informality.

Katya hummed, mischief in her eyes as she stared Lord Malcolm down. "Strange indeed."

"You realize there aren't many of us left to succumb to marriage," Marigold told Katya. "So when are you and Malcolm going to work out your differences?"

"Oh, we'll work things out, all right," Katya said in a purr.

Lord Malcolm chose just that moment to glance up at her. Lavinia expected to hear a thunderclap to follow the lightning that passed between the pair. She'd learned more about the sparks of sexual attraction in the six weeks since her marriage had started in earnest—the first two weeks didn't count, as she and Armand both agreed—to know there was much more going on between Katya and Malcolm than met the eye.

"As soon as he begs forgiveness for what he's done, then possibly I'll consider his proposal," Katya went on.

"His proposal?" Lavinia blinked. "You mean, he's already asked you?"

"Ten years ago," Katya said. "I haven't given him an answer yet."

Lavinia exchanged a glance with Marigold. The two of them burst into laughter. It was too delicious a story not to laugh at. Whatever was keeping Katya and Malcolm apart must have been mighty indeed to battle against the force of attraction between the two of them.

Lavinia was about to ask more when the freshly-hired butler she and Armand had just employed, a youngish, eager man named Mr. Resnick, appeared in the doorway of the parlor and caught Lavinia's eye.

"Do excuse me," Lavinia told her friends and crossed to see what Mr. Resnick wanted.

"A letter has come for you, my lady," Mr. Resnick said before Lavinia could ask what was wrong. He presented a silver salver with a small, thin envelope on plain stationery.

"For me?" Lavinia asked.

Mr. Resnick nodded. "Specifically, my lady. The boy who delivered it said it was to be delivered to you and not Lord Helm."

"I see," Lavinia said with a curious frown. She took the letter from the salver and opened it with her finger as Mr. Resnick returned to the hall.

Inside was a single, plain sheet of paper with the initials MG embossed in small, black letters at the top. The text was short and written in an impeccable hand.

"Dear Lady Helm," it began. *"I would like to thank you once again for the hospitality you showed to me at Broadclyft Hall, hospitality I was not entitled to, in spite of what others might have insisted. Hospitality such as that has rarely been shown to me, and so, I would like to return the favor. Below are some names my cousin and his friends might find of interest should they wish to remove the protections on a certain establishment. I only ask that if action is taken, I might be warned so that I would be unavailable to aid the proprietor of the establishment. Yours, Mark Gatwick."*

Lavinia stared at the list of six names at the bottom of the letter. She didn't recognize any of them. She read the letter again, understanding enough to know Lord Gatwick had come to her with an offer to help those opposing Shayles and that he didn't want Shayles knowing which side he was on, but not much else.

"I saw Resnick give you a letter," Armand said, walking up to Lavinia's side.

Eyes wide, without a word, Lavinia handed the letter to him. Armand took it and read. His brow shot up at the end.

"Malcolm," he called across the room. There was enough urgency in his voice that not only did Lord Malcolm come running, the rest of their friends did too. As soon as Lord Malcolm reached them, Armand handed him the letter. "Those names. They're Scotland Yard, aren't they?"

Lord Malcolm snatched the letter and read through it, his eyes going wide. "Bloody hell," he growled. "He's handed us the holy grail."

"What do you mean?" Lavinia asked, heart pounding.

Lord Malcolm glanced up at her, then to Katya as she joined the group. "It's Gatwick," he told her. "He's just given us the names of the cabal at Scotland Yard who's been keeping the Black Strap Club away from the law."

"Are you sure?" Katya asked, taking the letter from him.

"Who else could those names belong to?" Malcolm asked.

"But why would Gatwick hand this information over, and why now?" Katya asked.

"Because of Lavinia," Armand said, smiling at his wife. "Because, unlike the rest of us, she showed him kindness in spite of his connection to Shayles."

"But Lord Gatwick is Shayles's man, isn't he?" Captain Tennant asked from the edges of their group.

Armand shook his head. "We have reason to believe he's not."

"It's a long story," Alex added. He turned to Malcolm. "You'll have to research these names before you act," he said. "If Gatwick is being honest with us, these are the men we need to remove in order to go after the Black Strap Club for its crimes."

"And if he's trying to pull one over on us," Katya said, "then interfering with these men will land us in more trouble than we want."

"Then we'll have to investigate," Lord Malcolm said. "Quietly."

"Leave that to me," Katya said, handing the letter back to Lavinia. She turned to Lord Malcolm. "We've got work to do."

"Agreed." Lord Malcolm nodded.

"Oh, Lord," Marigold laughed. "If Malcolm and Katya are working together, things must be dire indeed."

"They will be," Lord Malcolm said. "For Shayles."

He and Katya stepped back into the parlor, putting their

heads together. The rest of the gathering wandered back to their tea as well. That left Lavinia in the hall with Armand.

"I have a feeling as though something big is about to happen," she said, tucking the letter back into its envelope.

"It is," he said, taking her hands. "And if and when it does, we'll be there to help in any way we can. Even if that means my medical skills will need to be put to use once more." There was a seriousness in his eyes that both frightened Lavinia and excited her.

"We'll beat Shayles," she said, full of confidence. "Together, I'm sure we can beat anything."

"We can," Armand agreed. He leaned in to kiss her, filling Lavinia with the sense that whatever happened, however dangerous things became, her wonderful husband would keep her safe.

I HOPE YOU'VE ENJOYED LAVINIA AND ARMAND'S STORY! YOU might not know this, but I'm actually an internationally certified cricket scorekeeper! So I'd like to give a shout-out to the guys on the team I score for, British Officer's Cricket Club in Philadelphia…many of whom may or may not have ended up in this book. … Okay, pretty much every cricket player I mentioned by name is one of my BOCC guys.

THE STORY OF THE SILVER FOXES AND THEIR FIGHT AGAINST Lord Shayles isn't over yet! In fact, things come to a head in Book 5, *April Seduction*. Are you ready to get the full story of what happened between Katya and Malcolm? How did two people who are so obviously meant to be together end up so much at odds? And can they put aside their differences to take on Shayles and defeat him once and for all? Find out on December 7th! But you can pre-order April Seduction now.

Be sure to sign up for my newsletter so that you can be alerted when all of these exciting books are released!

Click here for a complete list of other works by Merry Farmer.

ABOUT THE AUTHOR

I hope you have enjoyed *September Awakening*. If you'd like to be the first to learn about when new books in the series come out and more, please sign up for my newsletter here: http://eepurl.com/cbaVMH And remember, Read it, Review it, Share it! For a complete list of works by Merry Farmer with links, please visit http://wp.me/P5ttjb-14F.

Merry Farmer is an award-winning novelist who lives in suburban Philadelphia with her cats, Torpedo, her grumpy old man, and Justine, her hyperactive new baby. She has been writing since she was ten years old and realized one day that she didn't have to wait for the teacher to assign a creative writing project to write something. It was the best day of her life. She then went on to earn not one but two degrees in History so that she would always have something to write about. Her books have reached the Top 100 at Amazon, iBooks, and Barnes & Noble, and have been named finalists in the prestigious RONE and Rom Com Reader's Crown awards.

ACKNOWLEDGMENTS

I owe a huge debt of gratitude to my awesome beta-readers, Caroline Lee and Jolene Stewart, for their suggestions and advice. And double thanks to Julie Tague, for being a truly excellent editor and assistant!

Click here for a complete list of other works by Merry Farmer.